Waiting for Mr. Kim
*and Other Stories*

FLANNERY
O'CONNOR
AWARD
FOR
SHORT
FICTION

# Waiting for Mr. Kim
## and Other Stories

BY

*Carol Roh Spaulding*

The University of Georgia Press
Athens

Published by the University of Georgia Press
Athens, Georgia 30602
www.ugapress.org
© 2023 by Carol Roh Spaulding
All rights reserved
Designed by
Set in
Printed and bound by
The paper in this book meets the guidelines for
permanence and durability of the Committee on
Production Guidelines for Book Longevity of the
Council on Library Resources.

Most University of Georgia Press titles are
available from popular e-book vendors.

Printed in the United States of America

23 24 25 26 27 P 5 4 3 2 1

Library of Congress Cataloging-in-Publication Data
Names: Spaulding, Carol Roh, author.
Title: Waiting for Mr. Kim and other stories / by Carol Roh Spaulding.
Description: Athens : The University of Georgia Press, [2023] |
Series: Flannery O'Conner award for short fiction
Identifiers: LCCN 2023007054 (print) | LCCN 2023007055 (ebook) |
ISBN 9780820365268 (paperback) | ISBN 9780820365282 (epub) |
ISBN 9780820365275 (pdf)
Subjects: CYAC: Korean Americans—Fiction. | LCGFT: Short stories.
Classification: LCC PS3619.P3724 W35 2023 (print) |
LCC PS3619.P3724 (ebook) | DDC 823/.92—dc23/eng/20230309
LC record available at https://lccn.loc.gov/2023007054
LC ebook record available at https://lccn.loc.gov/2023007055

*To Roh Shin-Tae and Roh Jung Soon for the seeds,
and to Jacqueline Sung Ok Roh, for planting them*

# CONTENTS

# Waiting for Mr. Kim
## *and Other Stories*

# Day of the Swallows, 1924

I sit on my clean floor and count with little Joo. The child is almost too clever. I say one and two make three. He sees the pear and the apples in my hands and says, "Pear plus apples make fruit." No, perform the sum. He frowns to have to do it my way. "Three fruits equals happiness, Mama," he says. Outside our window, they are building a tower. From here on the floor, I see little men working on scaffolding way up in the sky. It is another day in America. Back home, it is the third day of the third moon, the day of the swallows' return. The day precisely one year ago my mother wept to see my younger sisters fighting among themselves over the few possessions I would leave behind and the private room I shared with little Joo.

Pieces of my memory of one year ago today add up to nothing whole: ship plus woman equals horizon. Yellow plus mountain equals sky. Salt plus hunger make wind. These sums are not the mysteries they seem. Here's a mystery for you: each year, a bird no bigger than a man's heart knows how to return home from across the ocean. Perhaps some of them return to the very nests of the year before, wedged between twigs in the treetops, the bits of straw and earth still crusty with snow and faintly scented with the puke and down and shit of the last crop of babies. Here is an even greater mystery: that my sensible head should have become cluttered with dreams.

What tremendous faith you place in the future, old Mun-ji had smiled with her crooked mouth. Get sick and die is what I ought to have said to her. Since I would be sailing across the ocean to join my husband soon, why not utter the very thing we all longed to say to her, troublemaking sorceress that she was? She would have cursed me, and although I never believed in her silly proclamations, she would have cursed my family, as well. Best not to set the table for trouble, which finds its own way soon enough. Still, it was breathtaking faith to promise myself to a picture of a man who came to me, married me, gave me a child, and promptly left us again with the promise he would send for us as soon as he could. He wrote to us, sent money. But we had already forgotten his face.

I thought the sky should have been coursing with swallows on the day of our departure. We spent most of the passage on the little deck outside of steerage where I wasn't supposed to be but that was the only place I didn't feel sick. Joo and I shared a windowless space with three other women, one of whom had barley breath and didn't wash her armpits carefully enough. The other two had the best pallets only because they had gotten there first. I could swear the last was a prostitute, sent for by her "Doddy" as she kept referring to him. Not that we weren't all being sent into the keeping of men we barely knew or had never even met. In that close cabin, steeped in the smell of anxiety, I thought I would go mad with sickness and restlessness.

On the steerage deck, the salt spray coated my face and throat and hair. Thank goodness my cabinmates were too sick or depressed to disturb us here. I had worn the light brown muslin Auntie had sent to me, but I stood hatless and gloveless so I could breathe. Joo wrapped his arms around my waist, his face burrowed into the folds of my skirt. Although I had been sick earlier, I leaned into the forward movement, into the wind and sky, urging the ship onward, utterly filled with, if blind to, my future. I licked the spray from my lips like tears.

I've been dreaming I am still my mother's only child. She bathes me, perhaps for the last time in the wooden baby tub. She will wash my scalp, as well. To calm me down, she loosens my braids by massaging her fingers up and down my scalp and behind my ears. As a young girl, I had a recurring dream of seeing my mother's body in the big wooden tub, her skin pale against the water-stained sides. I approach the tub always with the thought, here is my mother. She never rests, but here she is in repose. Then, upon closer inspection, I discover that of course she is not resting at all. That's not rest.

No one promises actual swallows on the day. Some years, snow still clings in patches, or the birds descend but nest further inland. The weather you can always count on however. In all the years of my life the day has featured a brisk and airy blue with a breeze that gallops down from the snowy peaks and sunshine, sunshine that makes your heart whoop and sing.

In preparation, we do the year's second cleaning. You take everything out—mats, lamps, grain sacks, babies, sandals, linens, and crockery into the courtyard. The older girls go in and wash everything down, sweep and pack the floor. The younger girls tend to the chickens and babies. Then we cook. Then we walk in the fields and eat flower-shaped cakes. Then we feast. Then we walk some more. If you make a sauce, it tastes better than ever on this day. If you plant a seed, it will grow strong and tall. If you take medicine, you are supposed to live a long life free of illness.

No one promises actual swallows on the day.

Joo and I were quarantined for four days, although they allowed Sin Tae in to see us. He waited with Joo while they performed my physical exam. Two male doctors, one old and one young. They lacked a Korean translator that day and only after much miscommunication did they realize that a Chinese translator would not do. After that, they didn't even try to explain procedures or why I had to urinate into a cup. Then a nurse tried to tug on my underpants. "Crabs," she explained, raising her fingers like little pincers. I shook my head no. "She has to check," someone must have said. When the nurse saw my soiled rags, she disposed of them and presented me with a box of new ones.

It is true that my husband is both hardworking and good-hearted, as his auntie had led me to believe. In my short time with him back home, I found these statements to be true. But you'd better believe I did not recognize him when he came for us at the port. Three years later, and he looked like somebody's grandfather, already stooped in the spine and graying fast. In my heart, I cannot blame him, this man who honored his commitment to me through letters over ten long years before we had even met, and three more after our marriage. He is not unhandsome even now, but he looks a bit used up for the age of thirty-four. I ask you, is that what this country does to a man?

In the night, when my husband turns and places his hand on my stomach, I am ready for him. He thinks it is his idea, but I believe that I can will him to place it there. I can will him to place his hand on me, but I cannot will his tenderness; that is his own. In this respect, I have been fortunate.

Be a bird! Be a bird! My father would shout to us as we ran around the courtyard, our arms flung wide, our hair flying, chickens pecking at our toes. He took great delight in us. We thought him strange and fascinating, this tall nonfarmer with tidy hands who worked all day shuffling papers for the Japanese and was hardly ever allowed to come home. That's why he died so far away, a man the age my husband is now, who spared us our way of life by leaving it. The missionaries gave him a Christian burial, which was all right with my mother because the missionaries had taught us to read. My teacher's name was Penelope Starling, a name I could never pronounce correctly. Penelope told me books were like birds because through them your mind could soar.

❋ ❋ ❋

Some days Joo and I head down Geary Boulevard toward the American produce and sundries stand instead of down Winnette to Chin's Grocery. There is so much to look at there, including a variety of packaged cakes and cereals, boxed antiseptic bandages for small wounds, and a number of products for styling hair. American women hold their heads up very high and rather forward, as though they are rushing to get to the next place. One yellow-haired woman in good shoes shops every morning at 10:00 a.m. I have observed her because we are invisible to her. Her little boy, a round eye with yellow hair, walks up to Joo every day and pulls at the corner of his eyes, saying, "Chinky Chinky Chinaman, riding on a rail, along came a cowboy and cut off his tail." Joo is terrified at the thought of growing a tail. The boy's mother seems exasperated with her son's behavior, but she never tries to do anything about it. So I asked Mrs. Ilah Flack, our sponsor, to teach me the English for "You look better that way."

The next time that yellow-haired boy pulled at the corners of his eyes, that's exactly what I told him: "You look better that way." It made him cry, but only because he was shocked that I could speak. His mother seemed equally astounded. "Aren't you going to do something?" she demanded of the shopkeeper. A gentle-souled *hajukin*, he merely shrugged his shoulders. The woman rushed her child away from us. Great, now I am a crazy woman.

❋ ❋ ❋

Once upon a time there was a king who had six daughters. When his wife was heavy with his seventh child, naturally he expected a son. Disappointed yet again, he sent the infant away with a servant instructed to leave her to die in the elements. The princess-child was found by an old couple who raised her as a healer. One day, they brought her a bowl filled with clear water. Look upon your father, child, they told her. She saw a very sick man. She returned to the valley where her father lay close to death, sent everyone away from his bedside, and nursed him from her bag of

5

herbs. In the morning, her father was restored to health. All the kingdom rejoiced, and the father begged forgiveness of his seventh daughter, welcoming her back with open arms.

I had always loved that story of the seventh daughter whose absence filled the household. My older cousins liked to act it out as a game. Pick me, I always insisted, in love with the idea of the princess's magical childhood. Banish me.

❀ ❀ ❀

Mrs. Ilah Flack says that the wives of missionaries and immigrants have something in common—we are both strong women. Don't speak to me of strong women. Where my mother comes from, there is a whole island of them, women with powerful limbs and voluminous lungs, who dive for their food in the ocean and can hold their breath for an unheard of duration. My grandmother was one of the *cheju haenyeo* of Chejudo, the Island of Wind, Rocks, and Women. She spoke a traditional dialect difficult to understand. Although she had sight, her eyes looked like those of a blind woman's, dark and deep, focusing on everything and nothing. My grandmother's eyes turned cloudy in her old age, seeing more than she could say. Mother said that's what comes from dwelling in the depths, holding your breath to bursting time and again.

Mrs. Ilah Flack tells my husband rather wistfully that when she was a girl she dreamed of sailing to France. To France? When I was a girl, I dreamed of sailing to the Island of Turtles and Children and the Island of Girls with Their Faces to the Moon. There isn't any Island of Turtles and Children my mother would say, so I never told her about any of the other islands—the Island of Scheming Sisters and Other Fools. Island of Lepers and Japanese Whores. Island of Mudangs and Other Pests. Island of Banished Princesses.

❀ ❀ ❀

Swallows return. There's not a year when they haven't. Your faith in them, or lack of it, makes not the slightest difference to them. They make it a point to get home. Only maybe what's home to me is away for them. Or wherever they alight is home. Or all places are away and no place is home.

It is almost too much. Three days ago, we all became aware of a smell in the apartment that turned from unpleasant to offensive to unspeakable. Neither Sin Tae nor I could locate the source. Perhaps a rat had expired behind the stove. Or something had happened next door. When we passed in the hallway, neighbors began to look at one another with questioning, troubled glances. Who was responsible? None of us contacted the landlord.

Three days ago, Joo had found a stunned bird on the sidewalk. Its wing hung limp, turned like an inside-out umbrella. One eye had been crushed or eaten; the other stared ahead unblinking and resigned. I scooped it up with a paper bag and threw it in a crate of refuse in the alley. At this, Joo let out a gasping cry I'd never heard from him. Still, I ordered him to leave it alone. Later, somehow, he must have retrieved the bird, his first act of outright disobedience. It was only when I was in tears at the mysterious stench that Joo led me to his little bureau. In the top drawer was the bird, wrapped in Joo's own paisley handkerchief with a wad of cotton to rest its head. After that, little Joo wanted to be held all day. He couldn't wrap his chubby legs around my waist tightly enough. It's because my waist is disappearing; I am expecting again.

Hunger is good. I feel hungry today. That's excellent news, Mrs. Ilah Flack will say if today is a day she will drop in on me. If I can, I make my way from one physical sensation to another. For instance, I lie here awake knowing that in about an hour little Joo will be up. Beside me, my husband's sleep is as steady as a train chugging through the countryside. In precisely forty-five minutes, before the sun has come up, he will jump into the back of a pickup with his friend Murillo and six other men and be driven through the flattest, driest, most disappointing landscape you can imagine to a field where he will pick the strawberries, green beans, heads of lettuce, and squash that we ourselves can rarely afford to buy.

I remember lying awake in our room at the back of my mother's inn, just before the baby started awake with little bleating cries of hunger. The anticipation of Joo's down-scented scalp, the baby-doughy scent of his pudgy limbs already tickled in my nostrils like citrus and set my heart to a faster beat. My nipples prickled awake and my breasts started to fill. I'd leak a little just lifting him to my breast and as his mouth opened and my milk let down, I was grateful for the sealed-off world of our making, for the physical trivialities of our day linking one moment to the next. The door to our world is so much wider now. I hand-over-fist my way through the sometimes busy, sometimes too-quiet hours.

Swallows return, always, always. But when you think about it, men almost never do. Centuries ago, a Dutch sailor took his ship around the Cape of Seopjikoji into the heart of a storm. The ship capsized, but Captain Hendrik Hamel, his crew of fourteen survivors, and a hound were found stunned and gasping with thirst upon waking on the beaches of Chejudo. All were fed, examined, restored to health, and then imprisoned, excepting the hound, for the sailors had entered the land of the Hermit King and unwittingly sealed their fate: the king did not suffer the departure of strangers.

Today, as they do every year, swallows alight in Pusan, in Pyongyang, in Seoul, on Chejudo. Today I became an exile. The Immigration Act has sealed the borders indefinitely to everyone on the globe. Those who are in the United States cannot get back with any reasonable expectation of reentry. If you left a wife behind, too bad. If you hoped your family might join you, think again. It is over for you, over for them, those days. I think of Captain Hamel, living out his days in a place he had never intended to stay. Of how he made do with the life he had found there, among people who took a long time to figure out how to accept him. What must he have thought as he floated on a broken piece of a ship's siding to the shore of his new country, birds swooping and flitting overhead, skimming the surf, alighting on his head or shoulder, his hair and clothing stiff with the salt of the sea?

# A Former Citizen

## Ghost House

Picture this fall. Above is a sky so blue it sings to the infant, the puffy fists of clouds so near to her grasp. She pulls up onto her feet, tiny fingers gripping the sill of the open window. The whole of her being strains toward that blue. Then the sill dissolves beneath her and she plummets a half-story—in a second of precipitous freedom her body will always remember—to the hard, hard truth of the ground. That child's name is Grace, who experienced descent long before she knew the meaning of gravity. If you knew too little, you might even blame me for that fall.

Grace is my baby sister. Although we have never actually met, I come to her in her dreams, my eyes shining. I am filled with my fate, solid as the weight of sleep. My name is Sung Maybelline, daughter of Sin Tae of the family Song. My father called me his Daughter of Good Fortune after the daughter of a successful American entrepreneur who had inspired the name of her father's cosmetics enterprise.

My baby sister shares some of my features—a tiny nose stuck between wide plains of cheeks rounding down to a small, dipped chin. It is our eyes that differ: if you look closely at my photograph, you may discern a gleam, but no depth. Mine was a bright, short life. Gracie's eyes, by contrast, are watchful and deep. She had been steeped in the juices of sorrow throughout my mother's gestation, a child called into the world in the name of my loss. As if losing one child hadn't been misfortune enough for Mother, out came yet another girl, Grace.

Mother would mourn for hours on the edge of the bed or chair until she slumped forward into the spot her gaze had burned into the floor. On such a day, she allowed her baby to slip from the open window. If it had happened in the land Mother came from, people would have gossiped that she was trying to kill off her daughters, that poor woman with only one son. During that first wrenching night, the infant's eyes were stuck in a glance heavenward, askew. There was talk of brain damage, experimental surgery, hematoma. By morning, however, her gaze was clear and straight and she responded to stimuli. Her limbs, more cartilage than bone at that age, had suffered no damage. Still, the sudden plummet caused my sister's mind to form itself around this event, such that even now Grace remains in a state of slight but constant anticipation expecting to be propelled into her fate by some unseen hand.

Gracie lives. I am a former citizen.

At only three years old, I held title to a modest brick split-level on Washington Boulevard fronted by a pair of crispy, tilting palms. Before Grace came along, I was the only actual American in my family and therefore the only one who could own American property. The house's former occupants, a Chinese family, had run off in the night, letting the house go back to the bank. That meant Father could obtain it for an amazing sum. Blinded by his desire to put his family into their own home years before he would otherwise have dreamed of doing so, he did not question the previous family's hasty exit. Mother declared that the house was taken over by spirits. It was entirely acceptable as far as she could make out, especially for Chinese people, and ghosts would be the only reason she could think of for why they would run off like that. No, it did not bode well to burden their Daughter of Good Fortune with the title to a Ghost House.

Having been converted years ago by the Methodist missionaries, and having never believed in ghosts in any case, Father insisted on the move. From his old friend Gilberto Murillo, by whose side he had once traveled from crop to crop on the back of a foreman's pickup, he borrowed the sum of $125 to complete a course in the barber's trade. His English had been barely enough to scrape by, but Father cut hair quickly and expertly so the school put in a good word for him with the examiner. Because he refused to work for one "Kenny" Kodahara, he had to settle for renting a booth in a shop a two-mile walk from home, run by a pair of Italian brothers who were related to every customer who had ever stepped foot in the place. He simply could not manage to turn a profit after he met the mortgage and his rent and shop fees were paid.

Grimly, Mother prepared cabbage soup with red pepper broth or on-ion, now and then a bit of meat or bone. The girls woke in the night, restless and murmuring from hunger. Joo, barely out of grammar school, took to the streets, sometimes bringing home coins or fruit or buns. No one questioned him. One winter, we went without heat and lived by kero-sene light. Everyone wore blankets against the chill and walked with their arms poked out in front of them to keep from bumping into things. Father must have watched sadly as Mother fed me from her slackened breasts. In desperation, he turned again to the Methodists, who in turn introduced him to Pak Jung Ku, an energetic young man in the process of forming the first Korean Methodist Church of Oakland. Thanks to Pak, we could quiet the gnawing in our bellies and meet our expenses. Having excelled in the art of thrift, Mother and Father could not bring themselves to dis-continue certain habits, even after my family's situation began to improve. The chilly fog of the bay had taken up permanent residence in our house, and still we lived by kerosene light. Nevertheless, I began to thrive. Moth-er called me willful and boyish in appetite, but I charmed Father with my constant motion.

All I can say in my defense is that I didn't mean to do it. I had been told to stay away, told that it was dangerous. Truly, it was an accident. In a dim corner, a kerosene light stuck out from the wall, half enclosed by a broken sconce. The light cast a jagged shadow onto the honey-brown crystals laid out on a small, chipped saucer nearby. They looked like rock candy, but sharp smelling, actually quite repellent. Even at the age of three, I knew as soon as I had eaten them that I had made a mistake. Then, through some childish logic I have tried and failed to understand, I repeated the mistake, fascinated. Awareness flowered in my veins: rats lived with us just inside the walls or under the floors, eating from their little rodent chinaware, reading their tiny rodent newspapers, and sleeping in their little rodent beds. Now and again, they would show themselves, noses twitching, and leave specks and trails of feces on the floor. But I don't think the crystals ever fooled a single rat.

After my death, my family's luck began to turn. Mother, now pregnant with Grace, insisted we leave the Ghost House. Our parents took jobs as tenant managers of a small laundromat and bachelor's hotel owned by none other than the local burgermeister, Kenny Kodahara. The twins started school, Joo went off to the army, and Grace was born, perfect and whole. At first, it was grief, then superstition: they would not speak of Sung Maybelline. Not until Grace was older. Not until she would understand.

## Bucksbaum Mary Janes

Even now, Mother and Father don't pinch pennies, they wring them. They make pennies bleed. Leftover portions appear at the table, sometimes recombined or disguised, until they are eaten. Shoes are worn until the soles of your feet make actual contact with the ground. Father graciously allows his children to accept gifts received from the kind Methodists on Christmas and Easter. Accompanying a giant striped candy cane or a basket of chocolate eggs might be a small gold cross on a chain or a white covered Bible stenciled with gold lettering. Aside from these, gifts are a frivolity.

This year, Grace is to receive her first real birthday gift. The twins, Sung Sook and Sung Ok, have taken jobs stacking pallets at the nearby docks after school. Their first few paychecks they handed directly over to Mother. But Mother doesn't know about their small raise in wages, or that they have been sneaking an allowance from their earnings to buy themselves the things girls like to have. Lucky Grace. She will have her first pair of brand new shoes. Only Austin Sung Chew, the youngest of us, but also the boy, ever gets new shoes. Nobody needs to tell Gracie that her choice must be sensible black or brown. It is enough for her that the shoes will fit and belong to her alone and that when she is done with them she will discard them, passing them down to no one. Gracie has never owned anything first, last, and all the time in-between except for pencils, paper tablets, and toothbrushes. Now she will have her own Bucksbaum Mary Janes of patent leather with a real brass snap at the cross strap and a heel that clicks as you walk.

She can hardly bring herself to take the money from her top drawer and step down to Earlham's to purchase the shoes for the pleasure she takes in knowing that she can. They are hers, those bills. She adores the slightly acrid smell of them, the texture part leaf, part paper. Any time she chooses she can shove her beefy little fold of cash across the counter to Mr. Atmajian and walk away with the goods. The dollars do the talking. Not that she cares to, but she could buy twenty packages of farina breakfast wheat instead of her Bucksbaum Mary Janes. Or fifty malt shakes at Bauder's Ice Cream and Drug. Or 300 packages of Beechnut gum—350 if she requests a bulk discount—enough to last her almost until her next birthday. The sheer anonymous authority of those bills! Of course, Gracie does not recognize the beginning of acquisitiveness growing ever more expensive and complicated. Soon, a plaid dress with a starchable Peter Pan collar will catch her eye. Now that she is too old for the Baby Betty with real fluttering eyelashes, it is finally on clearance. Satin ribbon has just been made available in streams of color you used to obtain only in specialty shops. Grace remains curious about the pleasure inherent in the potential of her unspent bills. Next to spending, however, she suspects it is a far inferior pleasure.

"Question number four: 'Independence from who?'" asks Mr. Pak. In the evenings, Mr. Pak helps members of his congregation study for the citizenship exam he and his wife have only recently passed.

Father is tired. A group of men has been picketing his barbershop all week complaining that he undercuts the price of a cheap haircut in their own neighborhoods. "From whom," Father corrects Mr. Pak. Long ago, at the university in Seoul he had studied English, Dutch, and, of course, Japanese. He had hoped to obtain a civil service position as a maritime examiner, but that was before the fall of Emperor Kojong and the annexation.

For her part, Mother simply waits for Mr. Pak's translation of the questions into her own language. She finds it ironic that they must prove themselves worthy of American citizenship when the Japanese have left them no choice in the matter. Father is not convinced that she truly understands the process, as she keeps referring to the day they will become American subjects.

"Independence from whom?" Mr. Pak repeats this time in panmal.

"From colonial rule, of Great Britain," answers Father in the language of his adopted country.

"Good, now in English, too, Mrs. Song, if you please."

"But they will allow you to serve as our translator, isn't that right?"

"Yes, but we mustn't make obvious your . . . limited proficiency. As—you'll excuse me—Japanese subjects, it is only this year we are technically free from enemy alien status." Ignoring my mother's harumph of displeasure, he continues, "Question number five, then. How many stars are there in our flag? And how many stripes?"

Gracie lifts her head from her schoolwork. "Forty-eight and thirteen."

Austin Sung Chew sticks his tongue out at Gracie. "Just ask our model citizen," he taunts, ducking Mother's cuff on the ear.

❀ ❀ ❀

For weeks leading up to Gracie's birthday, the Buckbaum Mary Janes sat perched on their pink velveteen pedestal, tilted slightly to the outside world as though they were hers already save for the formality of purchase. How could she have known that on her birthday they would no longer be there? They were fall shoes, the snug black patent leather meant for dresses of wool and heavy cotton. In their place on the pink velveteen pedestal sits a lovely pair of white Easter sandals. When it comes down to it, sandals light up a girl's fancy more than any fall styles can do. But Grace has come to Earlham's to complete a transaction begun in the fall, not to become distracted by an altogether different pair of shoes. The moon of Mr. Atmajian's face hovers beyond the glass. He seems to smile at her, but perhaps it is only an idea she has of him, refracted, as Mr. Atmajian does not smile. No, she decides. If they have no Bucksbaum Mary Janes, she will purchase no shoes at all.

Nevertheless, she will go inside to affirm her own resolve. The smell of things money can buy sweeps past her through the doorway. Mr. Atmajian glances up from the feet of a patron, offering Gracie a pained nod. He is very somber about the selling of shoes and equally somber about his purses, clutches, handbags, hose, and dress socks. Gracie feigns interest in the sale collection until, quite unexpectedly, an evening bag seems almost to wink at her from the clearance rack. This bag is two things that transport Gracie beyond any idea about evening bags she has ever had. First, it is an outrageous shade of magenta, the kind of color that sits coiled inside Sung Ok's stashed-away lipstick tubes. Second, this magenta is quilted satin, with a matching twisted satin cordon with which you sling the little bag stylishly over your shoulder, and a brass clasp. She feels as though she is standing in the bag's presence. That the item can be had at a 25 percent reduction only adds to its allure, even as it promises to expand Gracie's idea of herself. She believes that she can stretch to meet this idea, can become a girl who might have the sort of moments in life in which an evening bag like this would be required. In fact, the longer she stands there, the more clearly she sees that she must have it. Not now obtaining the item might even dim her chances of enjoying such moments one day. Besides, why shouldn't she have the cheek to purchase a magenta quilted satin evening bag? Her sisters would.

The haste with which Gracie suddenly parts with her bills after so many weeks of hoarding them is enough to convince Mother that the child is possessed by a spirit lurking among the merchandise. Grace has now but a half-dollar piece and three pennies to her name, and a purse bleating in magenta between two plaid school dresses hanging in the closet.

"You will have no money," is Mother's response when, inevitably, she finds the contraband. "Your sisters have no self-control, but I hoped it wasn't too late for you!" The jostled and unkempt bills Mr. Atmajian later counts back into Grace's hand lack the heft of her former tidy stack of singles. When she counts them out for Mother, she hardly even misses them. What she does mind is Mother's insistence that they now have a Merchandise Spirit to appease. From Mother's vague memories of a long-ago village shaman, she sets vases of cut marigolds and dishes of kimchi in the windowsills, muttering prayers to ancestors. For good measure, she keeps a candle burning, but Father draws the line. That's for Catholics, he tells her, and in any case, you'll burn the house down.

Grace bears herself, duly chastened, through schooldays and meal-times and the pressing, folding, and sorting of laundry. Then one evening, she slips into Sung Sook's bedroom where her sister stands laying out different combinations of outfits on her bedspread. "Are you wearing your new bed-jacket?" Gracie ventures. "It's an awfully pretty blue."

Sung Sook deigns to look up at Gracie in the mirror and then says over her shoulder, "Sung Ok says she's never giving you money again." Gracie eases down on the tidy bedcover. She fingers the worn but quality lining of a tweed skirt with a tiny bit of fallen hemline. Sung Sook can't resist: "That one's from the Army." She means the Salvation Army. "Look at this from the summer clearance at Gottschalks," and she holds up a crisp white blouse with a lace collar.

"I'll work for you. You know, be your assistant, if you let me earn the money back." She will always admire the utter smoothness of her sister's brow as she calculates costs and benefits. "Mom won't let you spend it on that evening bag. I don't know what you were thinking."

"I don't even want the bag anymore," Gracie replies, deciding it is true. Now she knows this about herself: she's a Bucksbaum Mary Jane girl.

Sung Sook eyes her sister appraisingly. "Fifty cents a week. Do my counter hours, my folding, and my tickets." She cocks her head toward the closet. "The dresses on the far right need mending. And dishes, bathroom, and sweeper are yours for the next month."

"A dollar a week?"

"Seventy-five cents, and don't get caught."

Gracie smiles. She's covered for her sisters more times than she can count. May as well get paid for it.

## Citizens

On the morning of March 25, 1943, Father instructs his friends and long-time customers, Sampa and Biersk, on the minding of the store. Then, dressed in their Sunday best, the Song family takes the number 47 line down Bay Street to the courthouse. As the women of her country have done for centuries, Mother follows several steps behind her husband and son, gripping Gracie's hand to slow her down. Across the plaza, through the twin lions and up the steps of speckled pink stone, they meet a beaming Mr. Pak at the Office of Immigration and Naturalization. As Mr. Pak assists their parents with some paperwork, Gracie and her brother perch side by side on wooden chairs. A sailor and a woman in a checkered dress hover, shoulders touching, in the frame of a clerk's window. The clerk shakes his head at the couple from behind the glass, tapping repeatedly on the paper before them. Across the room, a Chinese man hunches stiffly forward in his chair, his arms folded across his chest. The point of his beard grazes the rise of his belly. Austin nudges his sister. The man seems to slope forward almost to the point of rolling to the floor, at which moment they will be able to glimpse the queue down the length of his back. He appears to be sitting on its tip. The children watch the queue go slack then taut. When they are ushered away with the grown-ups, the Chinese man turns his head to look at them. The children are very surprised. They had believed he might be made of wax like Madame Fortuna.

Two gentlemen in identical ink-colored suits, a Mr. Voorst and a Mr. Campanelli, show them into a judge's chambers and ask them to be seat-ed together on the same side of a very long table. Mr. Pak uses his extra bright American smile with the gentlemen as they review the procedures for the exam. It is agreed that Mr. Pak will serve as translator.

"Holy cow!" shouts Austin Sung Chew for no apparent reason. Gracie feigns interest in her brother's coloring book on state birds and flowers.

"Now then, Mr. and Mrs. Song, can you tell us what holiday was celebrated for the first time by the American colonists?" asks Mr. Voorst.

Mr. Pak clears his throat. "What holiday—Day of Gratitude and Feasting—was celebrated for the first time by the American colonists—day of thanks—do you remember, Changmi?"

Mother and Father look at one another and nod. "Thanksgiving." Mr. Voorst furrows his brow and checks the question off his list.

Then it is Mr. Campanelli's turn. "What is the name of the president's official home?"

Mr. Pak turns to our parents. "What is the name—House of White—of the president's official home—white house, you know?"

"White House," replies Father.

Mother shakes her head. Everyone looks. "The White House," she smiles. Mr. Voorst and Mr. Campanelli exchange glances. The latter gentleman takes his glasses off, inspects them, and puts them back on again. Several more questions ensue, their answers woven seamlessly into Mr. Pak's translation. Before long, everyone stands to face the flag and recite the pledge of allegiance, Gracie and Austin bellowing out the words they know by heart over the voices of our parents, just as they have been instructed to do. There is much bowing and handshaking among the adults and even more documents to be signed. Everyone poses long and hard for a photograph. And then forty years and twenty-five minutes after the *Gaelic* sailed from the harbor of Pusan, Sin Tae Song and wife are U.S. citizens. They can now legally purchase in their own names the estate of Kenny Kodahara—his three-booth shop, hotel, and laundry with the apartment attached—all for next to nothing. Thanks to Executive Order 9066, American-born citizen Kodahara is going to Manzanar.

In the mornings, long before their workaday lives begin, Mother and Father take their breakfast together and recite to one another their dreams.

A gentleman of my father's acquaintance came to pay a visit. He had just come from Seoul. His teeth were gone and his hair was falling out in patches. The time for action has already passed, he said.

It was March, cold and bright, the day of the swallows. Oh, I was flying, Sin Tae, like a swallow, swooping and diving above the coursing waves.

I had eaten things people don't eat, silkworms, the eggs of a salamander, uncooked barley. These things made me sick not in my belly, but in my heart.

Because I missed my mother, I turned on the radio. She's been gone for years, but there she was, singing that funny song she used to sing to my brother as a child.

Sometimes Gracie awakes early and sits at the top of the stairs listening to a voice her mother does not use with the children and to her father's gentle chuckle. They are more than just her parents then. They are man and woman to one another. And then one morning: I was a firefighter entering a burning building. It was like no building I had ever seen, Changmi, with windows from ceiling to floor—palatial. I was trying to find . . . Sung May, only our Sung Maybelline. But smoke billowed throughout the rooms.

Gracie heard only Mother's silence followed by a scraping of chair legs, a light thump. Did you see her? Tell me, Sin Tae, tell me that you saw her. At this, Gracie creeps from the staircase, her heart pounding. Sung means a sibling of her own family. Smoke churns at the windows of a dream. Inside that building, a girl, given up for lost: our Sung Maybelline?

When Sung Sook and Sung Ok sneak up the back stairway at 4:00, Gracie plunks down on the lid of the toilet seat to watch them quickly and expertly scrub the makeup from their faces. Her sisters are black-haired versions of Lana Turner and Jean Harlow. Although none of them can imagine it now, in a few short years these beauties will be young wives so poor they will be asking to borrow Gracie's dresses on their visits home.

"Who is Sung Maybelline, anyway?" Gracie asks simply. One sister calmly blots her neck with a towel. The other wipes the vanity and the mirror until they shine. A look passes between them that Gracie cannot read. She waits.

In words that step carefully as though edging along a cliff, Sung Sook tells her, "Let us show you something." She leads Gracie to the bedroom window from which as an infant Grace had attempted to take flight. Down below, Sampa is cracking peanuts on the front stoop. Pigeons swoop and chitter around him. "You remember what happened here when you were a baby?"

Gracie nods, forgetting to breathe.

"Do you know why you fell?"

"It was due to gravity," attempts Gracie.

"No, I mean where was Mother?"

"Exactly."

Gracie bites her lip.

Into her hands, Sung Ok places the tabletop photograph of Gracie as a black-haired toddler with a tiny white bow in her hair. Gracie loves to tell herself a story about the portrait. How her mother bathed her and dusted her with sweet lilac powder, fussed over her wispy hair, swaddled her in a white knitted romper with silk drawstring booties. "That baby died, Grace."

Gracie shakes her head. "That baby didn't die. That baby is me."

Sung Sook unpeels Gracie's fingers from the photograph. "Her name was Sung Maybelline. Mom and Dad used to call her their Daughter of Good Fortune."

"Then one day she ate rat poison."

"She died," Grace utters wonderingly.

Adds Sung Ok, "And then Mother was expecting again so soon. And still mourning."

"And not paying attention."

"And leaving windows open."

"Guess the Daughter of Good Fortune was you."

Gracie muses, "I have another sister."

"Technically, no," helps Sung Sook. "You weren't, you know, born yet."

"There is another girl to us, to our family."

"Was," chorus her sisters.

Their faces are moons, empty rooms. "But why didn't I know?"

"It's Mother. She won't talk about it."

"No one talked about it," Grace accuses.

The sisters hang their heads.

This time, she tastes the words: "No one talked about it." She remembers a gentle weight, a pulling, in her sleep. "Was she hungry?" Gracie invents, stalling.

I confess that, even now, my hunger is a constant.

The girls shrug. "We were all hungry."

"She was jolly," Sung Sook chips in as though it's a puzzle they are trying to solve. "Joo was the one who could really make her laugh. He used to stand on his head for her."

"She liked his rooster crowing."

"And his pig and cow and sheep." The girls search Gracie's face to gauge their effect.

"She would dash to the window at the first sound of sirens, like it was some sort of parade."

"I think she would have been tallest of all of us girls."

"She turned blue when she was mad."

Grace picks up a mascara wand. Never in her life has she applied makeup. Now, sisters hovering, she leans closer to the mirror swiping lightly at her eyelashes. She wonders if Austin Sung Chew knows about this baby sister ancestor. It would be something she has that Austin Sung Chew doesn't. Then she draws back and blinks at her reflection. "Say her name."

"We told you."

"But you have to say it."

"Sung . . ."

"Maybelline."

Our sisters' eyes fill with tears. But Grace is watching her own eyes. How grown-up they look, she thinks. How knowing.

## A Gift

Surrounded by the whir and chug of laundry machines, Grace perches on the counter to study a magazine filched from one of Sung Ok's hiding nooks. The news that I existed, a sister she never knew, a sister from before she was born, feels to Grace like an infection. Her legs swing beneath her like any other day except that her cheeks feel hot and she squinches her shoulders. In one glossy spread, Joan Crawford reclines on a piece of furniture draped in the skin of a white-furred animal, her hand lilting at her jawline. She gazes out with those enormous eyes of hers through open French doors into a garden where bushes trimmed into the shapes of deer with their heads lowered drink from a black-bottomed pool. Opulent—last week's spelling word—is what a life like that is called.

Austin Sung Chew ducks his head in, his shirt collar askew. "Mom says to comb my hair."

"It won't do you any good," Grace says without looking up from her magazine. He flicks a bottle cap at her that zings off Grace's Joan Crawford shield and clatters behind the washers.

On the way to school, Grace has hold of Austin's hand until the next block, when, as usual, he dashes ahead, knapsack bonking. For once, instead of following dutifully behind, Grace ducks into Bauder's Ice Cream and Drug. What they all need, she has decided, is a little bit of opulence. Something beautiful that isn't good for much. After a search through Bauder's shelves of knick-knacks and bandages and then a disappointing stroll through the more reliable Ace Hardware, Gracie's resolve to find the perfect gift in honor of her parents' citizenship starts to flag.

After school, Austin Sung Chew takes what he calls the long way home with the Filipino boys. So Grace wanders into Rudie's Durable Buy-Trade-Sell. She eyes space heaters. Humidifiers. Orthopedic cushions. Lamps. Rubber-tipped canes.

Lamps.

She backs up to inspect a plaster-of-Paris creation studded with bulbous, amber-colored glass marbles of various sizes. It sits on the clearance shelf with a red tag tied around its electrical cord. Gracie tries the switch. The marbles illuminate in a gold-flecked hue, like cats' eyes, like the eyes of rats or dragons. It is no less than someone's idea of a decorative sconce, like something even Jean Harlow might own, and priced to sell. Even after splurging for gift wrap in customer service, Gracie walks out with her purchase placed in a sturdy shopping bag with handles and a still respectable stash of her several days' earnings from Sung Sook.

"She got something in that bag," Sampa calls from his front stoop as Gracie makes her way down the avenue. "Mmm hmm, something special in that bag, my little Gracie does."

Gracie gives Sampa a solemn nod, bears herself regally up the front step, and then dashes up to her room. In years to come, our Grace will knit for Mother sweaters of artisanal dyed wool. She will purchase all manner of tasteful wall hangings and decorative household items, the latest in small appliances, and make several rather good pieces of pottery from courses she will take at the community college while her children are in school. Nearly all of these gifts will be returned or refused by Mother, who will argue that she should save her money or at least spend it on her children. In later years, after a once-happy marriage ends in divorce, Mother will look Grace straight in the eye and ask, "What did you do to him?" Near death, when her lucidity becomes tidal, Mother will call Grace by many names other than her own.

This single gift, however, this hideous, indecorous lamp, will outlast both of our parents. Father will die many years earlier than anyone expects, leaving Grace to pass through her adult life with a peripheral ache she often forgets to name. Mother, on the other hand, will live long enough to see her children's children have children who will sport names like Kimisha and Tavian. Some will brand themselves like cattle with sinister looking symbols or sprout hair that glows in the dark. Some will strike sulking poses for the advertisements in slick fashion catalogs. The lamp will acquire a retro chic.

My vision is not superior however. It is merely timeless. I don't always see with the clarity that is my lot.

I confess that what follows is conjecture. Let's say Gracie presents the lamp to Mother and Father as a gift in honor of their citizenship. They are, at first, puzzled. Imagine that they watch as Gracie plugs it in, instructs Austin Sung Chew to kill the overhead light, and then flips the switch that illuminates the eyes of the sconce. Now, say that the suddenness of Gracie's actions, her surety, the unexpected and unusual gift—these things inspire hoots from Austin, who peers inside the bowl of the sconce declaring, "They look like rat's eyes!" Watch as Mother's own eyes fill with tears. Father takes the lamp away. Gracie allows Mother to squeeze her hand to a bloodless white as Austin Sung Chew hands them a box of tissues. He fiddles with the switch. "Holy cow!" he shouts. "It twinkles."

That is what I would will. Had I will.

## Gracie's Turn

Mother has been teaching Austin Sung Chew to count the weekly totals from the barbershop, linen service, and rooming house. One day, Grace watches them in the little room under the staircase, their heads bowed over the adding machine. Austin sits with his heels tucked under him, a lick of hair sloping across his forehead. Deftly, he counts and sorts. He is not yet ten years old.

Grace is in charge of the daily tally. On Monday, she is off by about five dollars. Tuesday, with two navy ships docked at the same time, business is brisk. But, again, the tally is short a similar amount. Keep your mouth shut and your eyes open, she tells herself. It was a line she had heard at the movies.

When Sampa or Biersk comes in with their laundry, she chats with them as usual from her perch on the counter. Biersk squints to see even with his glasses on, so Grace reads him articles from the *Chronicle* as he waits for his faded blue uniforms. In Austria, he had been an engineer. He can do calculations from Grace's homework in his head. From Sampa,

Grace learned to make folded paper cranes. An old girlfriend in China-town had showed him how. "Didn't your Chinese friend teach you how to make anything besides cranes?" Gracie asks.

"Sure she did, sure she did. You want a horse or boat? Or a house?"

"I'd prefer a houseboat. But I didn't know Chinese people made origami."

Sampa shakes his head. "I'll tell you the truth, Miss Gracie. Maybe she wasn't Chinese. Maybe I made that part up."

"But what was her name? That's how you could tell if she was a Jap or not."

"Really, now?" Sampa replies. He retained a mouthful of teeth, yellow and strong.

"Well, I can't tell you the name her mama gave her the day she was born," he admits. "But she called herself Miss Lily." Gracie frowns. Everything that ever happened to Sampa happened such a long time ago.

At the end of the day on Wednesday, Grace figures they are short about five to ten dollars from their usual earnings. Thursday is back to normal, but on Friday they are off again, this time by at least seven. On their way to school the following Monday, Austin slips his hand from his sister's as soon as they are out of view and pulls a box of cigarettes from his coat pockets.

"You little sneak. I'll tell Mother."

Austin shakes his head. "These aren't for me." He reaches back into his inside pockets and pulls out several packs of chewing gum and a fistful of wooden whistles. "Resale," he grins.

Gracie's mouth drops open. "It's you, isn't it? Stealing money from the till to buy all of that."

Austin curls his lip and stuffs the items back into his pockets. "Maybe it was Biersk."

"Don't you dare."

"Or Sampa." First Grace slaps Austin's cheek, then she gasps. Her brother is so startled his wad of chewing gum falls from his mouth. "Now you're gonna get it," he threatens, raising his clenched fists. Grace merely steps closer and towers over him.

"I just needed a little bit of capital to get my business started. Don't tell, okay?"

"You know what capital is?"

"Sure I do."

"You're a little thief."

"Not if I put it all back."

Grace eyes his bulging pockets. Better to let him get himself in trouble. "Well, I won't say anything," she tells him. "But I won't ever forget either."

He shrugs. What girls and women remember doesn't matter anyway.

When Gracie counts the shop totals that evening, she, too, sneaks money from the till—exactly the amount she forfeited to Mother after the return of the magenta satin evening bag. The change she pockets. Although the bills are unsuitably rectangular, she folds them as best she can into little half houses, one-legged horses, partially winged birds. She lines up the collection on her dresser in front of the photograph of me that changed everything.

"Now, you," she instructs me. "Watch." She pulls off Sung Ok's box of cigarettes from under the dresser drawer and replaces the wad of gum. She fishes out the matchbook shoved inside and, for courage, sticks one of the cigarettes behind her ear. At her bedroom window, she strikes the match and sets the tip of the flame to the first dollar bird. It eats quickly toward her fingertips, scribbling the air with black smoke. She repeats this process, lighting match after match. Last in the collection is a dollar house. She thinks about saving just one but changes her mind and strikes the last match, releasing the remaining wisps of charred paper into the air.

One day far into the future our Grace will have lived for so long that images from her childhood will flutter into her memory with lightness and abandon. But my photograph transformed from a portrait of herself into a portrait of a sister she has dreamt into being will never be far from her mind. One day it will occur to Gracie that everything she has ever known about me has been of her own invention. My impact is gossamer.

Death is a kind of birthday. There are many variations, but I can assure you there is nothing to fear. Your blood will probably begin to sing—a high, urgent whistling through your veins. Your mouth will have a funny taste and feel, as though you have eaten something furry and rotten. For a short time, your stomach might hurt, an acidic jolt, or possibly a dull throbbing, or your head might feel as though it is floating up and up. You will lie down so that you can watch this happen, and the ceiling will retreat, leaving you gasping beneath the quiet stars. Rising, you will try to follow the most silent and distant star of all, to nestle into its cold neck. But it will pull and suck at your lungs, asking to do your breathing for you. You will give yourself over to it. This part is uncomfortable but does not last for long. Then the bad taste in your mouth becomes a numbing sweetness.

I will always wonder: am I poverty's sacrifice? I don't know the answer, but I do think timelessness is overrated—the constant yearning.

Why did I choose Grace, the sister I never knew? I tried at first to enter Mother's sleep, to tell her how sorry I was for my mistake and that I really did not mean to go away at all. Her grief squeezed me. I could find no way in. After a while I no longer felt called to her. When my sister fell from the window I thought she might join me. She lived. So then it was Gracie I felt called to, Gracie who is dreaming me now. Go, I long to say to her. Claim your birthright. I've got nothing but time.

# Waiting For Mr. Kim, 1945

When Gracie Song's elder twin sisters reached the age of eighteen, they went down to the Alameda County Shipyards and got jobs piecing battleships together for the U.S. Navy. This was the place to find a husband in 1945, if a girl was doing her own looking. They were Americans, after all, and they were of age. Her sisters caught the bus down to the waterfront every day and brought home their paychecks every two weeks. At night, they went out with their girlfriends, meeting boys at the cinema or the drugstore, as long as it was outside of Chinatown.

Gracie's parents would never have thought it was husbands they were after. Girls didn't choose what they were given. But the end of the war distracted everybody. While Mr. Song tried to keep up with the papers and Mrs. Song tried to keep up with the laundry, Sung Sook slipped away one day with a Black welder enrolled in the police academy, and Sung Ok took off with a Chinatown nightclub singer from L.A. with a sister in the movies.

Escaped. Gracie had watched from the doorway that morning as Sung Sook pulled on her good slip in front of the vanity, lifted her hair, breathed in long and slow. Her eyes came open, she saw Gracie's reflection. "Co-

28

meer," she said. "You never say goodbye." She kissed Gracie between the eyes. Gracie had only shrugged: "See you." Then Sung Ok from the bathroom: "This family runs a laundry, so where's all the goddamn towels?"

When the girls didn't come home, the lipstick and rouge wiped off their faces, to fold the 4:00 sheets, she understood what was what. On the vanity in the girls' room she found a white paper bell with sugar sprinkles. In silver letters, it read:

CALL TODAY!

MARRY TODAY!

YOUR WEDDING! YOUR WAY!

EIGHTEEN OR OVER?

WE WON'T SAY NAY!

(MAY BORROW VEIL AND BOUQUET)

As simple as having your hair done. Gracie sat at the vanity, thinking of the thousand spirits of the household her mother was always ticking off like a grocery list—spirit of the lamp, the clock, the ashtray. Spirit in the seat of your chair. Spirit of the stove, the closet, the broom, the shoes. Spirit of the breeze in the room, the Frigidaire. Gracie had always been willing to believe in them; she only needed something substantial to go on. Now, in her sisters' room, she felt that the spirits had been there, had moved on, to other inhabited rooms.

Those girls had escaped Thursday evenings with the old *chong gaks*, the bachelors who waited effortlessly for her father to give the girls away. No more sitting, knees together, in white blouses and circle skirts, with gritted smiles. Now Gracie would sit, the only girl, while her father made chitchat with Mr. Han and Mr. Kim. Number three daughter, much younger, the dutiful one, wouldn't run away. If her mother had had the say, the girls would have given their parents grandchildren by now. But she didn't have the say, and her father smiled his pleasant, slightly anxious smile at the chong gaks and never ever brought up payment.

"Now we'll have a Negro for a grandson and a Chink for a son-in- law, Mr. Song!" her mother shouted, when the girls' absence was certain. She

29

cursed Korean, but had a gift for American slurs, translating the letter found taped to the laundry boiler into the horrors of marrying for love. Plates rattled in the cabinets, the stove rumbled in the corner, pictures slid, clanked, tinkled. Gracie and Austin pressed themselves against the wall, squeezed around the Frigidaire, sidled to the staircase. They sat and backed up one step at a time, away from the stabs and swishes of the broom. "Or didn't you want Korean grandchildren Mr. Song? You're the one who let them fall into American love. Could I help it there aren't any good chong gaks around? Thought we'd pack the girls off to Hawaii where the young ones are? Ha. I'd like to see the missionaries pay for that!"

Their father came into view below. Hurried, but with his usual dignity, he ducked and swerved as necessary. Silently, solemnly, he made for the closet, opened the door, and stepped in among the coats. The blows from first the bristled and then the butted end of the broom came down upon the door.

Austin whispered, "I'm going outside."

"Fine," Gracie told him. "If you can make it to the door."

"Think I can't manage the window? I land in the trash bins. Pretty soft!"

Gracie told him, "Bring me back a cigarette then," and he left her there. A year younger than she and not very big for thirteen, he was still number one son. Gracie stuck her fingers in her mouth all the way to the knuckle, clamped down hard.

She chopped cabbage, scrubbed the bathhouses, washed and pressed and folded linen and laundry, dreaming up lives for her sisters. From their talk and their magazines, she knew how it should go. Sung Sook stretched out by the pool in a leopard-print bathing suit with pointy bra cups and sipped colored drinks from thin glasses, leaving a pink surprise of lips at the rim. Somebody else served, fetched, cleaned. Her husband shot cardboard men through the heart and came home to barbecue T-bones. Every night they held hands at the double feature. Sung Ok slipped into a tight Chinese-doll dress and jeweled cat-eyes to sing to smoky crowds of White people from out of town. Her lips grazed the mike as she whispered, "Thank you, kind people, thank you." In the second act, her husband, decked out in a tux, dipped her, spun her, with slant-eyed Gene Kelly-opium flair. All the White people craned their necks. They could see for themselves that some Oriental women had great legs.

The girls had left Gracie and her mother with all the work. At first, her father tried to help out. He locked up the barbershop at lunch, crossed the street, passed through the kitchen, and stepped into Hell, as her sisters had called it. But her mother snapped down the pants press when she saw him and from a blur of steam shouted, "Fool for love! I'm warning you to get out of here, Mr. Song!"

Mrs. Song bowed her head at the market now. She had stopped going to church. Lost face. And there was the worry of it. No one knew these men who took the girls away. Maybe one was an opium dealer and the other was a pimp. Maybe those girls were in for big disappointment, even danger. Her father twisted his hands, helpless and silent in the evenings. Her mother clanked the dishes into the sink, banged the washers shut, punched the buttons with her fists, helpless too.

It was true. Her father was a fool for love, as far as Gracie could tell. Her mother slapped at his hands when he came up behind her at the chopping board to kiss her hair. Pretty brave, considering that knife. When her mother tried to walk behind him in the street, he stopped and tried to take her hand. Gracie and her mother were always nearly missing buses because she'd say, "Go on, Mr. Song. We're coming," and they'd stay behind as she cleaned out her purse or took forever with her coat, just to have it the way she had learned it, her husband a few paces ahead, women behind. Maybe the girls would never have gotten away if he'd been firmer about marriage, stricter about love.

Where her parents were from, shamans could chase out the demon spirits from dogs, cows, rooms, people. Maybe her father had had the fool chased out of him, because when Thursday came around, he sat in the good chair with the Bible open on his knees, and Gracie sat beside him, waiting. Life was going to go on without her sisters. Her life. Gracie watched her father for lingering signs of foolishness. Above the donated piano, the cuckoo in the clock popped out seven times. As always, her father looked up with a satisfied air. He loved that bird. Her mother believed there was a spirit in the wooden box. The spirit was saying it was time.

Austin was free in the streets with that gang of Chinese boys. She waited for her cigarette and his stories. Right now, he might be breaking into the high school, popping open the Coca-Cola machine, busting up some lockers. There weren't any Jap boys left to beat up on, and if there were, they might have gotten beat up themselves. Gracie sat with her hands clasped at her knees, worrying about him, admiring him a little.

First came the tap-tap of the missionary ladies from the United Methodist Church, their hats looking like squat bird's nests through the crushed ice window. They seemed to have taken such pains with their dresses and hats and shoes for their Thursday visits that Gracie couldn't think how they had ever lasted in the mountain villages of Pyongyang province. She had never been there herself, or been to mountains at all, but she knew there were tigers in Pyongyang.

Her father rose and assumed his visitors smile. "Everyone will be too polite to mention the girls, Gracie," he told her. That was the only thing at all he said about them to her.

The ladies stepped in, chins pecking. One bore a frosted cake, the other thrust forward a box of canned goods. American apologies. As though the girls had died, Gracie thought. Her father stiffened but kept his smile.

"We think it's wonderful about the war," the cake lady began.

"Praise be to God that we've stopped the Japanese," the Spam lady went on. They looked at one another.

"The Japanese Japanese," said the second. She paused. "And we are so sorry about your country, Mr. Song."

"But this is your country now," tried the first.

Her father eased them onto more conversational subjects. They smiled, heads tilted, as Gracie pressed out "Greensleeves," "Colonial Days," "Jesus, We Greet Thee," on the piano. And at half past the hour, they were up and on their way out, accepting jars of kimchi from her mother with wrinkle-nosed smiles.

The barbershop customers did not come by. Mr. Woo from the bakery and Mr. and Mrs. Lim from the Chop Suey restaurant stayed away. All the Chinese and Koreans knew about saving face, including the chong gaks, who knew better, surely, but arrived like clockwork anyway, a black blur and a white blur at the window. They always shuffled their feet elaborately on the doorstep before knocking, and her father used to say, "That's very Korean," to Sung Sook and Sung Ok, who didn't bother to fluff their hair or straighten their blouses for the visitors. They used to moan, "Here come the old goats. Failure One and Failure Two." Her father only shushed them, saying, "Respect, daughters, respect." Gracie saw that he could have done better than that if he really expected the girls to marry these men, but after all, the girls were right. Probably her father could see that. They were failures. No families, even at their age. Little money, odd jobs, wasted lives. A week before, they had been only a couple of nuisances who brought her sticks of Beechnut gum and seemed never to fathom her sisters' hostility. They were that stupid, and now they were back because one Korean girl was as good as any other.

Gracie could actually tolerate Mr. Han. He had been clean and trim in his black suit, pressed shirt, and straight tie every Thursday evening since her sisters had turned sixteen. He was a tall, hesitant man with most of his hair, surprisingly good teeth, and little wire glasses so tight over his nose that the lenses steamed up when he was nervous. Everyone knew he had preferred Sung Ok, whose kindest remark to him ever was that he looked exactly like the Chinese servant in a Hollywood movie she'd recently seen. He always perched on the edge of the piano bench as though he didn't mean to stay long, and he mopped his brow when Sung Ok glared at him. But he never pulled Gracie onto his lap to kiss her and pat her, and he never, as the girls called it, licked with his eyes.

He left that to Mr. Kim. Mr. Kim in the same white suit, white shirt, white tie, and white shoes that had never really been white but always the color of pale urine. His teeth were brown from too much tea and sugar and opium. This wasn't her hateful imagination. She had washed his shirts ever since she'd started working. She knew the armpit stains that spread like an infection when she tried to soak them. The hairs and smudges of ash and something like pus in his sheets. She could smell his laundry even before she saw the ticket. His breath stank, too, like herring.

Mr. Kim pretended to find everything amusing. "It's been too warm hasn't it, Mr. Song?" he chuckled. "I'm afraid our friend Mr. Han is almost done in by this heat."

"Yes," said her father. "Let me get you some iced tea." He called in the direction of the kitchen. "Mrs. Song!"

Mr. Kim chuckled again at his companion. "Maybe his heart is suffering," he said to his hosts. "Nearly sixty, you know. Poor soul. He's got a few years on me, anyway, haven't you, old man?"

Mr. Han lowered himself on the piano bench. "Yes, it's been too warm, too much for me."

His companion laughed like one above that kind of weakness. Then he said, "And how is Miss Song? She's looking very well. She seems to be growing."

Gracie hunched her shoulders, looking anywhere but at him.

"Yes, she's growing," her father answered carefully. "She's still a child." The men smiled at each other with a lot of teeth showing, but their eyes were watchful. "Of course, she must be a little lonesome nowadays," ventured Mr. Kim. Her father did not smile. To rescue the situation, Mr. Kim grinned, slapped his knee, and elbowed Mr. Han. Mr. Han merely squinted as if in some sort of pain.

If Mr. Kim hadn't been in America even longer than her father had, with nothing to show for it but a rented room above the barbershop, then he might have been able to say, "What about this one, Mr. Song? Are you planning to let her get away too?" But if he'd had something to show for his twenty or fifty years in America, he wouldn't be sitting in her father's house and she wouldn't be waiting to be his bride.

Then from the piano bench: "Lonesome, Miss Song?" Everybody looked. Mr. Han blinked, startled at the attention. He quietly repeated,

"Have you, too, been lonesome?" Gracie looked down at her hands. Her father was supposed to answer, let him answer. At that moment, her mother entered, head bowed over the tea tray. Gracie could hear the spirit working in the cuckoo clock.

Her father had told her once that he'd picked cotton and grapes with the Mexicans in Salinas Valley, and it got so hot you could fry meat on the railroad ties. But that was nothing compared to the sticky summers in Pyongyang where the stench of human manure brought the bile to your throat. That was why he loved Oakland, he said, where the ocean breeze cleaned you out. It reminded him of his childhood visits to Pusan Harbor, when he'd traveled to visit his father who had been forced into the service of the Japanese. And it reminded him of the day he sailed back from America for his bride.

Bright days, fresh wind. Gracie imagined the women who had waited for the husbands who had never returned. Those women lived in fear, her mother had said. They were no good to marry if the men didn't come back, or if they did return but had no property, they had no legal status in America and no prospects back home. Plenty of the women did away with themselves, or their families sold them as concubines. "You think I'm lying?" she told Gracie. "I waited ten years for him. People didn't believe the letters he sent after a while. My family started talking about what to do with me, because I had other sisters waiting to marry, only I was the oldest and they had to get rid of me first!"

Gracie imagined those women, their hands tucked neatly in their bright sleeves, their smooth hair and ancient faces looking out over the water from high rooms. And she thought of Mr. Han gazing from his window out over the alley and between skyscrapers and telephone poles to his glimpse of the San Francisco Bay. Where he was, the sky was black, starless in the city. Where she was, the sun rose, a brisk, hopeful morning.

On a morning like that, Gracie took the sheets and laundry across the street and up to the rented rooms. Usually the chong gaks had coffee and a bun at the bakery and then strolled around the lake, but Gracie always knocked and set the boxes down. Today, Mr. Han's door inched open under her knuckles. The breeze in the bright room, the sterile light of morning in there, the cord rattling at the blinds. Something invisible crept out from the slit in the door and was with her in the hall.

"Mr. Han? Just your laundry, Mr. Han." Spirits of memory—she and Austin climbing onto his knees, reaching into his pockets for malted milk balls or sticks of gum. "Where are your children?" they'd asked. "Where is your stove? Where is your sink? Where is your mirror?" Mr. Han had always smiled, as though he were only hiding the things they named, could make them appear whenever he wanted.

She pushed the door all the way open, and the spirits of memory mingled with the spirits of longing and desire. The bulb of the bare ceiling light buzzed mightily, as though it had been given permission to splurge. Mr. Han lay half-on, half-off the bed, one shoe pressed firmly, convincingly, to the floor. His spectacles dangled from the metal bed frame. That was where his head was, pressed against the bars. His eyes were rolled back toward the square of sky in the window, huge and amazed. And at his throat, a stripe of beaded red, the thin lips of flesh puckering slightly, like the edges of a rose.

Spirits scuttered along the walls, swirled upward, twisting in their airy, familiar paths. They pressed against the ceiling. They watched her in the corner. His spirit was near, Gracie felt. In the white field of his pillow. Or in the curtains that puffed and lifted at the sill like a girl's skirt in the wind.

Gracie squatted and peered under the bed. The gleam there was a thing she had known all of her life, a razor from the barbershop. Clean, almost no blood, like his throat. She knew it was loss of air, not loss of blood, that did it. She knew because she'd heard about it before. Two or three of the neighborhood Japs had done the same, when they found that everything they thought they owned they no longer had a right to. They'd had three days to sell what they could and go. She didn't know where. She only knew that her father had been able to buy the barbershop and the bathhouse because of it.

Wind swelled in the hall, with the spirits of car horns, telephone wires, shop signs, traffic lights, and a siren, not for him. The spirits were present at the new death—curious, laughing, implacable. They sucked the door shut, which gave Gracie a start. "Leaving now," she announced. "Mr. Han," she whispered to the chong gak. Then she remembered he'd become part of something else, something weightless, invisible, near. She said it louder. "Mr. Han. I'm sorry for you, Mr. Han."

Mr. Kim ate with the Songs that afternoon, after the ambulances had gone, and again in the evening. His fingers trembled. He lowered his head to the rice, unable to lift it to his mouth, scraping feebly with his chopsticks. Of Mr. Han's death, he had one thing to say that he couldn't stop saying: "I walked alone this morning. Why did I decide to walk alone, of all mornings?"

Mrs. Song muttered guesses about what to do next, not about the body itself or the police inquiry or who was responsible for his room and his things, but about how best to give peace to the spirit of the chong gak, who might otherwise torment the rest of their days. He didn't have a family of his own to torment. She'd prepared a plate of meat and rice and kimchi, saying, "Where do I put this?"

Jealous that Gracie had found the body and he hadn't, Austin offered, "How 'bout on the sill? Then he can float by whenever he likes. Or in his room? I'll stay in there all night and watch for him." Then he patted his stomach. "Or how 'bout right here?"

"Damn," her mother went on. "I wish now I'd paid more attention to the shamans. But we stayed away from those women unless we needed them. My family was afraid I'd get the call because I was sickly and talked in my sleep, and we have particularly restless ancestors. But I didn't have it in me. Was it food every day for a month or every month for a year? What a mystery. Now we'll have spirits 'til we all die."

"Girls shouldn't be shamans, anyway," Austin announced. "Imagine Gracie chasing spirits away."

Asshole, Gracie mouthed. Austin flipped her off. None of the adults understood the sign.

"You don't chase them, honey," Gracie's mother said to her. "You feed them and pay them and talk to them."

"Tell him," Gracie answered. "He's the one who brought it up."

"Not real money, of course. Just paper money," added her mother.

"Feed everyone who's here first," Austin suggested. Gracie flipped him off in return.

"What's that you're doing with your fingers, Gracie?" he shot back. She put her finger to her lips and pointed at her father. His eyes were closed. He kept them that way, head bowed, lips moving.

"Fine," her mother announced. "We can do Christian, Mr. Song. It's simpler, as far as I'm concerned."

Mr. Kim lifted his head from his rice bowl, looking very old.

Her mother eyed him sternly. "Cheaper too."

That night Gracie lay in her bed by the open window. Where was his spirit now? In heaven, at God's side? Or restlessly feeding on bulgogi and turnips in his room? Or somewhere else entirely or nowhere at all? Please God or Thousand Spirits, she prayed. Let me marry for love. Please say I'm not waiting for Mr. Kim. It's fine with me if I never marry and stay a chunyo forever.

They held a small service at the Korean United Methodist Church. Her father stood up and said a few words about the hard life of a chong gak in America, the loneliness of these men, the difficulties for Oriental immigrants, especially since the passing of the most recent exclusion laws. Gracie felt proud of her father, though she found him less convincing about heaven in Mr. Han's case. No one even knew for certain whether Mr. Han had ever converted.

Mr. Kim sat in white beside Gracie. "Thy kingdom come," he murmured. "Thy will be done." And he reached out and took her hand, looking straight ahead to her father. His hand was moist. She could smell him.

"And forgive us our trespasses," she prayed.

38

"As we forgive those who trespass against us," he continued, squeezing her with the surety of possession, though her fingers slipped in his palm.

Gracie never got to the "amen." Instead, she leaned into his side, tilted her face to his cheek, and brought her lips to his ear. "Let go of me, you dirty old bastard," she whispered. Then she snatched her hand back and kept her head bowed, trembling. She would pray for his death if she had to. From the corner of her eye, she could see Mr. Kim's offended hand held open on his knee. Sweat glistened in the creases of his palm. She would never be able to look into his eyes again. For a moment, pity and disgust swept through her. Then, as the congregation stood, she said her own prayer. It went, please oh please oh please.

Austin stuck his head in the laundry room. "Hey, you! Mrs. Kim!" Gracie flung a folded pillowcase at him.

"Whew. Step out of that hellhole for a minute. I've got something to show you." He slid a cigarette from behind his ear. They went out the alley-side steps and shared it by the trash bin. "The day they give you away, I'll have this right under your window, see? I'll even stuff it with newspapers so you'll land easy."

"Nowhere to run," Gracie told him. It was the name of a movie they'd seen.

"Isn't Hollywood someplace? Isn't Mexico someplace?"

Gracie laughed out loud. "You coming?"

"Course I am. Mama's spirit crap is getting on my nerves."

Gracie shrugged. "You're too little to run away. Why should I need help from someone as little as you?"

Austin stood on tiptoe and sneered into her face. "Because," he grinned and exhaled smoke through his nose and the sides of his mouth. "I'm a boy."

"Dragon-breath," she called him.

"Come on, Mrs. Kim. This way." They scrambled up the steps, took the staircase to the hall, then stepped through the door that led down again to the ground floor through an unlit passage to the old opium den.

It was nothing but a storage room for old washers now, a hot box with a ceiling two stories above them. It baked, winter or summer, because it shared a wall with the boiler.

They'd hid there when they were little, playing hide-and-seek or creating stories about the opium dealers and the man who was supposed to have hung himself in there. They could never figure out where he might have hung himself from since the ceiling was so high and the walls so bare. They looked up in awe. Once, Austin thought he'd be clever, and he shut himself in the dryer. Gracie couldn't find him for the longest time, but when she came back for a second look, the round window was steamed up and he wasn't making any noise. She pulled him out. He was grinning, eyes vacant. "You stupid dumb stupid stupid kid."

Austin felt for the bulb on the wall and yanked on the chain. Nowadays the old dryer was, somehow, on its side. Two busted washers and a cane chair hovered nearby. The air felt secret, heavy with dust and heat. Gracie moved her fingers along the walls searching for loose bricks, pulled one out, felt around inside like they used to do, looking for stray nuggets or anything else that might have been hidden and forgotten by the Chinese who had once lived there.

Austin got on his hands and knees. "Lookit." He eased out a brick that was flush with the floor. "Lookit," he said again.

Gracie crouched. He crawled back to make way for her, then pushed her head down. "Down there, in the basement."

She saw dim, natural light, blackened redwood, steam stained. The bathhouse. "So what? I clean 'em every day of my life."

"Just wait," he told her.

The white blade of a man's back rose into view. Austin's hand was a spider up and down her side. "See him, Mrs. Kim? Bet you can't wait."

The back lowered, rose, lowered again, unevenly, painfully. She saw hair slicked back in seaweed streaks, tea-colored splotches on his back, the skin damp and speckled like the belly of a fish. Austin's hand was a spider again at her neck. Gracie slapped at him, crouched, looked again. "What the hell's he doing? Rocking himself?"

Austin only giggled nervously.

The eyes of Mr. Kim stared toward the thousand spirits, his mouth hung open. Then those eyes rolled back in his head, pupilless, white, and still.

"God, is he dying?" Gracie asked. If she moved a muscle, she would burst. "Is he dying?" she asked again. "Don't touch me," she told her brother, who was impatient with spidery hands.

Austin rolled his eyes. "That's all we need around here. No, he's not dying, stupid. Unless he dies every day." Life in a dim bathhouse, Gracie thought. Deaths in bright rooms.

A door slammed hard on the other side of the wall. Her mother cursed, called her name. Austin giggled and did the stroking motion at his crotch, then Gracie scrambled to her knees and pulled him up with her. He grabbed for the chain on the bulb. Dark. "Don't scream," he giggled.

"Gracie! Damn you!" her mother called.

Then his hands flew to her, one at her shoulder, the other, oily and sweet, cupping her open mouth.

A letter arrived the next Thursday. Sung Sook had used her head and addressed it to the barbershop. Her father brought it up to her in the evening. Gracie was at her window, leaning out, watching the sky begin to gather color. "For Miss Gracie Song," he read. "Care of Mr. Sin Tae Song." There was no return address. The paper smelled faintly like roses.

With his eyes, her father pleaded for news of them. He said, "You look like you're waiting for someone."

She shrugged. "It's Thursday." She wanted him to leave her alone until it was time to go downstairs and sit with Mr. Kim. Instead, he came to the window and looked out with her. "Where's your brother?"

She shrugged.

Her father smiled. Then he told her, "Mr. Kim has given me money, Gracie. A lot of money."

She drew herself up. She couldn't look at him. "What money?"

"It's for a ticket, Gracie. He wants me to purchase him a ticket to Pusan and arrange some papers for him."

She sucked in her breath. "Alone?"

"Alone."

She smiled out at the street but asked again, "What money?"

Her father answered, "He will be happy to have a chance to tell you goodbye." And he left her at the window. His money, she knew. Her father's. She kept still at the window. With her eyes closed, she saw farther than she had ever seen. "Did you hear that?" she said out loud, in case any spirits, celestial or domestic, were listening. Then she carefully opened her letter. There was a piece of pale, gauzy paper, and a couple of photographs—a good thing, since the girls had stolen a bunch of family snapshots when they left.

> Dear Gracie,
>
> I hope they let you see this. You're going to be an auntie now. Sung Ok's the lucky one, but me and El are really trying. For a baby, you know. That's El in his rookie uniform and I'm in my wedding dress. We're at the Forbidden City, Joo's club in San Francisco. Louie, that's Sung Ok's husband, paid for everyone's drinks on our wedding night. The other picture is of Louie and Sung Ok at Newport Beach. Isn't he handsome? Like El. We all live near the beach, ten minutes by freeway.
>
> You'd love it here, but I guess you'd love it anywhere but Oakland. How are the old creeps, anyway? Maybe they'll die before Mom and Dad give you away, ha-ha.
>
> Be good. Don't worry. We're going to figure something out. El says you can stay with us. Sung Ok sends her love. I do, too.

The letter fluttered in her hand in the window. She pulled open the drawer at her bedside table, folded the paper neatly back in its creases, and set it inside. Then she took out the only thing her sisters had left behind, the sugar-sprinkled, silver-lettered, instant-ceremony marriage advertisement. Gracie breathed in deeply, as her sister had done with the hope of her new life—as, perhaps, Mr. Han had done with the hope of his release. Somewhere near, Austin laughed out loud in the street. Her mother banged dinner into the oven. Her father waited below, his Bible open on his knees, to greet the missionary ladies, to say goodbye to Mr. Kim. Below, a white, slow figure stepped from a door and headed across the street. Again, she breathed in, slowly. And what she took in was her own. Not everything had a name.

# White Fate, 1959

Not that he would ever allow himself to show it, and not that it would have made much difference in her upbringing if he had shown it, but the youngest of his three girls, Gracie, was Mr. Song's favorite. All morning, he had been dialing Gracie's number from the barbershop. She was probably out shopping with her sister Sung Sook and her baby niece, but he cleared his throat and kept practicing the right tone of hello, in case she answered. It had been a whole month since she had breezed into the front door with her new hairstyle, her new smile, and then stormed out again before she'd been home an hour, slamming the door shut behind her. A whole month since the argument with her mother and still not so much as a telephone call.

Song kept himself occupied between attempts to reach her on the phone. He swept up the black clippings from young Jasper Woo's haircut, and the steel colored clippings of Jasper's father, Elmer Woo. "Still have that daughter to marry off, Song?" Old Woo always asked when he came in. "What did you tell me she was studying? Was it science, hmm? Or mathematics?" Song just faked a contented hum by way of response. And then Old Woo had added—bit off the word and threw it at him—"Your daughter is ambitious, Mr. Song." Song never gave Old Woo the satisfaction of responding to his suggestion that his daughter was too studious, too masculine to make a good wife. What did Woo know about having daughters? Song put the linens in the hamper, rinsed the combs in the antiseptic, and went back to the telephone to try again. Gracie, he practiced. Your mother and I would like the chance to talk with you about this . . . young man.

That young Jasper Woo had turned out all right so far, thought Song. He was a former schoolmate of Gracie's who had taken over Woo's Bakery just like everyone had expected he would, married the tall, quiet Chinese girl his parents had found for him, and settled down and had two children. The boy was good to the old man, brought the grandchildren round on Sundays, helped his mother on with her coat. No denying it, Old Woo had done a good job with his boy. Every morning and every evening, if it wasn't raining and the fog wasn't too thick, Old Woo strolled around Merritt Lake, his hands clasped behind his back, his lips pursed contentedly like a Buddha's with a look that said, "My work in life is finally done."

He set the receiver back down and stared at the month of September on the calendar from Chong's Fish Market. A Chinese beauty in a fierce shade of yellow smiled knowingly from behind an embroidered fan. It was not without some satisfaction that Song polished the chrome in his barber chair and oiled the seat leather, wiped the glass door with the bell that jangled when someone entered and the windows until they were completely free of streaks. He liked order. He liked order's sameness. But this morning he felt a restlessness that belied the tidy appearance of his shop.

Why hadn't either of his elder daughters been interested in a boy like Jasper Woo? And why hadn't Gracie? Instead, the older girls had eloped in the very same week, one of them with a Negro and the other with a Chinese who crooned the night away at the Oriental clubs in L.A. At first it appeared his wife, Changmi, would never recover from her anger and shock but along came a grandson, plump as a steamed pork bun; and then a black-eyed granddaughter with skin the color of richly steeped tea.

They weren't the Korean babies Changmi had wanted her daughters to have, but at least everyone was on speaking terms again.

Although he did not express this opinion to anyone, least of all to Changmi, Song could not entirely blame his daughters for their disobedience, caught as they had been between the failure of an expensive matchmaker to find a suitable Korean boy for either of them and the American custom of letting passion decide your fate. Back home, the family would have been disgraced beyond repair at the loss of two daughters to an uncertain future. Gracie would have had no chance of marriage after that. But this was not Korea, and far from being out of the question, Gracie's marriage now seemed imminent.

Five years earlier, when she had been just out of high school, she had come in and sat before him on the footrest in front of his chair. Her deep blue dress was sprinkled with white dots of various sizes, and her shoulders shone like little moons. "I wanted to ask you first," she began. "If there's no chance you'll say yes, then there's no use bringing it up with Ma." She cleared her throat. "I want to . . . I'm going to college."

Song answered simply, "You're a girl, Gracie."

She bit her lip and looked toward the back laundry. "I'm not asking for your permission, Daddy, I'm asking for your help." Her chin trembled with determination. In the end, he had given his consent despite Changmi's protests, convincing her that it would be better to send Gracie to college themselves than have it be known that yet another daughter had disobeyed their wishes. Privately, Song hoped that Gracie's education would buy them all some time before the question of marriage was revisited in the Song household. Now his straight-backed, clear-eyed daughter was only one semester away from her university degree.

Song's gaze wandered the street outside the barbershop as he listened to the line ring. It was a bright and breezy morning, the kind of morning when his heart always lifted with a little a chirp of abandon, filling him with the brisk promise that some of the things he had always longed for could still be his. If he wanted to, for instance, he could lock up the shop, cross the street to the laundry, fetch his wife who would be pinning shirts about now, and take her out on the lake in one of those little green row-boats. He smiled to himself. The truth was he wasn't that kind of man.

He heard ringing, then a click. "Hello?"

Song's heart pounded. "Gracie?"

It was his daughter Sung Sook. Gracie was studying at the library, she told him. She reported that Gracie missed them both and would visit as soon as she finished her last exam. A moment of resentment lit Song's insides. It was Changmi who had announced that she would never step foot into Sung Sook's place while they housed that rebellious college daughter of hers, Changmi who was keeping everybody apart.

During her first couple of years at the university, Gracie had come home on weekends to fold laundry, clean out the baths, and sweep the barbershop. Slowly, it became every other weekend. Then by the time Gracie was a junior, it was difficult to adjust to her absence from home, because the Gracie that visited every other weekend kept changing in subtle ways. One day, there was something more confident in the way she held her shoulders, in the lift of her chin. Slim-fitting pants and pearl-buttoned sweaters replaced her handmade dresses and neatly starched collars. The telephone was always for her, and she answered with a special hello that Song had never heard her use with anyone else, a private hello, as though other people listening were not even present.

And then a month ago, a dozen white roses had been delivered to their door. Gracie had breezed in to help in the laundry, and when she kissed her father hello, a sweet scent broke softly open all around him. She stood in the kitchen with her mother, wrapping Sunday dinner's mandoo dumplings. At her lips was a small, secret smile.

"This *miguk* not realize white color means death for Oriental people!" Changmi complained to Gracie in dangerously pitched English. She spoke English when she wanted to get Song's attention. "What man do this sending white roses?"

"Of course I want you to meet him, Ma. His name is Wayne. Wayne doesn't care what white means to Oriental people."

"What, you ashamed being Oriental girl?" she shot back. "Let me tell you something," and she poked Gracie in the arm like she was testing the ripeness of a melon. "You. Oriental. Girl," she said. "You Chinese. You Japanese. You Siamese to this boy! Why he want to marry you?"

"Ma!"

"Why he don't like American girl?"

"Stop it, Ma. I am an American girl."

Song's teeth came together. The women's voices began again, low, but churning underneath, like the Beethoven pieces Gracie played on the piano that began solemnly and then crescendoed with little warning into a violent outburst. Song braced himself behind the *Oakland Tribune*, but in place of shouting, came a sound he had not expected. No broken glass, no spilled water, no tears. Only the thwack of twelve roses smacked against the wall by their stems, then a woman's high gasp, and white petals fluttering.

Gracie shot out of the kitchen, her handbag over one arm, a fist of bedraggled stems in the other. She slammed the door so hard that the old cuckoo clock donated to the Songs in their first year in Oakland by the Presbyterian Women's Relief Society sounded above the piano. "Kook," it yodeled, half in, half out of its little door.

Silence limped through the house for a few weary minutes. Finally, his wife came out, whipping at the back of his chair with her feather duster. "I hope you're happy, my husband. Ha! Sending her off to college!"

Song sat back down on the sofa, crossed his legs, and picked up his newspaper. "A white wedding," he said as the feather duster went off to attack the coat tree in the hall. "That's what they call it in America." What else would you call it if your daughter was planning to marry a White man?

Now Song hung up the telephone and sat down with a sigh at the little corner table in the shop where he counted receipts or wrote his Sunday school lessons between customers. How quickly it seemed his children had assumed this life of skyscrapers and cars with houses built right into them and burgers with thick slabs of cheese that shined. It was as though their fate had simply greeted them at the door. He had been a young man when he first sailed out of Pusan harbor only months before the long years of the occupation. If he was going to speak a new language, let it be English, he'd told himself, not Japanese. It wasn't until his hair began to gray and he was already exhausted that he had earned enough to bring his wife back to start a family.

As a girl, Gracie had worn a little blue pea coat that had been her sister's. It was an old but sturdy little coat and so becoming on her. They had had a tradition, Song and his youngest daughter. Every Sunday afternoon after dinner at the Korean Methodist Church, she would enter the shop and head straight to the cash register and ping it open. Out popped the drawer, and she would reach her fingers in and pull out two dimes for a ticket each to go to the Lux Theater. This was his cue to take off his white barber's jacket, hang it on its hook, and put on his coat and hat. Then the two stepped down the street, paid their dime each, and went in to watch the news of the war, and then the cartoons, and then Bette Davis or Frank Sinatra or Ingrid Bergman or Spencer Tracy, all the greats. He would slip his hand into his pocket and pull out a piece of taffy or a licorice drop, and Gracie would take each piece of candy one by one as though she had been brought to Earth to relish a piece of candy perfectly and completely. She was so sure of her toffee, her caramel, her peppermint, sitting there by his side in that strangely lit dark with the hushed and solemn carpet and the brocade covered walls, so sure that she never even had to look at him or at his proffered hand to know that candy was coming. And if the candy did run out when the picture wasn't over, she would eventually reach over and hold his hand and sometimes lean her head on his shoulder. Once or twice this way she even fell asleep.

Song opened his eyes, realizing that he had been dozing. He looked over the top of his glasses at the figure of a very large man filling up the doorway. The man had a good smile—a proper kind of smile—and improbably red hair. His handshake was so vigorous you had to admire his energy. "I'm Wayne Teller," he announced. Song knew who he was. He freed his hand from Wayne Teller's enthusiastic grasp, and because he did not know what next to do, he gestured toward one of the barber chairs. "Please," he summoned him, hoping to sound commanding.

As soon as the man settled in, Song whisked an apron around his neck and pumped the chair down with his foot. He had a reputation with some of the sailors for giving a good haircut, cheap, so he knew Caucasian hair. This Caucasian had freckles even on his ears and smelled of a tangy aftershave. He seemed to squint from sheer happiness while Song clipped above his ears, whacked away at the top. Song felt a little like a fly buzzing around an elephant. He straightened himself and pulled his own broad shoulders back. "Soooo. You work?" Song inquired conversationally.

Wayne's eyes slid in the direction of the clippers. He cleared his throat. "I'm studying city planning, sir."

"Yes?" Song replied. He combed. He clipped. He shaved the back of the man's neck and whisked away the stray hairs with his feather brush.

"Sir?"

"Yes?"

His hand rose when Song came at him with the Brillcreme. "Just—just a touch, sir." With an ill sense of timing in Song's opinion, Wayne looked directly at the reflection of his future father-in-law in the mirror and revealed, "Your daughter, Grace, and I are engaged, sir. We want to marry." Song stopped and looked at the top of Wayne's head. His scalp had his face's ruddy glow. "Yes?"

Wayne cleared his throat and half turned in his chair. "This is Song's Barbershop, right? Aren't you Mr. Song?"

"Yes," Song replied to the top of Wayne's head. Wayne hunched a little and tried again. "Sir, we intend to marry." He paused. "With your consent."

Song understood perfectly well what Wayne was trying to tell him but faking limited English might buy him some time. The less he said to the young man, the better he could watch him.

"I am a Methodist, sir," Wayne began again, rather carefully. "Grace told me I should be sure to tell you that." Song gave this some thought. No doubt the couple would have an easier time of it if they shared their faith. A White man and a yellow girl were going to need it.

"And," continued Wayne, "there is the matter of Mrs. Song's approval." Gracie had briefed him well. "So I would just like to say that I'll take good care of her. I'll take good care of your little girl."

Song could not remember when he had last seen someone so earnest. The men looked at one another in the mirror, both slightly amazed that they were about to become relations. Finally, Song closed his eyes. "Yes," he said. He tasted the word's little bite, its little promise.

For the rest of the day, the news sat inside him like a sprouted seed. He cut hair, lathered faces, trimmed sideburns, all the while moving lightly, carefully, as though part of him might spill. Once, he looked up at the bright flash of a streetcar and realized something was flowering inside him. Mrs. Chin lumbered past with her salmon and daikon radishes. She lifted the fish in greeting, the netted bag swaying from her arm. Song smiled, suddenly hopeful. It was true they knew nothing of Wayne Teller's family. But the young man had not expected his daughter to sneak out in the night with a stack of linens, half the family photographs, and a couple of jars of kimchi as her sisters had done. Wayne Teller had come to him; he loved Gracie.

Gracie would see, he would bring her mother round. Tomorrow, if all went well with Changmi, he would run out when he saw Mrs. Chin and say, "My daughter Gracie is getting married!" Then he could rely on Mrs. Chin to carry the news all the way down the street, to Jasper Woo who would be just getting back from delivering the teatime dim sum, who would tell McCoy, the *miguk* who hung out in Chinatown and picketed all the businesses that undercut the prices in White neighborhoods including Song's, who would tell Sampa, the old Negro bachelor who lived above the laundry who would shout out his congratulations from the second-story window down to the whole street.

But when Song pulled the key out of the shop door at 6:00 and double-checked the lock, he felt, quite unexpectedly, a stab of disappointment in himself. How was it that in all these years living and working right here on Winnette Boulevard he had never been the kind of person who would lock up at midday and go do something Changmi or Old Woo would have thought outlandish? That was Gracie's word for a certain kind of daring.

A blond American friend of hers had dropped out of college to marry a Moroccan prince. Russian astronauts had climbed aboard Sputnik to orbit the Earth. Out of this land, out of this world.

Once, as a boy, Song had been working the field alongside his father, when he decided to stand and stretch. He saw a gull sojourning inland, the white flash of the clay pots the women used during summer cooking, dried fish hung on a lattice of twigs. He stared so long these things began to shimmer around the edges. Then a *yangban* appeared, approaching slowly with his entourage, two servants on donkeys riding ahead and a young partner or son behind him on a steed. Song's father had told him about the yangbans, how sometimes they came around personally to collect taxes instead of sending their lackeys, and how the tax laws always changed when the yangbans had a daughter to marry off or wanted to add a new room to the house.

He had been quite unprepared for the magnificence of this nobleman in his wide-brimmed hat with the topknot made of gleaming horsehair, his quilted white coat, and lacquered button-up shoes. He stood and watched as the party moved past in a kind of shimmering stillness, made whiter and stiller by the backdrop of the mountains they moved toward. And then he watched his father watch the party, gazing after them with neither longing nor contempt. He realized now that even a self-important, overdecorated feudal lord was precious to his father, who would not live to see his country liberated from the Japanese. He saw the scene more simply now, its whiteness and stillness. Everyone, thought Song, is doomed to the present.

Squinting in the bathroom light, Song stood over the toilet patiently shaking himself off after urinating for the third time since he'd gone to bed. His bladder could not hold off like it used to. He had gone to bed before Changmi had finished in the laundry, his joints throbbing in the damp summer weather, and had been too distracted by pain to embark on the subject of Gracie's impending marriage. The next thing he knew he had been sitting up in bed, trying to remember his dream, but recalling only the sensation of feeling himself a child again, contented but untried.

When his eyes adjusted to the bathroom light, he noticed Changmi's bright satin bathrobe still shimmering on its hook on the back of the door. He shuffled out to the front room and lowered himself into his chair. Changmi was sitting up straight fully dressed on the sofa, her face as distant as a newly discovered planet. Something about the pastel terrycloth of her house slippers made Song lift himself carefully off the chair in which he had just sat down, kneel carefully first with his left leg and then with his right leg before her, and take her hand. "Changmi, please come to bed."

She would not look at him.

"The young man came to the shop today. They would like to have our consent to marry."

She shook her head. "It isn't for me to give my approval or not give my approval. It isn't my duty."

"But, Changmi, there is no other obstacle."

She sat in the dark and she would not look at him. She told him, "It isn't for me to say."

Song blinked at her, puzzled, then Changmi leaned to kiss him and placed a small something into his lap. He looked down for a long moment and then took up this thing she had given him, exquisitely soft and fragrant. White petals opened into his hands.

The next morning he rose very early, thinking that one remedy for his ailing joints might be more, rather than less, activity. Night had hardly begun to seep into dawn when he headed on foot down Ashland Avenue in the fog. The street was still so quiet he could hear the fog horns from the bay. Muted footsteps behind him, brisk but not urgent, seemed to be gaining. "Is that you, Song?" Old Woo called out when he had reached the park.

"I thought I would take some exercise," Song told his neighbor, noting that Woo's fists were pumping vigorously at his sides rather than clasped behind his back during his usual stroll. He was wearing white sneakers and a golf cap. "Yes, yes, yes," Woo replied. "My new American doctor say, 'If you want long life, you got to pick up the pace!'"

Song assumed the brisk pace of his companion beside him on the narrow footpath. He had to admit that Woo was looking very trim. "Is it true, Song, that your daughter is going to marry after all?" Woo inquired. "How do you Koreans call the White people? *Miguk*? Hmm?" Song gestured toward a park bench where he intended to sit and catch his breath. He sat. Woo bowed to him with a show of patronage. "Congratulations on your most happy good fortune, Song. May the obstacles to their happiness," Woo smiled indulgently, "be few."

Song sat watching a family of ducks huddled together in the fog, preening themselves and nipping at the loose back feathers. This morning, the news of Gracie's marriage seemed suddenly irrevocable. He sat forward, restless again. What if Wayne Teller did not make a suitable husband after all? What if there really was something odd, as Changmi suspected, about his wanting to be with an Oriental girl? A thought occurred to Song that made him stand quickly, scattering the family of ducks into the water. Then he turned his body, trembling like the dial on a compass, and headed toward home.

When he burst through his front door, he stood awkwardly in his own front room, his fingers twitching at his sides. But the next moment brought another sweep of courage, and he found himself marching through the kitchen, past the table set with the same chipped plates and the napkins snipped in two for economy's sake and the eggs gurgling in a pot on the stove. With a swift shove, the laundry room door flew open and Song stood before his wife, who held a freshly laundered sheet with her arms wide. Before she could give it that crisp snap, Song grabbed hold of the bottom corners and lifted them to see her quick look of surprise. Her hands came together, clutching the sheet at her chest, watching him more with expectancy than annoyance, which gave him hope. There in the laundry, with the pipes hissing heat and the scent of bleaching soap scrubbing the air, he studied the face of the woman who had consented to be his wife.

"Will you give them your consent?" he shouted over the spin cycle of twenty washers. He knew how he must look to her, sweaty and pleading.

He hoped that she was not going to ruin the moment, standing there staring at him with her mouth open, her eyebrows two exclamation points.

She merely shook her head, as though she pitied him. "You the one," she told him in English. "You the one need let go."

They did not speak again all day. In the evening, he ate his dinner in silence, the empty plate across from him gleaming in wordless accusation. Changmi was going to scrub sinks or empty lint trays or bleach sheets until midnight. He had tried to watch the news but trudged upstairs, his head muddied by thoughts of those U.S. soldiers that President Eisenhower had sent down to Arkansas to teach the White people that they must not keep those poor Negro children out of school. He pictured Gracie riding off with Wayne in a loaded-down station wagon, headed for a place like Arkansas for all he knew, where it was probably illegal for the two of them even to be seen together, much less live as husband and wife.

When Song had first come to California, he began working in the orange groves and vineyards and cotton fields of the Great Central Valley. He slept in bunkhouses and rode in trucks and ate at long tables under the trees with Filipinos, Chinese, Armenians, and Japanese, riding from Dinuba to Salinas, Gilroy to Coalinga, Reedley to Fresno. There were men he worked beside who had left their families, men who had lost them, men like him who were waiting for their families to begin. Missionaries came out to the fields. Because it meant clean used clothes and free doctors' checkups, he allowed himself to be converted although he had converted once before.

It was eight years before he had saved enough to marry and two more before he finally sailed home to claim the woman his auntie had found for him. Changmi. He remembered their first night together, his clumsy hands, scarred from years of work, and how he had felt himself going weak, weak in his groin, his skin sweating coldly, Changmi drifting from him in the ocean of their first bed. Her sturdy, trembling body. He had thought of how the breath could catch inside a woman if she didn't know the country of her own skin. How, if she were nothing but emptiness to herself down there, any touch would feel like a violation. So he had taken her hand and placed it on her body, making the first touch her touch. In the first new days, he had watched her, wanting to get to know her from afar too. She leaned out the window, her eyes half shut, her nostrils slightly flared, facing the horizon. He believed she would come to love him.

Pain woke him again, toward morning. Beside him, Changmi's breath was light and even, which calmed him. He felt, again, that he must move lest the pain overtake him. Not wanting to encounter Old Woo again on his morning jaunt, he started down MacArthur Boulevard. Already, delivery trucks were backing into alleys, fish wriggled atop the ice in buckets deposited on the sidewalk. Song did not make the mistake of trying to outpace his pain. He made it past the Polytechnic and the public library and all the new apartments going up on the east side of the expressway. When he got that far, he began to feel a bit looser in the limbs and decided he might as well continue on to Berkeley. He would pay a visit to Gracie. And while he was on his way over, he would think about some of the plans that he had never seen through to completion, like writing a sermon he had been invited to deliver at the Korean Methodist Church or starting up a Korean language school so that the young people would know where they came from.

He turned on to Telegraph Avenue and headed toward the university. Students riffled through the bargain boxes lined up in front of Cody's Bookstore or hovered around the kiosks that sold magazines and newspapers. Song noticed that many young women were now wearing their hair long and loose, like they were ready for bed. A young man in a raincoat stood outside a flower stall playing his flute. Song made his slow way through Sather Gate and across campus, past Campanelli Tower. On the square, a cluster of students listened to someone orating through a megaphone. The crowd alternately laughed or shouted something back to the speaker. Several in the crowd applauded or waved their placards. Song could not make out what the excitement was about, but people who were just wandering by kept drawing near.

He had seen it for himself, that White people had this pull. It wasn't just men like the orator or men like Wayne Teller. It was their belief in themselves. It was their things. Their moving pictures, their streetcars, their two-for-one sales, their big wooden radios that played the Mormon Tabernacle Choir at 9:00 a.m. every Sunday before church. It was their tea in little bags one-per-cup, their elevators, their shiny hubcaps. He felt it himself. He felt proud to be in the same country with ideas as good as these. How could a Korean language school compete with all of this?

Song continued past the commotion and then stopped, lifting his face toward what was now full sun. When he opened his eyes, he realized that he was not certain where he was. He knew that he had driven before on the street where he was standing, but on foot, he couldn't remember which direction would take him back to Oakland. He realized he was farther from home than he had ever been. It was not an entirely unpleasant sensation, but his practical side was beginning to make plans. You need to eat something and to drink something, his practical side explained, and you need to sit down. You might go into that coffeehouse where the young men sporting caps and sideburns are gathered smoking cigarettes and sipping from tiny cups and arguing. Or you might just as well go into the well-lit Chicken Pie Shop, where you will be certain to get food. So Song entered the Chicken Pie Shop, and his entire being responded to the warmth and the cleanliness and the doughy scent of the place. He was enjoying his hunger now, it made him feel alive. He would eat and eat and eat before he went home to Changmi.

Inside the restaurant, he spied an Oriental man in conversation with a young woman, her sleek hair tied back with a yellow ribbon. He saw that the young man was Jasper Woo, and the woman, a very pretty black-haired girl, was not his wife. Young Jasper's face was wrenched with sadness, utterly dejected. He looked as though he has been up all night. He looked so miserable he wasn't even bothering to blow his nose or wipe off his tears.

Jasper looked up from his coffee cup, and his eyes locked with Song's for just a second. Two things happened next. Song saw for certain that the young man was indeed Jasper, that it was Jasper with a woman who was not Chinese and not his wife hunched over a miserable cup of coffee in the Chicken Pie Shop, with a glistening rotisserie chicken twisting round and round just behind his back and some change on the table between them. And in the very next instant, Jasper turned his face to the wall, not in a gesture that shunned Song but in a gesture that submitted to his will. He had been found out. Song did not know the facts of the situation, nor did he need to know them. Jasper Woo knew that as well as he did. It was not the woman who mattered or the facts; he had lost face.

Song could not turn and walk back out without appearing merciless to his vulnerable young friend, so he continued to the end of the counter and deposited himself on a cushiony stool, saying very politely to the waitress that he would have a cup of coffee and a Danish but that he hadn't much time. He learned that he could have the coffee in a cup made of paper and take it with him. So he poured in his sugar and stirred it until it was quite dissolved and fixed the lid back onto the cup. Then he walked back out the way he had come, looking straight ahead, and let himself out into the street.

He found an out-of-the-way bench under a civic-looking aspen, brushed the pigeon droppings off with someone's old newspaper, and sat down so as to cause the gentlest disturbance to his joints and his muscles and his bones. He let his breath out slowly. Again, he lifted his face toward the sun. "Cast the net," his father used to remind him gently when they would sit together in the rowboat on summer afternoons. "Don't simply fling it." And Song would nod, squint into the blazing blue above them, and then fling the net with all his might. His father would shake his head at him, but Song didn't know any other way. Later, the boat would drift under the shade of the paulownia trees, where the cove was thick with mackerel. He could hear the wooden clonk as his father lifted the oars, algae stained and dripping, could taste the chewy, salty strips of fish his mother would hang out to dry. He squinted into the old, old sunlight, sweet ache of memory warming his bones.

A student whished past him on a bicycle with a transistor radio blaring at his ear. It was one of the very few times in many years that Song was not at his shop on a workday morning. The first time was the day he had learned of his father's death, by letter, months after the fact. Then the belief that he had sailed away with at the age of eighteen—that he was going back, that he was most certainly going back—quietly died in him in a day. The second time was on a Monday morning in that same year of his father's death, a few weeks after Gracie was born. It had been a day like this one, with a dauntless sun. He had asked Changmi to strap the baby to his chest the way women wore them. She had complained that he would drop the child and that it was improper for men to be wrapped with their babies anyway, but he had made her do it. Then he had climbed the steps that led from the second floor to the attic and from the attic onto the roof. Wind gushed straight at them when he lifted the trap door; he had to hang on to keep from toppling. Although he kept one arm around the baby, prudence required that he head straight back downstairs. But he had wanted to show his daughter the new bridge that was completed in the year that she was born, the bridge they called the Golden Gate.

Whitecaps scudded along the surface of the bay. Across the water rose the green coastal mountains of Marin with its hushed forests of ancient redwoods. He stayed up there just a minute or two and talked to his daughter in the serious way that people talk to infants when they are alone with them. He pointed across the water and told her about a place that he had once called home. Gracie's little eyes and nose peeked out from the tightly done wrap and blinked, he thought, comprehending. This tiny person! He could not begin to imagine her fate. But here, just for this moment, he was never going to let go of her, this child for whom the whole world was nothing but a tightly wrapped cloth and his beating heart and, above it all, this wild blue.

# Typesetting, 1964

The day I became Lotus Blossom to my employer, Alan Nicks, I was wearing a sleeveless maternity blouse in what now seems to me an exclamatory shade of pink. Tired of donning my husband's big shirts or the prissy, impractical maternity clothing of those days, I had purchased the bright fuchsia sateen with my first paycheck and taken it to my friend Sophie, who took in sewing for extra income. "Look at you," said Sophie, "ready to pop any minute and Wayne expects you to bring home the bacon." I shrugged. "Don't make it sleeveless. This is for work."

Alan Nicks liked to stroll the shop floor wearing his cocked beret and glance with a proprietary air over the shoulders of his girls. Sometimes he paused behind one of us, thoughtfully stroking the little point of his goatee. Punching keys takes real stamina. We five girls sat staring into our light tables for eight hours a day operating a type disk that spun, clattered, and stopped, one revolution per character. When I felt Nicks behind me for a longer than usual moment, I turned slightly to see him making strange postures on the other side of the glass. He dropped to his knees, snapping "photos" of me from various angles with an imaginary camera.

"Don't move!" he shouted. "That's perfect, peeking out at me like that. You need a little fan." The other girls snickered from their cubbies, all except Joan Banks. A blushing geisha, Nicks made mincing fanlike movements of his hand as two almost womanly mounds of flesh jiggled like a pair of pork chops under his wrinkled turtleneck. "Every Oriental beauty needs one," he suffused, hands stroking the airy waist and hips of the imaginary female form before him. "And what a delicious . . ."—he waved his hands around until he caught a word—"oxymoronic color is that pink you're wearing, at once emboldened and demure. Young woman," he continued, plunking a pointed finger onto my exclamation point key, "you are the reason men symbolize." CEA!SAR SALAD read the words on my light board, right in the middle of an hour's worth of text.

Mistakes had to be pasted over by hand.

Toward the end of my pregnancy, fluid pooled in my ankles and my back ached from hunching forward to see my light table. But a blanket folded over the hump in my belly muffled the type disk racket. I hummed lullabies. I ate protein—boiled eggs, canned salmon salad. Things were going to get much better once Wayne passed his bar exams and I could stay home with little Mitchell and the new baby.

❊ ❊ ❊

Early in our marriage, Wayne had taken a snapshot of me in his graduation cap studying with mock-seriousness my red-and-white-checkered *Better Homes and Gardens* cookbook. My heart actually pounded with enthusiasm at the idea that I would create for my family an everyday linens-and-chilled-salad-fork-at-dinner kind of life. Wayne had been driving a Wonder Bread route and contemplating his next professional move. Then came that afternoon in December when the country fell silent before the grainy image of Kennedy's benumbed widow and her two young children. Suddenly, the future looked much closer. Law school became the wagon to which Wayne hitched his star. Time to put my typing skills to work. Wayne couldn't study with Mitchell under foot all day, so we tried a crash course in potty training and enrolled him in preschool. He was just too little. One day when I picked him up after work, an exultant Mrs. Kloberdanz plucked his soiled underpants from the nail she had used to hang them on the wall for all the other children to see and said, "I'll bet he stops wetting his pants before the week is out." Also before the week was out, Mitchell stopped singing at the top of his lungs as I got him dressed in the morning, and he stopped looking people in the eye.

For my second child, Dr. Stabile planned to induce my labor on a scheduled date and time, like clockwork. This idea struck me as convenient for everyone except the baby. When I inquired about the possibility of having natural labor, I got a "Tsk tsk, Mrs. Teller, the next thing I know you're going to say you want to try breastfeeding again too, hmmm?"

Perhaps because Dr. Stabile had written me off as irrationally opposed to the advances of modern medical science, in walked a tiny, freckled woman with round spectacles and sandy colored hair in a long, loose braid down her back. "Mrs. Teller, meet Miss Standeford. She prefers to be called Isabella. Miss Standeford calls herself a midwife." He raised his eyebrows at her. "There is no need to be alarmed, however, as she is merely a nursing intern like all the rest of them." Then he left us alone so Isabella could take my vitals and draw blood.

She murmured, "You can do it without drugs, it's true, especially if this is your second. That trail's been blazed, as it were." She looked around and then spoke into my ear, "Now, in case I never see you again, let me give you one piece of advice: don't take it lying down."

"Don't take what lying down?"

"Childbirth." She breathed at me and smiled. "Two words, Mrs. Teller. Stand up."

❀ ❀ ❀

"Her cloudy hair is sweet with mist," Alan Nicks intoned one morning in lieu of hello. "Her jade-white shoulder is cold in the moon." When I blinked at him, he asked me, "Li Po or Tu Fu?"

"I don't even know what you're talking about, sir."

"Why won't you call me Alan? Joan calls me Alan. Cynthia and Patsy and Louise and Eileen call me Alan. And the answer, young lady, is Tu Fu, great poet of the Tzu Dynasty. I would think you would be familiar with his work, Lotus Blossom."

Joan Banks over in cubby five bit her lip hard. Here was a woman who sported what were arguably the first pairs of dangly, homemade bead-and-wire earrings in the entire city of San Francisco. She knew her dashikis from her daikon radishes long before either had become trendy.

TWO For ONE I typed. THIS WEEKEND ONLY AT THE SANDS! I'd toyed with the idea of asking Wayne if we could afford a little getaway like that for our upcoming anniversary. "Don't you parry, mademoiselle?" Nicks smiled broadly and struck a fencing pose.

I turned entirely from him, back to my work. "I'm no mademoiselle."

He clutched his heart, pierced, and then straightened. "Fair enough. But I thought you said you'd studied poetry in college."

"I studied English literature, sir."

"Alan!" he warned, finger unfurled.

"Wordsworth, Coleridge, the Brontes, George Eliot, and so forth."

"Tu Fu was altogether more of a romantic, wouldn't you agree?"

"Than William Wordsworth?" I squeaked, taking the bait.

"Than Li Po." He took a moment to savor this tiny triumph. "Was Li Po, then, a more accessible poet to the common reader? Yes, in fact," he conceded, his eyes scribbling up and down the pillow cushioning my belly. "But what is wrong with accessibility? Give me access! Poetry to the people!" he shouted, reassuming his guarde. His eyes narrowed. He stepped even closer. "You want a love poem to really kick it, don't you, Mrs. Teller?" From his back pocket he produced a slim volume, *Poetry of the Tzu*. The cover featured a drawing of the cold, white-shouldered girl of the Tu Fu poem gazing out over a moonlit landscape.

"I dropped out of college before I had a chance to complete the requirements for my degree," I told him.

Nicks left the book atop my Vari-Type screen as if it were any other work order. "A certain 'Lotus Blossom' has submitted some excellent Tzu-like verse to the *Fringe*. I believe she wishes to remain Anonymous." Then his breath, minty masking fetid, actually brushed my cheek. "There's too few of us in the world. I want to share my love of poetry with," and here he passed a glance across the room as though all others were pedestrian souls, "like-minded women."

Joan Banks eyed me with a viciousness that could have started a Volkswagen. She had once bragged that she'd met Kerouac at a party in Brooklyn. He had squinched her shoulder affectionately with his big hand, she told us, and shouted into her ear, "So how do you like teaching high school French?" To preserve the moment, rather than attempt to explain that she was merely a typist, she'd nodded. If a woman could be Beat or hip at all, Joan was that woman. Too bad the scene she wanted in on was a boys' club.

Patsy, one cubby over, handed me a stick of cinnamon gum. "You know you really should put your foot down," she advised. I was pasting over an entire line—The RENO! The GOLD RUSH! The SANDS! ALL FREE!—that I had inexplicably typed in italics. I shoved the stick of gum in my mouth, savoring the spicy distraction, and rested my eyes. Always, in negative imprint, a blackboard marred with white font. In my sleep, lettering scribbled the open field of my dreams.

❁   ❁   ❁

"You know what's happening, don't you?" Sophie said when I told her about Nicks and the Oriental fan. "You're giving off some sort of signal you're not aware of. It's probably the baby. You know, an excess of hormones or something."

"Well, I can't stop being pregnant. He can stop what he's doing." Sophie had a complete set of the new frosted pastel Tupperware. You just pressed in the middle and the thing sealed shut. Her white sandals clicked across her spotless linoleum as she tucked sliced cantaloupe and chicken salad back into her gleaming fridge. "Maybe he can stop, maybe he can't," she answered. "But don't you blame yourself for it."

Sophie caught my glance. "I don't blame myself." She was a friend of my heart—had been since grade school and always would be. Whenever such moments arose between us, we clung to the belief that our differences were really just some kind of conjugation of the same verb. We stepped across the impasse toward one another and went on as if nothing had happened. We had to. We had the same face.

She grabbed me up in a sisterly embrace, waking Mitchell. "Gosh, I wish so badly you didn't have to work," she confessed. "I wanted us to raise our babies together."

I reached for Mitchell's naptime bottle to stop his cries. "I thought we were raising our babies together." Mitchell wrestled himself off my lap and stepped off to find Louise and Mary Sue. Sophie nodded vigorously, her eyes teary from withholding judgments about me she would never share.

Sophie didn't know about the perfect moments. When Mitchell slept, I held him in my arms, breathing in the talcum-scented sweat of his scalp, the applesauce sweetness of his chin. I had attempted to nurse him those first days in the hospital, although I never let anyone see me try to do it. It hurt and nothing came out but a bit of fluid the color of earwax. Before I knew it Mitchell was hungrily sucking formula from his bottle and they were showing me how to bind up my breasts to stop the ache and catch the flow.

❀ ❀ ❀

For our fourth anniversary, Sophie and Dan took Mitchell for the night while we drove out to North Beach where you could get five courses for amazingly cheap, including Peking duck, at the Golden Dragon. Poets from City Lights bookstore, the famous Beatnik hangout where Ferlinghetti ruled the roost, were said to have written the fortunes in their fortune cookies. Wayne filched a couple of them before our meal. His cookie read: A man who never tires of explaining himself is a thief. "I hate it when they give sayings instead of actual fortunes," he said, still brooding about the B- on his quarter terms that had put him out of the running for some sort of law firm sponsorship.

Mine read: One inch of love is equal to one inch of ashes. "They're kind of unusual. Not what you'd expect in a cookie."

"Yours is sorta bitter. Love and ashes and all that."

I shrugged. "'One inch of love'?"

Wayne squinted at me suspiciously.

"Okay, what would be a fortune, darling?" I tried. "Not a saying? Not bitter?"

"Anything I want?"

"It's your fortune."

"That tonight will be, you know, great."

"A fortune can't be something that everybody already knows," I smiled. Then I recited from memory, "A gold toad gnaws the lock. Open it, burn the incense." For a flash, there was that little gleam in his eye that he'd carried for me in our college days when I recited sonnets across the blanket to him, sprawled in my capris and sandals out on the quad.

He poured us more tea.

"A tiger of jade pulls the rope. Draw from the well and escape."

"Where'd you get that? Sounds a little ominous."

"Risky, anyway. I think it's saying take your chance, seize your fate."

The waiter set a covered dish in front of Wayne, lifting the lid to fragrant steam. "Is that some new sort of poetry, then?"

"No, that's spring duck." I countered the glance he shot me with a playful smile. "Not new," I obliged. "Ancient. From the Tzu Dynasty."

"You wanna fok?" asked the waiter, jabbing his finger toward the egg foo young.

Wayne's chin lowered and came forward. "I beg your pardon?"

"Fok," he insisted, his hand stitching the air in an eating motion. "Or chopstick?"

Chastened into clarity, Wayne replied, "Chopstick, please. Make that two." The waiter darted off, shaking his head incredulously. We looked at one another and burst into laughter. "Not that I have anything against forking," he joked. "So," he tried again, "ancient poetry of the Shoe Dynasty? What happened to 'ol Wordsworth? 'Thou still unravished bride,' and all that?"

"That was Keats, dear. It's just a little book of Chinese poetry in translation that I picked up." And there lay the off-white truth between us that kept tilting and shading the mood.

At home, we exchanged gifts sitting cross-legged on the bed in our stocking feet. He stared at the contents of the box. "Grace, I do love you," he said. "Happy anniversary and all that. But what the hell is this?"

"It's a Wernacke compass," I answered. "The finest you could own." That show of blinking incredulity he could summon was going to serve him well in the courtroom one day. "Okay, so I bought it back when you were thinking about teaching geography." It was a sore subject. I had been against his getting a teaching certificate but had purchased the gift as a sort of consolation prize. "You can still own a really nice compass, can't you?" I peered at him. "You're truly angry with me?"

"Not at all, Grace. Why should I be insulted with a gift from my wife that says, 'Darling, you're terribly lost. This will help you find your way.'"

"And you tell me I read too much into things?" I screeched. "My poetry professor would have loved you, Wayne. It's not symbolic, it's just a goddamned compass."

He threw up his hands. "You're the one who said everything is symbolic, but thank you for the goddamned compass."

"You have to put it that way?"

"You just put it that way."

"In self-defense, Wayne."

"The compass. How's that?" He handed me the Macy's box.

"Wrapping's pretty."

He looked away; I would need to like this gift. Pale ballet pink shimmered between sheets of delicate tissue. I fingered a strap of slithery satin.

"Take it out," Wayne commanded. "You don't even know what it is."

A pink satin baby doll with spaghetti straps, a single pink rose clasp between the breasts and matching satin panties. "I've been waiting all day to see your little rosebuds poking through."

"It's not going to fit right now, Wayne. You know that."

"Come on. The top'll fit, barely," he grinned. "You can skip the underpants."

"Wayne, I'm too big for it. It'll have to wait until after the baby."

He turned me and began to unzip the back of my dress. "I don't want to wait until after the baby. I want you to be my little baby doll right now. My little China doll."

I wheeled back to face him. "What the hell's gotten into you?"

"Just cooooool it." He did a little swag and shuffle. "You can swing, can't you? You can kick it, baby."

"You've been falling asleep in front of late night again." He had been unimpressed with television in general until that day the entire nation sat down to watch the Kennedy funeral procession. Now it was on even during Mitchell's bedtime story. He had set up a card table in there, where we could take our meals if we wanted to dine with him.

"This ain't television, baby, this is the Thing, and I've got it." Once we went dancing downtown at Joo's old club, the Forbidden City. The band got a little crazy and some of the crowd let loose with moves that weren't so much dancing as shakes, jiggles, and twists. Wayne insisted on waltzing me that night, but now he let loose like the folks we'd seen. He scrambled to the hi-fi and put on a big band record with lots of thumpy bass and jaunty horns. He lifted out the baby doll top and jiggled it in the air. I did pirouettes around it and the mambo under it until we collapsed onto the bed, gasping with laughter. He reached behind me again, panting. "Come on." He tugged on the zipper. "Be my little China doll. What's it been, like two months?"

"It's been never. I've never been your little China doll."

"You know what I mean, Gracie."

I lay back, arms crossed behind my head like a kid looking up at the stars. "Your sister said to me before we married that I wasn't being fair to you. She said my Oriental novelty would wear off, and that it wasn't fair to our children to mix the races."

Wayne lay there blinking, finding other routes. "My dad's from another time. What about what your mother had to say about me?"

"My mother only wanted to know why you didn't like Caucasian girls."

He put his hand on my belly. "I like beautiful girls. We have beautiful children."

"So, why don't you?"

"Like Caucasian girls? This is a trap. And on my anniversary too."

"Oh, so case dismissed? And now it's time to play China doll for you?"

"Hell, I'll play Superman for you."

I flipped the strap of the nightie around my finger. "Do I put this on and then tip toe around the bedroom in my bound feet, or what? Where's my chopsticks? Where's my fan? I mean for Chrissake," I shouted. "I'm not anybody's Lotus Blossom, okay? I'm a muth-er and a wife and an employee, Wayne. I'm supporting my family. And doesn't anybody notice that I'm pregnant here?"

Wayne turned on his side to face me. "Who the hell is Lotus Blossom?"

I blinked at him. "You know what I mean." We lay through two whole torch songs until the hi-fi needle started bobbing in the free space. Finally, Wayne got up, undressed to his boxers and went to lift the needle. The baby readjusted itself with a couple of decisive thwomps, after which I felt seriously better. I rolled onto my back, still in my makeup and dress and stockings and let my eyes fall shut to the sound of Wayne brushing his teeth in the bathroom. Then suddenly he was at my side in the dark. His hand found my cheek, my elbow, my belly. I lifted his hand and kissed his fingers open.

❖ ❖ ❖

Monday morning a different and startling-looking Joan was making the same bad coffee in the break room. She had plucked her naturally bushy eyebrows into near oblivion. Now they were penciled in, but poorly, so that they resembled a couple of sentences scribbled across her forehead rather than a pair of graceful arcs. Gone was her usual roller-set shoulder-length wave, replaced by a straight bob with severe bangs high on her forehead. She wore a white wrap blouse with a red satin frog-clasp at the throat. An orchid tucked behind her ear would have finished off her China doll look, but I wasn't interested in her story.

"These are bad, aren't they?" I asked her, handing over a sheaf of poetry Nicks had given me to look at. I had taken the papers from him only because I'd thought it was a work order. They were his attempt at verse in the Tzu tradition.

The percolator quieted. I filled Joan's paper cup and pushed the sugar shaker across the breakroom table toward her. Then I linked my thumbs into twiddling position across my belly and kept a watch out for Nicks.

> Dark clouds up in the sky
> Yellow leaves down, down on the ground
> My heart is lost in the mists of autumn
> Your head is buried in the sands of time.

Her lips parsed the lines with a hunger that gave her away. She knew whose they were and how I'd gotten them, although she hadn't seen him touch me. "Do me the honor, won't you, Lotus?" he had said, coming up behind me and placing a folder down, his hands on my shoulders. "I'm not Lotus," I told him. "Really, I'm not."

"Yes, yes," he murmured. His fingertips traced the sides of my arm, massaged my neck a little. I stiffened with the weight of knowledge suddenly upon me that Nicks had crossed the line and I had done nothing to prevent it. I had failed to be vigilant and this was my reward—his fingers creeping from my neck to my throat. Since I made no protest, his fingers slid down my front to the collarbone. "You're so full," he whispered. "Ripe and full." And then his hands lifted and he was gone.

> My little skiff bobs where I tied it this morning
> The whippoorwill sobs miserably overhead
> I cannot sail to your home so far to the east
> This river doesn't wind as far as that.

Joan handed them back like they were currency I'd tried to bribe her with. "Why are you giving these to me?"

"You told me once that your parents were missionaries. You were born in Shanghai, isn't that right? I thought you went to school there."

"Until I was five," she snapped. "Do you know what they taught us?

70

American propaganda about the evils of Communism. We were educated by the Foreign Service. So why should I know anything about Chinese poetry? And what are you up to, anyway?"

"Look," I countered. "I know we're not bosom buddies here. I just really want to know if you think these are as bad as I think they are."

She, too, looked around for Nicks and then picked up the cup of coffee I'd poured for her. "Are you kidding," she muttered. "They stink."

"Good. I thought so," I told her, snatching the papers back. "You're Lotus Blossom, aren't you?" When she merely pursed her lips, I added, "You'd think he could see that."

She glanced heavenward. "It's not like I'm trying to be obvious."

"Oh, I won't blow your cover. I just meant I like what you've done with your hair."

Nicks knew he was no Ginsburg. Better to try out his poems on someone whose opinion didn't really matter. He may truly have believed I was Lotus Blossom. He may even have respected what he thought was my work. But I wasn't one of them and didn't, like Joan, aspire to Beatnik status. If he shared his poems with Joan, she would show them to his cohorts. He'd be laughed off the *Fringe*. Lotus Blossom was their détente, Joan and Nicks.

"He's not the same man outside of this place," Joan insisted.

"Thanks. I feel ever so much better."

She shrugged. "He just thinks you look the part."

I leaned across the table at her. "I am the part," I told her. "I just didn't sign up for it."

I thought about this statement on my next visit to Dr. Stabile's office, where Nurse Isabella Standeford went about her work like a brisk and capable Mother Superior. I wondered if some man at home loosed that braid at night, admiring the ripples. She checked my urine and found my blood sugar high. "He's going to give you a pill called Vlandine," Nurse Standeford explained. "It'll get your sugar count back down but it's really not good for your kidneys. Drink tons of water and try upping your grains." She caught my puzzled look. "Fiber, Grace. May I call you

Grace?" I smiled at her. Of course she could call me Grace. "You can get whole grain bread at that little gourmet store on Beaumont, the one with the Cheshire cat on the door? You should also try their breakfast cereal. It's good but crunchy. It's called granola."

I nodded, feeling unduly grateful to this woman. I worried that I might become confessional. Nurse Standeford was so very who she was. Her presence felt safe as a warm bathtub. "I'm glad you know you can get away with this with me," I told her. "But it seems awfully risky."

She untied the blood pressure strap from my upper arm and shrugged. "Don't worry for me. Things are changing."

❀ ❀ ❀

The year I started high school my parents allowed me to spend a week with Sophie at her grandparents' farm in Stockton. They grew lychee, bok choy, and other Chinese produce on a few acres nestled in the coastal range. Every day that week, we put our lunches in a pail and went for long walks with her grandfather's dogs over the crispy grass of the hills dotted with manzanita, granite, and scrub pine. One afternoon, we hiked up to Serrano's Pass, where you could catch a glimpse of the mission nestled between slopes and, on sunny days, the ocean. The dogs barked crazily when they saw two sheep from someone's pasture bleating and hollering near a barbed wire fence. The bloodied ewe kept trying to right her front hooves as the ram pushed her raggedly into the barbs, its hind legs doing a wild balancing dance.

Sophie screamed with something like outraged delight and ran downhill, the dogs bounding after her. I stood watching the pair, the impassive face of the ewe. Later, I found Sophie sitting on a rock picking at the inside of her sandwich and feeding it to the dogs. "Aren't you having any?" was all she said. That night, we lay wordless in the dark. Lately, I had begun to wake to find that I had been touching myself during my dreams, lust bent in my gut like a dirty spoon. Now Sophie's whimpering awakened me. She clutched her pillow, her back to me, in a fetal position.

"Sophie!" I whispered. "Are you all right?"

I dreaded hearing some bitter confession from her, some raw truth that would make things never again what they were. I lay back flat on my pillow staring into the caving dark. As far as I could tell, Sophie was fast asleep.

That was the same loneliness I felt on the last day Nicks walked up behind me. I'd been finishing the Hungry Tiger dessert section—"topped with creamy caramel" in 14 point New Roman—when with nearly ox-like stoicism Nicks reached over and cupped his hand over my left breast for what was not two seconds. He didn't squeeze. He said nothing. My breast might have been my shoulder. The mundanity of the gesture seemed to present the option of behaving as though it hadn't happened at all—a tempting option. My husband and son depended on me. My world would tilt to something that required a huge readjustment and resettling. Nothing would be like it was, like when you changed the font on your document and all four margins had to be adjusted. Line breaks, hyphens, punctuation, orphans, and widows had to be checked and rechecked.

Nevertheless, some other part of me began to act. I could not both eat whole-grain breakfast cereals on behalf of my unborn child and let this man frighten and insult me. These were not the same woman. Besides, it was becoming clear that Nick's transgression was merely an early paragraph in a story it was my job to keep him from writing. Thus, at the end of the day, I told Patsy that I was leaving early and gave her instructions on the menu job I had left unfinished. She hugged me and gave me her fresh, unopened pack of cinnamon gum. I filled an empty paper box with my few personal belongings, typed up my resignation, and left it on Nicks's desk under his pipe stand.

I watched myself with a distant curiosity as I went to pick up Mitchell early from preschool. Uncharacteristically, I lingered to chat with Mrs. Kloberdanz, who told me Mitchell was speaking in two-object subject-predicate sentences. I drove the few miles to the Weinstocks' tearoom in Oakland, where Mitchell and I shared a slice of pineapple cake and a glass of milk. He sat next to me in the little booth, his ear at my belly so he could listen to the baby. I stroked his head. I watched myself stroking his head. I became aware that the maternal scene we made was touching to look upon. Vaguely, I hoped that if I could imprint the scene on enough hearts—of the waitress, Velma, and the hostess, Charlene, and the manager in the tie and shirt sleeves who didn't wear a name tag and the lunching ladies all around us and the shoppers who wandered in looking for something cold to drink—then perhaps the momentum of that feeling would serve as a tide against whatever was going to happen next.

For three days, I lived a secret, unhinged life. I got up in the mornings on the pretense of going to work, kissed my husband goodbye, and took Mitchell to preschool. On the first day, I wandered the shops, waddling with a purposeful click down one street and up another, as though I had a long list of errands and little time. When I caught my reflection in a storefront or the window of a passing bus, I nearly gasped at the unconvincing picture I made. I had visions of backing out of rooms with my son under my arm as Wayne upturned furniture in his rage. I wandered into a diner, lowered myself onto a stool and ordered a ham on rye, my face tucked self-consciously into *Poetry of the Tzu*. According to the radio newscaster, they had found the bodies of those three young men who had gone down south to teach in the newly integrated schools. A Jew, a Yankee, and a Black man.

> Petals fall
> in flowing water spring passes—
> Within a dream, my body forgets
> it is a prisoner:
> A flash of greedy pleasure
>
> Sorrow of parting.
> Cut it, it does not sever.
> Sort it, it ravels more.
>
> To heaven? Or on to others?

Once upon a time while waiting for the birth of my son, I indulged in a frenzy of cleaning and organizing, putting my house in order. I made the landlord climb a ladder and wash the outside windows in our second-floor flat. I labeled things in closets and medicine cabinets. I used toothpicks on grime. What inspired industry could I promise my husband and children now? At best, I must continue on gratefully with the trivial tasks of the day and somehow use the momentum to propel myself forward.

I went home and made chicken à la king for my family.

The next day I pretended to be a tourist. I strolled through botanical gardens and boutiques and natural history museums, keeping my chin at the appreciative, inquisitive tilt of someone from out of town.

On the last day, I knocked on Sophie's door. She told me she'd been thinking. She handed me her gorgeous penny-colored wool cape that fit over my bulk and, together, we plotted the downfall—the literary downfall, anyway—of Alan Nicks.

Wayne and I had browsed at City Lights a few times; he loved their history section, but we'd never been to a poetry reading, never rubbed elbows with actual Beatnik types. Using up my remaining store of postanniversary goodwill, I had talked Wayne into accompanying me to a *Fringe* reading but decided not to tell him about the "open mic" portion after the program or about the little sheaf of poems I had tucked away in my purse. Instead I told him that, being the clean-cut law student from Arcadia, California, that he was, he might as well expect the unexpected. I wore Sophie's cape, which deep down I had believed only Sophie could pull off. Now with the fog already settling thickly for the evening and my husband on my arm, I swept it over my shoulder, enjoying the space it took up just getting into it.

Pipe smoke haloed an aloof Ferlinghetti stooped behind stacks of new and used books. A jazz trio was playing. We followed the music up a staircase to a room set out with old couches and coffee tables and a few folding chairs in rows. A Chinese fellow bald on top but with hair to his knees perched atop a paisley cushion playing a recorder. A noncommittal-looking percussionist in a baseball cap and a smiling bassist in a purple and green dashiki rounded out the trio.

Wayne gulped. A microphone stood in the corner near an elongated music stand. Several women with a Joan-like slouch, and Joan herself, chatted while either guarding or proffering the wine and cheese at the table, I wasn't sure. Nicks strode in from what looked like a closet with a toilet in it, touched Joan's arm lightly, and lit her cigarette. This was their world. A few of the couples there looked like Wayne and me—foreigners with visas. The Asians in the room had already scoped one another out and turned back to our respective business. I was the only noticeably pregnant woman there. An Asian man and a White lady chatted with a couple wearing matching fisherman sweaters. A very tall but stooped and kindly looking White man in what looked like batik-print pajamas accompanied a regal-looking Black woman draped in jewel tones. Several university types hovered, men with scraggly beards and White women dressed like Chairman Mao down to the black cloth Chinese sandals that had recently become the rage. There really were lots of different kinds of White people; it was easy to forget that.

Too self-possessed to do a double take when he saw me with Wayne, Nicks squinted a knowing smile our way and cocked his chin in greeting. We took folding chairs in the second row and had just begun to sip our cups of Chianti when Nicks sidled over to us bearing copies of the *Fringe*. My former employer and my husband had a moment to recognize that they were entirely different animals. Nicks was perfect, no insinuations. "Magnificent, aren't they?" he said of the journals. "Spread the word." He handed us a stack of four or five and then winked at me and made an el with his thumb and index finger. Lotus, I guessed. I nodded, my face pulsing hot in anticipation of the moment I had come for.

After the jazz trio solemnly wiped and packed their instruments, Ferlinghetti materialized at the makeshift podium, puffing on his pipe. He gave a little talk that seemed less exciting than it should have about the importance of the *Fringe* and journals like it for the counterculture, and by association, for mainstream culture. Then he read from his new work. My husband perspired at my side. Next came a fellow named Dunbar, another named Croy, and a few others who began to blend together. People started getting up to use the john between poems, instead of between poets.

The evening's claim to fame was a dark-haired Swede, Krieger, and after Krieger, still more poets. People started getting up during poems. I was one of them. The baby's position hurt in a way that made me want to elbow people with a hard jab in the gut to clear my path.

Finally, came open mic. Nicks urged me toward the podium with a little scoot of his hand, causing Wayne to raise his eyebrows first at Nicks, then at me. Nicks believed I had come to own up to my true identity as Lotus. Hawk-eye Joan trained her glance on it all.

Here was an occasion when I actually enjoyed the comedic aspect of my late-pregnancy waddle. I removed my pillbox hat—I had worn a hat! Sophie had thought it would be just the right touch. I looked over to Wayne, who wore a look of sympathy mixed with horror. I hadn't stood in front of a sea of faces since my marriage. Pins of sweat pricked my upper lip. I breathed in carefully through my nose. "I am not a poet," I began. "It is my understanding that participants may read from work they admire by poets who are not . . ." I cleared my throat and tried again. "It is my understanding that we may read the work of others. Therefore I would like to say that I am the humbled and grateful recipient of several poems penned by a man who I am sure you all respect and admire. Please allow me to share with you some poems by Mr. Alan Nicks, producer of the *Fringe.*"

A wicked smile spread across the face of Ferlinghetti. There were murmurs of interest and curiosity and a knowing little buzz from Nicks's compadres. Nicks narrowed his eyes at me in what everyone else thought was a smile. It was after I read the "Little Skiff" poem that I felt my first contraction, a wave that caused my knees to tremble behind the podium. I gripped the sides, smiled at everyone, and read the "Sands of Time" poem. Someone snorted. Another fellow chuckled behind his fist. I'd timed my reading for twelve minutes, forty seconds. Another contraction before I finished would mean this baby was ready. A couple of short pieces later and still in the clear I figured I had just enough time to wrap up with Nicks's pièce de résistance before I waved my husband over and, leaning heavily into his side, made my exit.

I pulled back the curtain and there you were
My Lotus, my Blossom, my Prize
What color is the hair that runs down your
back?
No matter
We've snuffed the candle, Baby
It's black as night.

As for Joan, if she ever decided to play her trump card—that she was Lotus, the real poet of the two—her triumph would be all the more satisfactory after this evening.

At the hospital, I tried to stand up as Isabella Standeford had advised me to, but they gave me an old warhorse of a nurse who believed that beds were for lying in. By that point, I quite agreed with her. The nurse did make me get up and walk to the bathroom once, bringing on considerable progress. On the way back to the bed, I paused and sank to my knees as earth and heaven thundered through me. No more of that; I was going back to lie down. Dr. Stabile arrived when they announced the baby's head was crowning. The nurses changed shifts and—joy of joys—it was Isabella Standeford. She placed my hand in hers with calming surety but was unimpressed with my progress. She had to be made to accept by Dr. Stabile that no one was making me stand up again for anything.

Isabella simply breathed in, closed her eyes, and concocted her plan B. "Grace, I'm going to tell you something that should make all this much easier. Now, with the next wave"—her word for contractions—"don't try to push the baby down or out. Push back. You'll rip yourself wide open if you push out, and you'll give yourself a nice, fat hemorrhoid or two if you push down. Push back, Grace. Save yourself the stitches. Now, try."

I tried.

"You call that pushing? Come on!"

I hissed at her through gritted teeth.

"Pretend it's a big wall trying to close in on you, and push push push against that wall. Don't let it squeeze you. Push!"

I pushed so hard something clicked and came loose in my temples. In-sect-like lines and curls of various fonts arced and burst at the edges of my sight, wiggling and illegible. It was almost comical how all that effort made so little difference in my progress. Between contractions, I dropped into a profound, momentary sleep still gripping Isabella Standeford's hand. Someone seemed to be speaking a foreign language. I woke to a glint of stainless steel on a surgical table they'd wheeled in. "Step aside, Miss Stan-deford," ordered Dr. Stabile. Forceps.

"You don't need those, Grace," she warned. "Your baby doesn't need those. You don't even need to tear if she comes out gradually."

Dr. Stabile switched on a very bright light. "Isabella," he intoned.

After my next forty-second nap, I tried to sit up. "She?"

"I'm almost never wrong."

Dr. Stabile shook his head.

"And you don't need to look at me like that either," Isabella told him. "I didn't learn all this from the witch at the edge of town. I learned it in the army."

"You just keep it up, Miss Standeford. Just keep it up." Were they lovers, I wondered helplessly? I didn't get it, the kind of pushing she was asking for. "She?" I asked again and fell into another forty-second dream, this time of a clear, fontless, light board. I woke screaming my husband's name in outrage and elation and pain. Wayne was somewhere where they kept the fathers. This push was for him. She, if it turned out to be a she, would be born with a clear light board, no squiggles and loops hovering over her bright future.

"Yes!" screamed my formerly becalmed midwife when my daughter's head emerged. The hardest part was finally behind me. I hadn't been able to take it standing up; I was no Isabella. But finally, finally, with an im-mense shuddering sense of rightness, of relief, I began to push like I meant it. Back.

# Do Us Part, 1973

We're all sitting in a circle, knees touching, wind and sand whisking around us as Reverend Bill Boone blesses the fat glass chalice of grape juice and the hunk of sourdough bread. Am I the only one who can picture myself wrestling that loaf out of my neighbor's hands and stuffing huge chunks of it into my mouth? Morning has broken, as the song goes, but only just. We were lucky to get three kids out of sleeping bags and up this sand dune in the dark, much less get anybody breakfast. Plus, this would all seem holier to me if they'd given us time for coffee first.

Bill Boone is our handsome new ski-tanned minister, a young guy with a vegetarian wife, Paula, who rode with him across the country on her ten-speed for their honeymoon. This weekend, it's communion in the dunes at Pismo Beach. Next month, it's family backpacking at Kings Canyon, and the month after that a couple's retreat. Wayne has signed us up for all three. He and his best friend since high school, Steve Leach, led the committee that hired Bill Boone. It had come down to a woman who graduated at the top of her seminary class at Harvard Divinity School, and Bill, whose credentials were not quite as shiny but who, people felt, would "energize" the congregation.

Turns out Steve and the family Leach don't even make the sunrise service, nor do half the slumbering families of our congregation back at the campground. Wayne, in contrast, seems determined to keep up with Reverend Bill. After we hold hands and Bill Boone starts strumming his twelve string, Steve and Maddie Leach finally straggle up the dune, their pair of alternately sheepish and glowering long-haired boys bringing up the rear. Not quite finished with his benediction, Bill Boone opens one eye, waves the family over as though they are joining us all in a hot tub, and leads us all, a cappella, in "Shalom Shavarim."

Judging from the crumpled-up tissues in her hand, I suspect Maddie Leach has been crying. She has not found time to style her hair. It lies flat against her head with cute bangs, making her look ten years younger. By the time he crests the hill, Steve's looking as brisk as ever in his perma-press jogger and white sneakers. The wind keeps lifting a page of his hair over his temple, revealing the depth of his widow's peaks. The Leaches are aging faster than Wayne and me, but they're still better looking.

Services over, my three children scuttle down toward the surf. I take off after them, the wind full in my face and ears sans the protective windbreak of the dunes. The children unleash screams of delight. A skein of some kind of shorebirds winds overhead, echoing the creatures below with screams of their own. My kids are already brown as nuts, their sun-glossed hair growing long and wild. My God, I think, look at how beautiful they are. It hits me that given their screams, the wind, the surf, and the ups and downs in the dunes almost like soundproof rooms, I could scream too. I could deliver primal shrieks unto the wind, which would dispatch them with the same effortless disinterest as the call of gulls across the skies and over that swelling, anonymous ocean.

❀ ❀ ❀

When I'm not accompanying my family on Bill Boone–inspired excursions, I'm taking a class at the local community college as a sort of warm-up for returning to get my baccalaureate in literature, primarily British, of the twentieth century. The professor's pet, a young man named Harley

Blindt, has deigned to befriend me. Having indulged in the vanity of be-
lieving he found me smart, I'm now unable to shake him. He strikes me as
nice enough, although maybe a bit preoccupied by the labor of normalcy.
He's not the only one in striped bell-bottoms or puka shells; there's just a
sense that some slight, ubiquitous distortion in his head takes effort not to
succumb to. He's in his midtwenties. Friends of his have begun to settle
down. This troubles him, he shares with me as he walks me to my car.
Not that he has any intention of settling down. His friends have sold out,
he believes, to a life of station wagons and large-pawed dogs. My life; he
must know that.

❀   ❀   ❀

White lights twinkle in the manzanita as we whir down the concrete paths
of Rancho las Palmas Resort and Convention Center in the golf-cart tram
toward the Oasis Room. It's a starry night, with a moon that clears the
peaks like it's taking extra gas to get the job done. The Coachellas loom
like the dark rims of a huge bowl. It's been a long day of "encounter"
sessions led by Gil and Sharon Diego-Halcyon, first in couples, then in
small mixed groups, then in gender-specific groups, and finally back in a
large group. If the flame of your union wasn't already flickering when you
entered the over-air-conditioned Room of the Three Palms this morning
and sat down in front of your name tag, workbook, and complimentary
Enhancement Weekend retractable pen, it is likely pretty wobbly now. The
theory is that your resistance to change will be ground down to an insignif-
icant little nub if you get no snacks, meals are Spartan, and more than one
bathroom break is frowned upon. Never mind that you did not necessarily
sign on for change per se, especially since the brochure advertised couples'
enrichment, enhancement, a love investment. Dinner, at least, turns out
to be both tasty and substantial. It includes expertly prepared and subtly
aphrodisiacal foods like asparagus with béchamel sauce and pulled ginger
duck served with individual soothing hot lemon cloths. We need it. Men
cried today. Spouses uttered things to one another that will echo down the
corridors of their future. One woman who goes by Stormy stomped out

and wasn't seen again until Games People Play, right before Sharing and Evaluations. Why does it not surprise me that Bill and Paula Boone are not even here? According to Steve and Maddie, they have already done the Rancho las Palmas and the week-long advanced couples' session in Yosemite National Park. This weekend they are drywalling their addition.

"Why do you think I've 'disinherited my ears'?" I ask Wayne while dressing for dinner. I mimic the reasonable tone that the Diego-Halcyons use with us. "Well," Wayne replies, "were you trying to run up your 'forbearance deficit' with me when you said I play 'Yes, Dear?'" Our hearts aren't in it. In fact, if it takes a full stomach to make me forget what irks me I'd just as soon let it go. Maybe that's the trick. Say Wayne was out splitting the wood that would cook the animals he had hunted and the water I had hauled and the nuts and berries and edible plants I had gathered when I wasn't beating our linens clean on the broadest, flattest river rocks I could find after sweeping out our cave, with Mitchell and Evie afoot and Ben on my back. Who would have time for marital discord?

Maddie isn't speaking to Steve either, and it appears she has a bigger bone to pick. During Couples Encounter, spouses were supposed to write a letter to the man or woman each had been on the day they were married. Gil Diego-Halcyon wouldn't let Maddie see Steve's letter, saying it would "rupture the trust" they had built together; this infuriated both Steve and Maddie, although for different reasons. Now Steve is driving the golf cart with the kind of military precision that is above reproach, and Maddie is after him like we're headed down an ice chute. At dinner, she weep-talks about normal things. Her older son made varsity diving, she announces, dabbing at her cheeks. Then she tries to explain how the chef might have done a better job with the fish course, but the end of each sentence disintegrates into moist chokes that everybody is too disheartened to do much about except stare with downcast eyes at their melting scoops of sorbet.

It isn't until the next day that I learn of the, in my opinion, legitimate source of Maddie's misery. In the I'm Ok, You're Ok session, clearly meant to be the uplifting finale, Maddie and Steve shine like the most fully attuned couple (to employ the lingo) there. But on the six-hour drive home, Maddie writes on the inside jacket of the Enhancement workbook, underlined three times, "I'm NOT OKAY!!!" I pat her on the arm. Directly under her previous declaration, she writes the letters O.M. which stand for the two words that strike terror in the heart of every woman of that era still with her husband after the seven-year itch: Open Marriage. She points at Steve, her arm locked secretively against her side. Up front, the men keep taking turns trying to find the football scores on the radio as though a new hand on the dial might produce fresh results. Not Steve! Then Maddie sticks her thumb in Wayne's direction, her face a question mark. I stare at the back of Wayne's head (looking straight ahead is mandatory for the carsick). Several thoughts come to me at once, and in this order: not my husband. Vindictively, a few beats later: who would have him? And finally, alarmingly: someone perhaps. Who?

The weekend the kids go to Lifestream camp, Wayne begins leaving his *Playboys* in a stack on the bathroom floor instead of bothering to hide them in the closet. Is he communicating to me some sort of new bridge he's crossed, or is this simply a more relaxed attitude after fifteen years of marriage? His father displayed *Playboys* on the coffee table for young children to thumb through, so I suppose it was inevitable but also pretty tame of Wayne to stack them neatly in the corner behind the toilet. I haven't yet sat down and had a good look; I'm saving that for when I'm really miserable.

The basement's damp in the building where we go to pick up the kids, which wouldn't be so bad except it's where they've put the playroom and nursery. Toyoko, aka "Chelsea," Shinoda, the counselor who designed and painted the murals of Noah and the Ark and Jonah and the Whale down there, is popular with the kids. On our last visit, I found them all wearing daishikis and eating fried plantain dipped in peanut sauce, world beat thumping in the background. "Ah, Africa night," one mother remarks, to which, in a preview of her adolescence, my daughter Evie snorts disdainfully, "Africa is not a country." She has just gotten glasses and probably figures that the best offense was a good defense. The little ones have just learned the word "nincompoop," practically a rite of passage in childhood, I've noticed, and the rest are telling one another "you need to get Rolfed" or just "get Rolfed" for short, which is the kind of thing kids of Lifestream parents pick up on, I suppose. Evie threatens to puke if she has to make one more God's Eye. Mitchell has a crush on pert, round-bottomed Toyoko, so he's fine with whatever she cooks up. But Ben, only four, trots up and announces in an obvious imitation of stated policy, "Here, we poop with no doors." Eerily enough, none of the children even laughs.

❀ ❀ ❀

Harley Blindt telephones me at home. He wants to check if I'm getting the difference between realism versus naturalism because he can help me out with it if I'm not. I tell him I think I'm okay there. Okay, then, he says. By the way, do I know Carolyn Jacobi, the busty red head in class? He warns me about Professor Swilken, who has a PhD although this is only a community college, and who is known for getting women like Caroline alone in his office for serious tête-à-têtes. Because Harley is from Kentucky, this comes out as tit-a-tit. Have I seen the new musical *Jesus Christ Superstar* yet, he also wants to know. Also, how do I know about the band Jethro Tull, to which I made reference in class the other day? Finally, where am I from and do I speak a "native language"? It's like he was working his way down a list that trumps any principles of conversation people normally rely on. I tell him I have to go. I have a stiff pet guinea pig to bury and kids to bathe before my day is done.

❀ ❀ ❀

When Bill Boone rises, everybody rises. "It's the COD!" he calls into our tent, which stands for crack of dawn. We have climbed a six-thousand-foot peak. We have eaten Ramen noodles and freeze-dried chicken à la king with vacuum-packed peas and carrots and nonfat dry milk. We have fetched water and squatted over suspicious-looking plants with fists of bio-degradable toilet tissue in hand. None of this merits sleeping in according to Bill Boone, not when you have fifty-pound backpacks to hoist onto your aching shoulders, still higher peaks to climb, even more miles to cover.

Maddie's tears have become a sort of fixture. And yet no one will talk about it. Steve is attentive to her, even solicitous. Others are sympathetic in a distant or sometimes misplaced way. For example, Bill Boone has Maddie recline atop a boulder at Tres Pinas Point, where he treats her for altitude sickness. This diagnosis is the result of a joke Paula Boone whispered to Maddie, who keeps repeating what is evidently the punch line— "Gee, that's a hard one!"—slapping her knee and doubling over in painful-looking guffaws. Hard, I gather, is a double entendre. Less obvious is what any of us is supposed to do here. Marriage is like an organism consisting of many vital and interdependent systems. Sometimes it can be dealt a direct and fatal blow, but more often parts just die off until the thing collapses. I assume that in Steve and Maddie Leach's case, if not in every case, Open Marriage is the last gasp of a failing traditional marriage. Steve attempted to see if he could have it both ways and the answer was NO, so on to plan B—divorce and remarry.

Maddie curls up on her boulder and, turning from us, vomits a spittle of her breakfast of powdered eggs over the edge. One of her boys, Wilson, leaps to her aid, pulling her hair back tenderly from her face and speaking soothing words to her as though no one is there but the two of them. The other boy stands with his hands in his pockets, his acne-ridden cheeks behind his long hair, announcing the obvious to all gathered. "My mom's sick. My mom's not doing so good." His dad has that look he's been wearing a lot lately, the half-puzzled, half-concerned expression of a guy who can't make the thing run, who hasn't got the tools and would just as soon pay somebody to fix it.

"I'm fine," Maddie insists, straightening herself and dabbing with thumb and ring finger at the corners of her mouth. "It must have been the MSG." We all look to Steve, who is watching Maddie with a beseeching look that could be staged but could be genuine too.

"Monosodium?" asks one son.

"Glutamate," finishes the other.

Progressive bunch that we are, Bill and Paula and their flock have driven all the way out to our place in Navelencia for what I'm calling my Evening of Oriental Flavors. Everyone is game enough to try my kimchi and namsook and bulgogi, wielding their chopsticks with an acquired ethnic panache (except for the veterans, who use them better than I do) and sitting with their knees tucked under them as they sip barley tea from the mock celadon cups I splurged on. I went all out, purchasing lacquered chopsticks in hues that match the vinyl cushion squares everyone's sitting on. I set out rice candies and moon cakes, dried lychee and tamarind twists, sesame squares, and, of course, fortune cookies. Seeing our friends lined up on cushions around coffee tables in the living room, scooping rice from bowls, dipping bites of food into sauces they can't identify, I feel something more than mere gratitude for their interest and support and their appetites. And I am more than just relieved that the evening has come off without a hitch. I confess I feel a sort of smugness, even a smidgeon of superiority around this group of such well-meaning White people. I can't help noting that Bill Boone, originally a midwesterner, is skittish about Oriental food. He's using his chopsticks like a probe. He tastes something, then chews, then stops, then brings a napkin to his lips. I expected more from a guy who has rappelled down granite and ridden the Blue Crush.

But that's what I get for lording it over anyone, even for a moment. My Evening of Oriental Flavors is the night the Boones and Leaches have picked to make the unofficial announcement that will become official at services the next morning: Steven and Madelyn Leach are getting a divorce, and the Reverend Bill Boone will lead them in one of the very first rituals of its kind—a divorce ceremony. There goes my sweet bean pastry surprise.

"What in the Diego-Halcyon is going on?" I hiss to Wayne in the kitchen. He's been running a forbearance deficit all evening by sitting with Toyoko aka "Chelsea" Shinoda during dinner and feigning interest in each and every charm on her charm bracelet.

"Honey, I am so sorry," says Wayne. "It was all just talk. You know Steve. I thought he was joking, honest. I had no idea he was such an idiot."

For the third time in only a year, Bill Boone has made the local paper. The first was when he and Paula had moved to town and made something of a splash because they had become spokespeople for the Chinchilla Rescue League in order to address the unique and growing problem of the unusual animals' abandonment and abuse. Next was an article about their hand in starting up the Lifestream House, where the children of refugees can learn and play with American children. And now Bill Boone is making the biggest splash of all:

> . . . "I was really glad to have this opportunity," says Boone, 35. "The couple felt they needed a ritual to end their marriage—and since it began in the church, it should also end in the church. It's wonderful to be able to provide a healing service for them—rather than having only a civil statement to mark the end of their marriage." When asked why the couple feel such a ceremony is necessary, Boone explains, ". . . there certainly is a lot of wilderness, pain, and confusion round about people caught in divorce." But perhaps it need not be seen as having "fallen off the edge of the spiritual earth." Adds Boone, "And could we possibly talk about the religious aspects of it—all those broken vows, for instance—in the same way, as some form of spiritual journey?" Divorce is not "falling off the path of life; it is taking a different one." How would it work? "You and your ex-spouse could each take the time to write down what you honor about your years together, and then read these things to each other. You could give back your wedding rings to each other at the conclusion of the readings. After this ceremony, you would each leave with your respective friends and family to gather somewhere private (like people do after a funeral or wake) where grieving would be supported."
>
> —from the *Fresno Bee*

I'm not sure how I feel about being a member of a church like Bill Boone's. At a recent children's service, releasing balloons and doves was such a hit that far from becoming stale the new feature has served as a gateway to further adaptations on the traditional hymn-sermon-hymn-benediction routine. Last week was a slide show of smiling third world children set to music, and another Sunday a demonstration of some vaguely Native American–influenced form of Christian "movement worship" called Spiritdance complete with an amplifier and four-piece band. What happened to passing out illustrated children's Bibles? My hackles rise when it becomes clear that everyone is expected to join in and that we will look like fools if we don't. Maddie saves the day when she leans over and whispers, "You people start swaying together and I walk."

She pulls a pack of cigarettes from her purse and motions for me to follow her outside. "You want to know what's going on?" Maddie conducts an air symphony with her as yet unlit cigarette, bracelets jingling. "It is never never never just about yourself." So she doesn't love Steve per se; she loves the life they have—had—together, the boys, the boat, the vacations. How come you can never fix just the parts that are broken? Why won't he even give her a chance? There's been no trial, only a verdict, and who made Steve the judge, in any case? Maddie lights her cigarette here, takes a puff, and hands it to me pinched between her thumb and forefinger. I look at her funny; can't I just have one of my own? I have to admire her robust sense of having been wronged. The summer before Ben was born, I took the kids and slept in the guest room at my sister's place for three weeks. Not for good. Just to think. My mother phoned from her apartment in Oakland: "What'd you do to him?"

❀ ❀ ❀

On Swilken's realism and naturalism final, I get the highest score in class. I ace the four-pager on Hardy and Hopkins, as well. During break time when I head down to the vending machines for a four-ounce coffee-decaf-white, Harley is holding forth in the stairwell to a small gathering on William Morris's idea that we ought to hang real art on our walls or none at all. He slides his arm behind me on the handrail as though he's just propping up his slouch and then very slightly around my shoulder. My classmates seem not to find this alarming—troubling in itself—but I am so startled I don't, at first, know how to respond. Then, with the sense of entitlement I have discovered accompanies an exam score of 98.5, I do precisely what I am inclined to do at the moment I am inclined to do it—an odd feeling indeed. I shrug Harley's arm off of my shoulder, duck away from the crowd, and head back upstairs. After class, he walks me to my car as though nothing has happened. I remind him that walking me to my car is something I have never invited him to do. It is a rosy, breezy evening in late spring. Harley's lip curls. "Don't get all stuck up with me. I was lowering myself for you anyway." At first, I figure that's the end of it. He takes off, unlocks his bike in front of the student union, and then rides back past me. "Chink bitch," he calls and then fast pedals to make it through the stoplight.

Perhaps it's our equal and opposite reaction to the Leach's disturbing announcement, but on our fifteenth anniversary, Wayne and I have a weekend as close to perfect as we are ever going to get. We find a little inn on the coast near Carmel perched out over a rocky cliff with breathtaking close-ups of the crashing surf. The owners fuss over us like VIPs, even comping us a not-cheap box of chocolates and champagne on ice in our rooms with a note that says, "The 15th Anniversary is the best one!" although there's no explanation as to why. We have the kind of night that no couple—not even Bill and Paula Boone—could handle all the time. An argument starts us out, followed by bungled dinner reservations that practically have us convinced we should just give up and drive home. Instead, an extremely contrite maitre d' makes it all better and then some.

That success carries us through a little bit of dancing at a swanky nightclub and a moonlit stroll through town so that by the time we get back to the room and drink champagne it feels more like our honeymoon than anniversary number fifteen. There is even some of that fumbling awkwardness in getting each other's clothes off that you have early on as lovers. And we end up talking, going way past kid stuff, house stuff, job stuff to my dreams about teaching and Wayne's confession that he shouldn't have let me drop out of college so close to being done, and other talk about teenage dares and childhood peccadilloes and enduring philosophical questions, punctuated by more and more tender silence, until we become almost shy with one another, although it's different from dating shyness, so that when we finally are undressed I feel a nakedness I've never felt with Wayne, or ever, a shivering vulnerability that I like, that makes me feel more married than I've ever felt. Wayne, too, I think, the way he lies there on his side facing me, listening, smiling and still, like he's seeing the part of me that loves me in unalterable ways, like God slipped up and we've been given an accidental glimpse into one another usually reserved for more qualified souls. Then follows a similar lovemaking, fumbling because we try things we've never done (a sizeable list), which brings mixed results but also occasional, awe-inspiring success. In the morning, sunlight even streams in on us through lilting white curtains puffy with the ocean breeze. Maybe we got our money's worth out of the Diego-Halcyons after all, or maybe they had nothing to do with it. Whatever the reason, we're headed home with a satisfied sense we've just swallowed a healthy dose of super vitamins for our marriage.

Mitchell has made up a little menu and pretend restaurant for our return. Evie has set the table with my good linens and china and has penned the menu in her adorable fat cursive strokes: salad, to which Mitchell has added the modifier "tossed," followed by "baked" lasagna and "scrumptious" three-layer cake. An ambitious bunch. Ben has even stuck cut peonies from the backyard in our water glasses.

Such a homecoming should have been a wonderful finale to the weekend—Mitchell with a kitchen towel folded neatly over his arm, Evie wearing one of my chiffon aprons, a pencil stuck behind her ear. But Wayne's first priority is going to the bathroom and then checking on what he hopes is not an oil leak in the Pontiac. He doesn't see how nervous the kids are about getting everything just right. Evie is on the verge of losing it. I go outside to the driveway and say to the legs sticking out from under the car, "Wayne Steward Teller, get in there now."

Wayne won't look at me across the tablecloth covered card table the kids have set up in the living room. The chanting coming from the kitchen is Mitchell, Evie, and Ben trying out the meditation practice their Aunt Elin taught them during her stay. Suddenly, it becomes clear to me after all these years of marriage that what I'd thought was an annoying tendency is in fact a pattern. On the way home, while still aglow with the previous night's magic, I made the mistake of being frank with Wayne about something we'd done together the night before, almost as a way of bringing it out into the open so there'd be no shame between us, no way for it to go sour. Wayne turned monosyllabic on me. That's how I know I'm in for a week, minimum, of the silent treatment. This is what happens. I don't mean after weeknight sex; I mean whenever we've managed to edge toward something real. So, in the hope of not losing ground, I venture while unpacking later in the bedroom that night—"Should we see someone?" I'm thinking his avoidance of my glance speaks for itself.

"See someone?"

"You know, talk to someone."

"Talk to someone, Grace?"

I drop it. If I push, I won't even be able to salvage what's left of the weekend. My couple-enhanced gut tells me to go into it. But you can't drag someone. And isn't that what we've been doing all weekend—getting really into it? Good Lord, I chastise myself, is nothing the man does ever good enough? I nurse that little lozenge of guilt and shame through the night, hoping with any luck things will be good as new in the morning. Instead, I'm woken by the sound of a rhythmic thwomping coming from the laundry room. Wayne is already up and gone. Ben often puts things in the clothes dryer that don't belong there, like tennis shoes, fruit, and paperback books. So the thwomping, though persistent, doesn't alarm me. That comes later, when I go in to fold clothes. To find a stiff, more or less deflated cat in your dryer after a romantic anniversary weekend excursion is such an abrupt welcome-home-to-your-real-life that it not only mitigates it downright dismantles any gains achieved in the "foundation of your marriage" department.

Wayne calls when the kids are setting the table for dinner. He claims he has to be at work really early in the morning to prepare for his big trial, so he's just getting a motel room in Fresno to avoid being slowed down by the tule fog.

Can you save a marriage if you're able to pinpoint the beginning of the end? I don't want to look closer. I just don't. Not until some kind of truth comes oozing out at me with the clarity of flesh and blood and bone. Maddie's right: How many people who split up really want to lose the whole banana? The house, the kids, the tax breaks, the his-and-hers towel set, the social standing? But I say it, anyway—throw it like a stone into the lake of our marriage to watch it plump the depths. "Open marriage without your wife's consent is just adultery, Wayne." There is a possibly damning pause, followed by the line men on TV use when they are lying about their affairs: "Is that what's got you so upset lately, Grace?" What's the thing that, years from now, I'll tell myself I should have done? What is it? Murder Toyoko Chelsea Shinoda? I hang up and dial the number for Harold Blindt listed on the class roster. My hand is shaking. A man answers with a bored and indolent hello that is and is not Harley. "You're a sick, mean prick," I tell him and hang up the phone. In the bathroom, I pile Wayne's neatly stacked *Playboys* in a paper sack and stick the paper sack in the garbage bin because, as Sharon Diego-Halcyon told our women's group, the marriage you save may be your own. I am banking on Harley K. Blindt's knowing too many possible candidates to deduce the originator of the phone call. As for Wayne, if he squawks about his magazines, I'll phone Bill Boone. I just pray Bill Boone doesn't have a stack of his own.

❁   ❁   ❁

Outside the sanctuary on a baking hot afternoon, I can see I'm not the only one who can't watch Steve and Maddie Leach utter meaningless words to one another about how "til death do us part" had really meant "til the death of our love." That's just cheating. Steve and Maddie's boy Wilson bounces a handball against the "He's got the whole world in his hands" mural that the fourth through sixth graders painted as a Sunday school project one year. Wilson had been in that class. The handball isn't doing any harm, so I keep my mouth shut. He ignores my approach, but in case he might get in trouble for bouncing the ball off the mural, he begins rolling it down the length of his arm, letting it drop off the tip of his fingers and then catching it before it falls to the ground. I sit on a ledge in the dappled shade and watch him. "You're pretty good," I say. It comes out more parent-y than I intended. Without looking at me, Wilson says, "This is bullshit. There's no way I'm going back in there and standing up with them."

I take a deep breath. I'm on the kid's side, but it's not my place to say so. Without warning, he tosses the ball to me, which I catch accidentally in my attempt to shield my face. The ball has a nice fleshy give in my palm.

"It was my mom, you know."

"I don't know."

"I just mean she was the one seeing someone. She was the one who wanted, you know, the open marriage."

My mind works its way through possible suspects. Maddie Leach and Wayne? It can't be.

"The guy's really nice; I've met him already. He and Mom both say there's no way they're getting married again." Wilson looks at me. "What do you think, Mrs. Teller? Should I believe them?"

Distracted by the realization that my own marriage is not completely out of the woods given Wilson's comment, I ask a lame and selfish question. "Where does he work, your Mom's . . . friend?"

Wilson's at the age where you don't know how much he really understands. "He bags groceries," Wilson says. "When he's not running the store."

I mask my curiosity pointing a stick of chewing gum at him and watching him pull it from the pack. "And your dad? Is there anybody?"

Wilson gives me a look of consternation.

"You care about your folks a lot, I can tell," I offer, trying to get back to my parental feet. I bounce the ball in front of me once or twice. Wilson jumps in, catches it, and dances away twirling before shooting it back at me, like he expects me to follow. We stroll down Bachman Parkway's wide concrete sidewalks in front of banks and chain restaurants, the kind of street no one walks down because people don't walk in Fresno. In order to have something to say, I reveal inexplicably to Wilson that Evie has a terrible crush on him.

Wilson smiles, apparently pleased with this information but then adds without a trace of animosity, "What kind of mother reveals something so private? You really shouldn't do that, you know."

Am I ready for this conversation? Am I prepared to dialogue with someone being so real? "I was just filling space with words," I confess. "Nerves, I guess."

"What have you got to be nervous about? Your family's not over." That's the way this man-child would see it. The marriage isn't over so much as life and his family as he knows it. He puts the ball right into my hand, like he's done bouncing it. "How come marriage isn't something this species can get better at, Mrs. Teller—you know, like space flight or dentistry?"

"Ask me when I'm a hundred," I answer.

"You know, it kind of gives me hope that you're out here instead of in there listening to that asshole spout off about how people change."

"Wilson."

"Like we're not supposed to see how my mom and dad are failures to each other. Like what they're doing is the right thing, like change is good. I wish they'd stand up there and say they screwed up, they blew it, and it can't be fixed and they're really really sorry." He looks at me carefully. "It's a pretty ordinary failure, don't you think, Mrs. Teller? Isn't it kind of embarrassing they're making such a case of it?"

Completely disarmed, I can think of nothing better than to put my hand on his shoulder. "Just wait until you have to explain yourself to your own kids." Fair to middling. Sufficient anyway. Wilson shrugs his shoulder out of my grasp. "You're pretty cool, for a mom. I don't suppose . . . can I get you high?"

I wince. "Really, Wilson, we grown-ups can only take so much." A city bus pulls up at our corner.

"Depends on the grown-up," he grins.

"Wait a second, where're you going?"

"Not far. You don't need to worry anymore, Mrs. Teller." He strides to the very back of the bus and lifts his hand to me in goodbye.

I try to imagine Evie and Wilson on a date. They were like twins, leggy, pimpled, hair hanging in their faces. And I consider Wilson's question—why isn't marriage a perfectable institution? The Diego-Halcyons believe it is. But what if they're wrong? What if, despite all of their degrees and certificates, they are simply unaware of the depths to which a marriage can sink? What if their optimism is so robust precisely because it is sheltered from the wind and rain of complicated people and exceptional circumstances?

The Leaches are holding their divorce reception in their as yet intact home. Shouldn't people who can manage throwing a reception together for a hundred just stay married? On the other hand, what if these two are on to something? They'll be living within a mile of one another, will share custody of the boys and remain within the school district. Each will move into a little condo where somebody else does the yard upkeep. Each will enjoy a wide open life in which to start over. They're amicable. They can hang their own stuff on the walls. Damn those Leaches. Even divorce they've pulled off with enviable flair.

Bill Boone is handing round cups of coffee and lemonade at the hospital where my eldest son, Mitchell, is sleeping peacefully, seventeen stitches later. Now that the danger is past, Steve and Wayne are trying to find the game using the faulty waiting room remote. Bill Boone's wife, Paula, is on the floor coloring with Bennie. One minute my babies are slumped in front of the After School Special pulling goldfishy slivers of kimchi from a huge jar they call the Vat and downing them with big cups of ice water. The next thing I know a swarm of neighborhood preteens alights on the porch and everyone is out on the front lawn for a game of tag football. I'm cleaning out cat litter boxes in the laundry room, a task I just want checked off my list, when little Doug Woody pounds on the door, yelping incoherently. I dash out front to see a cluster of boys hovering around my son. Ben is crying and pacing the lines of the basketball court on the driveway; Evie is nowhere to be seen. I can see inside Mitchell's knee through a neat, broad split in the skin. It's anatomy-class clear, and impressive. Bumpy, glistening fat-colored flesh, not much blood to speak of, a limp tendon, and a kneecap the color of good teeth peeking through. The next time I breathe, it's when I'm watching my husband come through the hospital doors, Evie's hand in his and Ben slumped, asleep, over his shoulder. Evie had been hiding in our bedroom closet, scared for Mitchell and scared that the neighborhood boys would laugh at her if they saw her tears. Is this the same man I'd sworn at on the telephone the night before?

"Has he lost weight?" Maddie asks, legs crossed to show off her new silver sandals.

I realize that I already forgive him, and myself, for whatever happens. I have evidence of nothing. I feel one hundred years old. It is just a glimpse, like that peek inside my son's torn open knee, but I do see that there are workings beyond us. Maybe Wilson is right; maybe the end of a marriage is only the most ordinary of failures. But who we fail and how we fail them is the most important story when it's happening, if only to us.

Home, I gaze from the kitchen window onto a patio strewn with wood burning wands sans the kit they came with, lidless ant farms, Barbie paraphernalia, and a junior astronomy lab. Wayne and the kids are assembling an enormous piece of outdoor play equipment, an addition to the jungle gym, perhaps, or some kind of patio furniture. Contraband cans of soda dot the picnic table, and they have broken into the new bag of Doritos without finishing the old one first. All of them, even Ben, wear that look of intent focus ready to break into delight as they see the thing come together with their own hands. They have their moments of befuddlement as they flip through pages to find the instructions in English. Wayne utters a shit or dammit under his breath. Ben imitates, and though they're not supposed to, everyone laughs. Evie starts jumping up and down when they begin to see evidence that these bolts and screws and labeled parts will indeed become just like the picture on the box.

There's no small triumph like the triumph over Directions for Assembly. Now they've got it, although I'm still not certain what it is. They begin to stand the thing upright, faces flushed with pleasure at their handiwork. Then I realize, a heartbeat before my beloveds do, that it's put together wrong. In another heartbeat, Evie's face will collapse in disappointment. Mitchell will register no expression, although inside his stomach will drop. Ben will acquire the expression he sees on the face of his father, earnest and concerned puzzlement. Something has gone wrong; it is backward or upside down, something.

But that's not the moment I'm interested in. I'm talking about that precious, slightly elongated piece of time in which they survey their handiwork and they believe that all is well. Look at them, beaming with pride. Let's pretend that moment can be as long or as brief as you want it to be, that it can stand apart from the consequent moment of dismay. That is our moment. That's us: all is as it should be. So far as we know.

# Made You Look, 1979

Mr. Chou has not bathed in three days. His hair has stiffened into odd-angled tufts and the white shirt he has worn since his arrival has wilted to an unhealthy shade of yellow. Sometimes we hear him brushing his teeth or the obligatory whir of an electric razor, but these seem more like sound effects instructing us to keep our distance than evidence of his personal hygiene.

Mom is taking this eccentricity in stride. "Oriental people have certain rituals surrounding the bath," she explains. "He is probably just observing some sort of waiting period." She has no idea what she is talking about, but being Korean American, she believes it is her prerogative to comment on the behavior of other Asians, even when they are Chinese and have been in the country for five minutes.

"No, it's about our filthy bathtub," I counter. Mildew is practically encoded into the grout and spackling, and the fiberglass siding has acquired geological layers of scum. "We're disgusting, and he doesn't want to touch our smut."

My mother looks at me, alarmed. "Touch our smut? What kind of word is that—smut?"

"Dirt," I shrug. "Yuck. Filth. Ick."

She hands me the Comet and a scrub brush with a suspicious look and says, "Get in there and clean out that tub."

I wasn't the one who agreed to take on a houseguest during the holidays, so at least I am getting some satisfaction out of the fact that he is turning out to be a bit difficult. This guy is nothing like the other international students we've had over the years, like Purnama, the former beauty pageant winner from Indonesia who sang Broadway tunes and taught us flower arranging. Or Sakura, the violinist from Japan with her bangs always a little in her eyes. Or poor Moon-li, who ate kimchi even with her scrambled eggs and whose fiancé was a GI killed in Vietnam. Mr. Chou is a biologist from Huangtan province participating in an exploratory mission of goodwill exchange organized by the state university. While our other international guests cooked their native dishes for us and brought us things like moon cakes and good luck symbols to hang on the door, Mr. Chou works long hours at the laboratory where he studies the dung of snails.

We are slogging through that cold and dreary limbo-week between Christmas and New Year's, when everyone is too lazy to take down the tree and put away the ornaments and there's more gristle than flesh left on the turkey. I spend a lot of time in my room listening to my new Supertramp tape on the eight-track and reading my magazines ("What's Your Beauty IQ?" and "How You Should Look If You Want Him to Look"), but I'm supposed to make more of an effort to get to know Mr. Chou since we are taking him with us to Hugh and Estee's for New Year's.

One evening after dinner when Mr. Chou retreats to his room, I knock on his door. Something thuds. It takes a moment before he opens up. I peer in at his utterly tidy space, wondering what has fallen. Then I smile. "Do you want to watch *Jesus Christ Superstar* with us?" We are told Mr. Chou is a Christian, so I hope it won't upset him, like it did with *Godspell*, that this version of the story ends before the Resurrection.

Mr. Chou nods and smiles. His white shirt is unbuttoned down the front.

"You call me Chuck?"

"Okay," I answer. "Chuck." But it doesn't stick. The only other Chuck I know of is Chuck Conner, of *The Rifleman* fame, Mr. Chou's opposite. Then I ask, "Is there anything you need, anything we can do for you, Mr. Chuck?" I make a motion like I am turning on the faucet in the tub, remembering as I do so how tricky it is to both turn it on and get it to the right temperature. Mr. Chou's face takes on its familiar pained expression. I bite my lip. "Can I . . . may I just show you something?" I ask and motion for him to follow. I push back the shower curtain, get into the tub in my pajamas, and yank up and to the left on the big knob. When the water gets hot I adjust the temperature. "Ah," says Mr. Chou. He puts his hand into the stream of warm water, nodding and smiling.

I smile back. "I'm Evelyn," I say. "But don't call me that. Call me Eve."

Later that night, I kneel down beside my bed in the light of my Snoopy lamp and pull out the two magazines I've filched from my Dad's stack. New ones. I study the pictures, keeping one ear cocked in case Mom or Dad comes home or Mitchell or Ben comes down the hall. Nude cyclist Miss Carina Bourjaily (5'4", 110, 38–23–34) is so mesmerizing that I do not hear the footsteps until they come right up to my door. I cram the magazines back into the slit between the baseboard and mattress and snatch up *My Friend Flicka*. My heart knocks inside my chest. The footsteps head into the bathroom; then the tub water gushes on.

❀ ❀ ❀

The cactus and juniper are twinkling, while overhead, the dark rim of the desert mountains spills its bowl of stars. Here come the Teller kids, whirring down the walkway in Hugh's electric golf cart. I'm squeezed with Mitchell and Benjy into the rear-facing seat, singing "We Three Kings" as a round (this isn't working) and taking in the lighting displays of all the condos along the golf course. Heat still pulses from the concrete lining the endless, trimmed, rolling green.

One family has overdone it a little, at least in comparison to the other homes on the course. It's the guy who lives in the caretaker's bungalow, the guy who makes golf a daily reality for the tanned retirees of Rancho Paseo

Springs. A plastic interior-lit Santa, a Rudolph, and a penguin wearing a real scarf march in formation across a crispy square of turf toward a near-life-sized nativity scene in which a baby Jesus, looking more perplexed than beatific, blinks on and off at unpredictable intervals. The caretaker's name is Timo. I've had a crush on him since the fifth grade. He comes round digging, mowing, and fixing things in his caretaker's cart (a golf cart minus the fringed top shade) with a rosary and his prayer beads swinging from the dashboard. I don't know what bothers Hugh and Estee more, the fact that Timo is Mexican or the fact that he would drive around announcing his religion to everybody in this way. "And why is he always so dirty?" Estee will utter, unprovoked, as though she's keeping a running list. "The least these people could do is jump into their jacuzzi."

Tonight we get to stay up until past midnight to bring in the New Year. Estee serves leg of lamb with mint jelly on gold-rimmed china. She cannot believe I won't eat lamb, and I am not helping matters because I cannot even claim to be vegetarian. Everyone has animals they will and won't eat, I try to explain. For example, would she eat a dog? "Oh, pish-posh," is what Estee has to say to that. She is annoyed. She never had children with Hugh (she's wife number two) and she is thankful she didn't.

Estee serves homemade raisin pie with ice cream for dessert. It's a hit with the boys, who, at first, wrinkled their noses. My mother is explaining to Mr. Chou something about scoring in golf, a game she does not play, in loud, baby-talk English. I get up to use the restroom, but on the way back to my pie, Hugh corners me in the kitchen holding a little jug of half-and-half in one hand and something behind his back with the other. For a man who pees from a hole in his side into a little bag, he can really get around. He tells me a joke about three nuns and a priest on an airplane that I do not even get, and then laughs a laugh like the sound of a car motor trying to get started on a wintry morning.

"Where is everybody?" Estee sings. Mom, Dad, Mitchell, Benjy, and Mr. Chou are assembled at the table, so she means the two of us. Estee gives me a sharp, anxious look. Still sore about the lamb? I squint at her like I can't quite make her out.

"Doll, have you ever had a girl pie?" Hugh asks conspiratorially.

"What is it?" I have always wondered why the people who need to be humored cannot see when you are humoring them.

He winks and produces a fig from behind his back. He peels the fig and places it into a little bowl. "Now you watch," he says. With a spoon, he squishes the center of the fruit. The greenish-brown flesh spreads, the seeds ooze. Then he dribbles cream over the pulpy mess. "Mmm," he says and winks at me again. "You try that." I look at him to see if he is serious.

"Hugh!" Estee calls. "What is the holdup in there?"

"Honey, I was just fixing a little something special for my granddaughter. Can't we just have a minute, please?"

I edge away from the girl pie and back into the living room. It is only 10:00 and I am already agitated. Mom and Estee and Mr. Chou are examining Estee's prized African violets in the greenhouse attachment that Timo built. Mitchell and Benjy are sprawled across the sleeping bags playing Battleship. Dad wanders into the kitchen with Hugh to endure a lecture about the best performers in the Fortune 500 and laughs too loud at Hugh's dirty jokes. Everything is a joke to Hugh. He laughs until his eyes water or laughs so hard a cough starts in his chest and Estee has to come and whack him between the shoulder blades.

I call my friend Kara Cupola back home. I sense it before she does, although I don't sense it tonight, that we won't be friends for much longer. Her cleavage is not her fault; it just means her path in life is going to be different from mine. Tonight she is going to a New Year's Eve party with a nineteen-year-old electrician she met while she was at a Christmas party with a carpenter-framer. Her mother is letting her do this. She is going to wear her new platforms and her Chics, her tightest pair. I am not exactly jealous. I am, in fact, a little concerned for her safety. I have never even been asked out by an eleventh grader, much less a skilled tradesman.

Fanned out on the glass coffee table are copies of *Gourmet* magazine, the *Smithsonian* and *Playboy*, several months' worth of each. Mitchell is sixteen, and, like Dad, he can pick up a *Playboy* whenever he likes. No one ever says a word. I have to sneak my peeks, so they are much more irresistible to me. I stick an issue between the pages of a *Smithsonian* all about King Tut and assume an indifferent air as I flip through the photographs of bronzed limbs and frilly lace that I'm dying to study. There's the Santa-and-nubile-nymph cartoons. An article about dirt bike racing and another about the debate over women's colleges going coed. And then there's the jokes page.

"Gee! That's a hard one!" Hugh says in dumb blond falsetto from the kitchen, wheeze-laughing at his own punch line. Dad roars, Hugh wipes the tear from his eyes. Now I know where he gets them.

Estee comes out of the bathroom with a troubled look and whispers to my mother, who looks over at me. "We have a problem," Mom says importantly. She and Estee close in, their expressions part beseeching, part accusing. "Evelyn, are you on your period?"

"What are you?" I whisper, hotly. "The Voice of America?"

Mom closes her eyes in prayer. "Please tell me you did not flush your maxipad down the toilet. Again!"

Estee has already rushed over to the phone to call Timo, miming to Dad and Hugh to sit down and shut up.

It simply is not possible for me to see Timo under such circumstances, so I step over Mitchell and Ben, who have not allowed themselves to lose focus because of this "women's matter," and out onto the patio. A moon that doesn't really look like it's trying has crested the San Angelos. Across the green, I count seven parties in full swing. It suddenly occurs to me that Timo might have an opinion about having to get out of bed or interrupt his own festivities to come and fish out my maxipad from the toilet. Would normal people wake the plumber on New Year's Eve if the house wasn't actually flooding? Would they shout the word "maxipad" in front of their male relatives and international guests?

Pretty soon, Timo comes riding up the walkway in his cart. He's wearing khakis, sandals, and a Hawaiian shirt. Looks clean to me. He fetches his toolbox and goes up and knocks on the sliding glass door. In the second before Estee pulls the curtains aside, he stands and slicks his hands back through his hair. I shiver with adoration. Estee shouts out either "Our savior!" or "Por favor!" and lets him in. She throws her hands up likes she's been jolted or goosed and then clutches them to her chest. I settle in behind the manzanita bushes between condos, figuring I'm in for a long wait.

Mr. Chou comes out to the front step and lights a cigarette. He squints and takes a deep, deep drag, exhaling the smoke like it contains his whole long day. Before ten minutes have passed, Timo steps back outside holding a jar of the preserves Estee gives away at Christmas, tied with a red and green plaid ribbon. Mr. Chou offers Timo a cigarette, which he accepts, and the two men stand there quietly conversing. I can't make out what they are saying, but at one point, Timo holds up the jar of fruit and makes a twisting motion with his hand. He says something that causes Mr. Chou to nod and then practically double over in a belly laugh. I feel myself blush in the dark, sure that they've connected fruit preserves and maxipads in a way I'd rather not know about. Neither Timo nor Mr. Chou speaks what anyone would call fluent English. They come from different hemispheres. They have never even met. And yet here they are in the middle of the desert on New Year's Eve, conversing like old buddies. I edge closer, but by the time I get close enough to make out the words, metal heads rise, sputtering, from the lawn at strategically placed intervals all around me and water begins to shoot me—chit-chit-chit-chit—in the hip. Timo slaps Mr. Chou on the back and is on his way. I didn't even know Mr. Chou was the joking type. What language could they possibly be speaking with one another? And why don't they ever talk with us like that?

I am not alone. I am not by myself in the house with Grandpa Teller. Mr. Chou is only about five feet from me, on the other end of the couch reading one of Estee's *Gourmet* magazines. I have, of course, been watching to see whether he will pick up one of the *Playboys* but (perhaps because I have been watching) he has not. I have even arranged the July issue that's on the top of the stack a little askew over the partially bared breasts of Miss October directly underneath it, to see what will happen if I leave the room. However, Mr. Chou seems absorbed in reading about the making of chocolate fondue. Midnight has come and gone with some this and some that, some whoop-de-do. Now, Mom, Dad, and the boys are out for the annual postmidnight New Year's drive up Mount La Blanca to see the lights of the city. Mr. Chou, who begged out of the trip, has tucked an afghan over his legs. Estee is long since in bed. I've stayed behind, still a little embarrassed by the maxipad incident and reluctant to feel crampy and too far from a restroom on the first day of my period.

Last New Year's Eve, I'd been winning at Solitaire, my aces all neatly aligned on the glass coffee table, when Hugh padded out from the den in his black satin brocade robe and velvet slippers, puffing on his pipe. I call it his Hefner getup.

"There's something I'd like to show you, dear," he said. "Just a little something I think might interest you." I followed him to the hall closet where he reached toward something on the topmost shelf. "You're growing up so fast," Hugh said. He pulled down a stack of three or four magazines called *Massage Couples*. On the covers, happy-looking pairs of nudes were arranged in various poses beside pools or on the beach or, in one case, inside a hot tub, kneading one another's flesh. "I just wanted to share these with you, dear. Just wanted you to see how beautiful sexual pleasure can be." He shook his head sadly. "We never had this kind of opportunity when I was young. My folks were so damned uptight about such a beautiful thing." A woman with breasts splayed like what's for breakfast lay back on a fluffy white animal skin of some kind with her arms above her head and legs spread in front of her partner. Their glasses of Chardonnay glistened in the light of the fire roaring behind them in the fireplace. The woman was in some kind of heaven as her partner massaged her inner thighs. "You strike me as a liberated young woman," Hugh said, flipping through and stopping at various photographs. "I'll bet you've already had some pleasurable experiences. With that little bit of Oriental flavor from your Mom, those boys'll make a beeline for you." Another woman kneeled on all fours on a redwood deck overlooking the characteristic cliffs of Big Sur. The man behind her massaged her buttocks, his scrotum dangling soft and huge. "You see," Hugh pointed to the man, "it's not just about intercourse. This man is not even erect. Look at that. And this. These people aren't doing anything but enjoying one another's bodies."

I managed a nod and an interested-sounding "hmm." He returned the magazines to the shelf. "I just want you to enjoy your youth, pretty thing," he said, tweaking my nose. Then he went back to his program as though he had just paused to ask me how I was doing in algebra.

This New Year's, Late Night Classics is on, featuring the beautiful Grace Kelly in *To Catch a Thief*. Hugh pads out to the kitchen, same slippers, same robe, leaving a trail of cherry-flavored tobacco smoke. He has Hefner's bushy eyebrows and very large nose. He comes back out with a tin of Almond Rocha and offers me one. "Does your mother's friend want one?" he asks through the pipe in the corner of his mouth. Mr. Chou bows his head politely and reaches for the foil-wrapped candy.

Hugh takes the pipe out of his mouth and stands there pursing his lips, looking at me as if he is about to say something.

"There was this frog who walked into a bar," I say. Mr. Chou is busy experiencing the tooth-rotting pleasure of almond brittle. "The bartender says, 'What's that?' The frog says, 'I don't know. Last time I looked it was a bump on my butt.' Ha-ha. There was this horse," I continue, "who was feeling depressed. He goes into the bar for a drink. Bartender says. . ."

I wink and nod at Mr. Chou, trying to get him to laugh. He does me one better. "Why long face?" he says.

I look at him, amazed. "Yes. 'Why the long face?' How'd you know?"

He shrugs, pleased with himself. "American on plane telling to me during flight."

We look at Hugh. "Just swapping jokes," I tell him. "Mr. Chou and me."

❀ ❀ ❀

Years before I started my period, Mom and I had read a book together titled *The Wonder Called Life*. I give her an eight out of ten for the "you're a woman now" talk I received, with points off for expecting me to use the brand new and unused but by now archaic sanitary belt (sort of like a bra strap for the hips) she'd been saving for me since I was ten years old. Still, I figured out early on that information about the things worth knowing in life is best obtained by stealth. I sneaked into her room and studied her things, wondering what it was I was looking for. A leopard-print bikini with pointy bra cups, which I never saw her wear. The slightly stained rubber cap she kept inside a blue plastic case that snapped shut like a compact, with the accompanying tube of jelly in its own little blue case. The stack of letters folded inside a piece of embroidered satin, all of them addressed to "Pug" (?) from "your little man" (!). The box under the sink cluttered with cosmetics destined for obscurity—panty-hose-look leg makeup, crusted bottles of nail polish and eyebrow-plucking wax, men's cologne in a ship of glass. I filched things, of course. Stuff that, according to my image of my mother, she was never going to miss.

It is on an expedition into my parents' closet one summer afternoon that I first find my father's magazines. A dusty stack of *Playboys* and *The Joy of Sex* have been fixtures of the living room bookcase for as long as I can remember. But one year, a loose stack of other kinds of magazines appears on top of his shoeshine case, their titles consisting of words you never heard ordinary people use: *Hustler, Penthouse, BreastMan*—and some of the words like nasty little slaps—*Swank, Jugs, Cum, Oui*. This stuff is a far cry from *The Joy of Sex*. There isn't much joy. There isn't even that much sex. It's mostly just ordinary-looking women (not counting the *Penthouse* and *Playboy* goddesses) pouting or smiling or sometimes looking at you from the other side of a rounded body part, or across the gaping, glistening divide of spread-open thighs, taunting you, daring you, as if to say, made you look.

Every now and then some of the issues get taken away (does he tire of them? does she toss them out?) and new ones appear. There's never more than five or six in the stack, but there's plenty of turnover. I read the stories, fascinated. A trucker is so driven by lust for a teenage girl on his route that he kidnaps her and teaches her the pleasures of sex on the open road. A babysitter seduces the children's daddy every time he drives her home. A cop comes upon two women making out in the back seat of a car, takes off his gunbelt, and joins them. The women seem to be in charge of the sexual goings-on, while the men, just decent guys, average joes, cry out like babies, wounded, beside themselves, helpless with lust. What fascinates me the most is that the only way to have this sort of power over men is to have nothing or nearly nothing on.

❂   ❂   ❂

Kara and I are reclining in lounge chairs by the pool. Mom has dropped us off with Mitchell and Benjy and Mr. Chou, and we are giggling about what Mr. Chou is going to look like in his swimsuit. "Ah, so!" Kara says, jutting her front teeth out over her lower lip. "I come from China. Want to see bee-keen-ees!" She jiggles the contents of her underwire bikini top. "Ah, so!" I answer, bugging my eyes out and cupping two imaginary giant breasts in my hands. "You biggee girl! Verrrry beeg!" I realize it is my Korean grandmother who says these words to me every time we go to visit her, but that is in an entirely different context.

My brothers are adorable. Reddish hair on one, blondish brown on the other, both of them entirely easy and alive in their own skin, brown as nuts and it's only January. Mr. Chou follows. At first, Kara and I guffaw into our fists, pretending to be having coughing fits. He's wearing a tight black Speedo and yellow jackflaps. "God, look at that," Kara says. "Does a guy like that even have a marital status?"

"Kara, everybody has a marital status. His would be called single."

She is working the ching-chong-Chinaman thing into the ground, acting now like a buck-toothed, slant-eyed, apoplectic Chink clutching his throat like he is choking on something, perhaps his lust for American girls. "All right, already," I say.

In my opinion Mr. Chou doesn't look half bad. He actually has a chest and compact but well-formed shoulders. He steps out of his jackflaps, unrolls his towel, and then strides to the high dive. Apparently, he has a whole routine. Front to the edge of the board, bow it a little. Back to the ladder side, working his shoulders in forward and backward circles, then high-stepping his legs, pulling his knee to his chest. Then a deep breath, bows his head, and steps forward without the slightest hesitation, up into the air, a complicated-looking flip, and into the water with hardly a splash. The lifeguards on either side of the pool actually clap for him.

"Hmm," Kara muses, looking from me to Mr. Chou back to me.

"What."

"Strut for him."

"I am totally sure."

She bows her head and looks up at me. "Strut, Evelyn" she commands, cocking her head toward Mr. Chou.

"What for?"

"Because you've got to show off that sweet little ass of yours."

Kara would know. She's always checking people out. So I stand, adjust my bikini bottom, and walk toward the diving pool, crossing my feet with each step in a bad imitation of a runway model. Mr. Chou is still in the water, bobbing at the edge. He brings his arms up to rest on the ledge, watching me, breathing. When I turn at the corner and start back, I walk normal and then almost break into a run before I get back to my towel. I sit down and look back his way. I see that I am being taken seriously. Before I can decide how I feel about this, my brothers come running up and jump in on either side of him. Mr. Chou grabs a boy with each arm and dunks first one, then the other. Ben is squealing, delighted. Mitchell regains control and climbs to Mr. Chou's shoulders. Down up, down up, goes Mr. Chou, opening and closing his mouth like a fish.

If you're fourteen and female, I have discovered, pretty much all you need to do to get men to look at you is walk down the street. Kara and I are walking down the street, in halter tops and cutoffs. The sidewalk is way too hot for our bare feet, and she refuses to run, so we are sort of leap-stepping our way to Thrifty's for ice cream.

Even when we are shod, however, and even when Kara is not with me, men do look. Men in delivery trucks, men in Datsuns, men in Lincoln Continental Town Cars. Some look unabashedly. Some wait until they've driven past and then check you out in the rearview mirror. Some whistle and say things that make you feel good even though you're not supposed to like it. Once, a guy stopped in traffic, turned to me, and said, "What are you looking at, you little cunt?"

"I mean, what is it they see?" I say to Kara.

"Fuckability," says Kara. "Not old, not fat, not ugly."

I look at her. I don't think she is very smart, and I don't like her all that much anymore, but she's got that one down cold. Thrifty's air conditioning buffets us like cool gel. The floors gleam beneath us. "Please don't steal anything," I whisper to Kara.

"They just need to spread their seed," she says.

"God, you are so right," I tell her.

I get mint and chip, Kara orders a double rum raisin thinking she'll taste some rum. We wander to the magazine aisle and purchase our own copy each of *ROCKIN* magazine with a foldout of Peter Frampton and some good concert shots of Stevie Nicks and Linda Ronstadt. I shoot Kara's neck, under her lifted hair, with Shalimar. She does my wrists and back with Love's Babysoft. "I have to make a tampon run," I say. I have never used tampons. We study the various brands. "It doesn't break your cherry to use these, did you know that?" I whisper.

Kara makes a face.

"What? I've always wondered where they get the KOT—and the TAMP—that they add to the -EX in Kotex and Tampex. And where do they get the -EX?"

Kara says, "What would I care about a broken cherry?"

"Shhh!" I say. "Jeesh, Kara." Then I look at her across the vastness of two steps away and already my stomach is a big lump of dough for her, a flattened apple, her mother's giant plaid bean bag ashtray.

"What do you think I've been doing, you doink, giving him hand jobs?"

An arpeggio of emotions sounds inside me, like those organ notes in old silent movies. Jealousy. Shock. Loss. Plus, the way she says hand job, the little minor organ chord realization of that, too, the thought of which suddenly seems dirtier to me somehow than the idea of plain old intercourse.

Despite my recent discoveries, I am still easily shocked. In a way, I am more easily shocked than ever because now I know that the most innocent or ordinary of terms can refer to something illicit. Amateur housewives, for example. (Are there professional ones?) Watersports. Upskirts. BSDM.

(BSDM?) To think that people know what these things mean, that they do them. Scat. Celebs. Golden showers. I figure out "celebs" easily enough and "golden showers." I can even halfway deal with the concept of golden showers, relative to some of the other stuff I'm finding. But "scat"? I mean what is that? Some sort of sex game? Slang for a woman's body part? Something that comes out of you? Then I'm watching an episode of *Wild Kingdom* on Sunday. About grizzly bears. I am sitting on the couch between my mother and Mr. Chou with my bowl of mint and chip ice cream and realize with a chilling sense of befuddlement that yes, okay, Christ, it is something that comes out of you. And?

Me and Timo strolling on the beach together at sunset, looking for shells. Me and Timo surrounded by laughing, well-dressed couples all speckled with light, dancing close. Me and Timo snuggled under a blanket, a fire crackling at our feet. Me and Timo holding hands at the movies. Me and Timo making out in his white convertible. Me and Timo sitting in bed in our pajamas doing a crossword puzzle. Me and Timo drifting on a rowboat in a hazy afternoon. Me and Timo, always in panoramic. Timo and I.

At meals, I sit across from Mr. Chou and practice the pout, the come-hither. He always raises his eyebrows at me with a look that is neither discouraging nor particularly inviting. It's more like the look you have when you're waiting for someone who stutters to get it all said.

I practice on Mr. Chou because I get the impression that as far as sex is concerned, no one takes him seriously. There are "Oriental chicks," usually a pair of them lathering up the hairy White guy sandwiched between them in the tub. There's an occasional hard-bodied Latin Lover or Saucy Senorita. There's always Black guys with White women, Black women with White men, Black women with White women, and so on. But there's never an Asian guy. Ever. Not even a Kung Fu stud. Aside from my uncles and my cousins, who actually are Kung Fu studs, I know two other Asian men—Mr. Mori, the dentist who lives across the street from us and does laps around the block at midnight when his wife and kids are asleep, and Mr. Fukeyama, whose kids I babysit and whose wife is German. Mr. Fukeyama reads only *Hustler*, he's a *Hustler* man. His stack is right next to the toilet in the bathroom, in plain sight. Nothing adds up to anything else.

So the next time I have the house to myself, I head to Mr. Chou's room instead of to my usual destination, my parents' closet. I knock on the door even though I know he's gone to the Hofbrau with Mom and Dad and Mitchell and Benjy. The air in his room is possibly a little stale, but other than that, there is no evidence of Mr. Chou's presence in our household. No tie clips or fuzzy cough drops or eraser nibs in the dresser caddy. No papers on the desk or even in the wastebasket. There's nothing at all in the wastebasket, and I'm the one who takes out the trash. What could that mean? I slide open the closet door: shirt, shirt, shirt, jacket, striped shirt, jacket, trousers, trousers, hanger, hanger, trousers. Inside is his suitcase on the suitcase stand, which contains a few folded T-shirts, Calvin Klein briefs in assorted colors, several pairs of black dress socks, and a couple of crumpled hankies. The only items in the dresser are an expensive-looking bottle of cologne with Chinese lettering on the front, a good-quality wooden comb and brush set with natural bristles, a manicure set in a sturdy zippered pouch of what may be real crocodile leather, and my mother's red-satin embroidery box full of unsorted snapshots (ah-hah!), which I then realize she must have forgotten to clear out when she was preparing Mr. Chou's room. A guy like this would make a great spy, very low impact.

I sit down on the bed to strategize. It is only a matter of time before I find something. Everyone, even a guy from Huangtan province who specializes in snail scat, has something. I spy a neat stack of Mom's paperbacks on the hanging shelf between a vase of peacock feathers and our baby portraits. Mom often moves piles of books to different locations around the house for reasons that are clear to her, like a cat moving her kittens. There's *I'm OK, You're OK*. There's *Summerhill* about an alternative boarding school in England where the children arrive tense as boards and leave with their own mantra. There's *Future Shock, The Jungle Book, The Moviegoer, Nausea, The*

*Second Sex, Alan Watts: The Way of Zen* and *The Joy of Sex*. I always associate *The Way of Zen* and *The Joy of Sex*—those smug little know-it-all titles—and because the picture of Alan Watts in *The Way of Zen* looks just like the drawings of the bearded guy doing all that lovemaking in *The Joy of Sex*. Did my mother put these here, or has Mr. Chou been browsing?

I consult with Kara. If anybody knows where to look for the dirt on Mr. Chou, it's a girl whose mother reads dog-eared paperbacks with titles like *Torrid Belle*, in which southern plantation men rape lusty slave women, who enjoy it, and the lady of the plantation is so insatiably horny when her husband is off killing Yankees that she has sex with anything that moves, including a donkey. And that's just the stuff she leaves on the coffee table.

"Did you check under things?" she offers. "Bed? Dresser? Stuff sitting on the shelves?"

"Of course."

"Under stuff in drawers?"

"Yep."

"Mattress?"

"That was the first place I looked."

"Well, I dunno . . ." I can tell she is bored. "Butch is coming over in an hour." This is the seventies; hair takes an hour. "My advice to you?" she says and pauses. Kara picks at food with her fingers; I can hear the little sucking noises she makes when she's cleaning off each fingertip. "Is to quit looking for it in his room."

In his week off from the state university, we take Mr. Chou sightseeing. Everywhere we go, he has something to say about the experience, something that strikes us all as succinct and apropos. Of Yosemite in winter: "Half-a-dome mountain fill my whole soul." Of the giant sequoias: "How can we ever know such height?" After riding the Pirates of the Caribbean at Disneyland (or is this just about Disneyland in general?): "Jolly, jolly thieves!" We call these Chou-isms, and all week long we look for excuses to say things like, "That's the Chouth!" or "Tell the Chouth, the whole Chouth, and nothing but the Chouth, so help you God!" Mom points out that we are mocking Mr. Chou in a "Confucius Say-chop-suey-fortune-cookie" kind of way. She keeps a diary; she's writing this all down.

"So, what made you interested in snails?" I ask him outside a gift shop in Sausalito, where Mom and Dad are buying felt banners and snow globes and ashtrays of quartz for Mr. Chou to take home to friends and family.

Mr. Chou laughs a private little laugh. But then he looks me straight on, and I can tell that he deems me worthy of a real explanation. "Actually," he says, "snail is so fascinating. Because they are very low"—he squats and raises his hand about snail height from the sidewalk and looks back up at me—"they can tell us many thing about their habitat, okay? Like residue—you know pollution? Age of decompositions of various substance, toxin, and so on."

I nod; I am getting this.

Encouraged, Mr. Chou continues. "You know—how do you say—the little trail leave behind? The glisten?" I assume he means the focus of his work, the snail's waste. Yes, I nod. The glisten. "When you don't see the glisten, it is a very bad story." A Chouism if I ever heard one. I see now that I should have started our acquaintance with snails. Who knows what might have happened had I started with snails?

"And you?" he asks. "What is your interest? You want to be . . . ?"

"A Motorcycle Mama," I say. "Either a Motorcycle Mama or a killer whale." He laughs and keeps laughing—doubles over in laughter, in fact, just like he did with Timo. I look at him and I start laughing too. Mom and Dad come out with their loot and distribute pieces of saltwater taffy. They make the boys huddle on the bench behind me and Mr. Chou, who puts his arm around my shoulder, and we all squint into the sun and say "greased leeches."

We all feel so good that now I feel bad about what I've done.

One night, sometime between hand jobs and half dome, I was babysitting for the Fukeyamas, checking out the *Hustlers* in the bathroom as usual after I'd put Dierdre and Johan to bed. I was studying the Classifieds, where I imagine most people who read girlie magazines don't bother to look:

My Daughters Want to Pull Down Their Panties for You.

Dial for Photos. Discreet. Legal.

Free Bloody Photos of Women on the Rag.

Lesbians.

Housewives.

Sexy Teens on the Rag.

Hermaphrodites, Older Women, Torture,

Dressing Room Hidden Cameras,

Fat Women, Lactating Women, Hairy Women,

Women with 4 Breasts.

Like the circus was coming to town. I sneaked the issue into my purse and brought it home with me. After some dictionary consultation, I selected Hermaphrodites, Lactating Women, and the shots of women with multiple breasts. I knew enough to stay away from ads that listed only a phone number or had to assure customers of product legality; I wasn't trying to get anyone in trouble. With several nights' worth of babysitting money—this stuff is not cheap—I purchased three separate money orders at the 7–11: one for Mr. Nicholas R. Craven, L.S.P (L.S.P?); one for Aquarius Associates; and one for Deadpan Dames, Inc. All promised plain brown wrappers. All said allow four to six weeks. Three times I signed the line swearing that I was an adult and that I was at least eighteen years of age. They ask you in different ways just to be sure. The name on the order blank looked so simple and exposed, like eyebrows suddenly visible after a haircut.

Mr. L. Chou.

Mr. L. Chou.

Mr. L. Chou.

I don't even know what the "L." in his name stands for. Poor Mr. L. Chou. But there's nothing we can do now except wait.

# The Inside of the World, 1997

Grace supposed she could allow herself to become alarmed at the way this day—Christmas Day—yawned open before her. She couldn't run her usual Saturday morning errands to the bookstore, the farmer's market, the drugstore. With an eight-week medical leave beginning right after the holiday season, she had no papers to grade or courses to prep. She wasn't supposed to be looking forward to foot surgery. Her doctor had warned her that her bunions were severe and would involve not only cutting the bone but realigning ligaments and would be more painful and take longer to recover than most. "Don't be such an optimist, Doc," she had joked, only to be met with a tolerant squint. What was wrong with people? It was Gracie's little secret that she liked or could handle almost everything about living alone, except that she missed having someone to complain to on a regular basis. You expected loneliness, even the occasional dark night of the soul. But what a luxury it would be to have someone waiting at home to whom one could say, "My doctor is such an ass." Of course, that someone would have to be willing to listen. Her daughter Evie was due to arrive in on New Year's Day to help her through recovery. Too bad she didn't qualify.

This Christmas morning, Gracie could see all the way up to the snow-caps of the Sierras from her kitchen window. She breathed in deeply, imagining that she was inhaling the stark, clear air of those peaks deep into her lungs. A couple such breaths made you feel vibrant, almost light-headed. Eartha Kitten coiled herself into her favorite sagging spot in the faded canvas chair while Grace scanned the *Fresno Bee* opened before her on the counter and half listened to the television on low. Why not forced blooms? Martha Stewart suggested. The program encouraged viewers to adopt just one new LIVING idea in the New Year for a lasting sense of satisfaction at having cultivated even a small change. This from the new and improved Martha, although Grace was one of those who had always liked her. The quince-currant jam and five everyday-elegant napkin folding techniques (yikes) seemed like genuinely good ideas, if a tad fussy, to Grace, but the bulbs made sense like nothing had in days. Why not forced blooms, indeed, she thought and slowly ate her breakfast—freshly squeezed grapefruit juice and leftover fruited kuchen from her friend Eileen's Christmas Eve get-together.

Eileen, her longtime colleague at the adult education building, had invited Gracie to the gathering at her place up in the foothills. Her family lived in one of the nicer new housing developments the contractors were throwing together up there. Eileen had insisted that Grace should spend the night and leave whenever she felt like it the next day. The invitation did have its appeal. The drive up to Coarsegold, just above the fog line, was a pretty one, and she could escape the gloom for a spell. Eileen couldn't entertain often, living forty minutes from the valley floor, so it was only right that Grace try to put in a showing. After all, if she did not, Christmas Eve would consist of her getting into bed early with a hot cup of decaf cappuccino and a novel. On the other hand, Gracie did not look forward to making conversation with well-meaning strangers, even if some of them were otherwise alone on Christmas Eve like she was. This year was so different without the kids and grandkids. Christmas was for family. So at the last minute she decided to make the drive up to Eileen and Vic's. "Yes, I do have family," she practiced answering in her head as her Corolla negotiated the twists and turns of the mountain highway. "They're with their dad this year. Busy. Couldn't afford the plane tickets." Which was close enough to the truth. The truth was that Gracie wasn't sure which, if any, of her children was still speaking to her since she had threatened to sell the house and leave Navelencia once and for all. When she finally stood before the plum-studded wreath at Eileen's front door, her sugar dusted gingerbread balls and a tin of Almond Rocha in hand, she peered through the window panes at a lighted tree and a crowd larger than she had anticipated. Gracie felt for a moment like the little match girl, born to be on the outside of things. She shook it off, put on a smile, and knocked.

To her surprise, she had felt surprisingly cozy with Eileen and her family and their circle of friends. There had been hot mulled wine, spiced nuts, all manner of sweets and pastries. A really nice spread was laid out in Eileen's handmade crockery, simple, not trying to make a big statement. Vic played carols on the piano including "O Holy Night," which always gave Grace goose bumps even in a roomful of people she didn't know. One woman about her daughter Evie's age had adorable twin toddler girls dressed in white knitted getups with red bows in their hair and little red tights. They shouted out "Rudolph" with appropriate glee, while Eileen's daughter, who was at that wonderful, poised age of prepubescent girls, looked on approvingly. At one point, Grace felt very flushed and set down her glass mug of hot wine with the cinnamon stick in it. She felt moved to say, "What a perfect evening" to Eileen, but her tongue felt less than reliable. She'd let the moment pass but later remarked to Eileen about how pretty Amanda was becoming.

After the singing, she took the plaid wingback by the crackling fire, tucked a bright throw over her lap—her legs got a chill so easily—and decided she was staying put. There seemed to be so much good will in that house, and warmth, and, well, Christmas cheer, that instead of becoming the evening's wallflower, Gracie found that people kept coming to her to chat, offering to warm her mug, bringing her things to eat. Now that she thought about it, she realized it was because they saw her as old. Grandmotherly. In need of solicitous attention. Grace straightened and took one last cold sip of coffee. Well, you are old, she told herself. Old for your age. Other women her age were out running marathons across glaciers and single jetting over the Serengeti, she knew. Even her own mother had crossed an ocean knowing she would probably never return home. The funny thing was if she went far enough back in her memory to the days when her body was young and strong, she could imagine having lived a life that led to flying airplanes in your sixties. That had not been the life she ended up living of course. But she liked to think she knew something of the adventurousness those women must have felt inside because, although it didn't count for much, she had always felt some untapped part of her waiting in the wings. She didn't feel like the old women other people saw, the woman who has already become everything she was destined to become.

Those twin girls must have thought she looked the part of grandmother because they spent a lot of time in her lap, alternating with Amanda or their mom. The girls had sensible, womanly names—Catherine and Francesca—not cutesy twin names and not abbreviated into Cate and Fran or, worse, Cathie and Frannie. The mom was one of those extremely together earth-mother types dressed in a loose ankle-length cotton dress with a pair of quilted doves appliquéd on the front. She was still nursing her daughters. They climbed onto her lap, confidently tugged at the doves on her chest which turned out to be a cloth panel that opened into discreet nursing slits, and nursed away. Very clever. Women with sense had designed such clothing.

Unfortunately, such women hadn't seemed to be around when she had young ones. Back then, of course, the only women you ever saw nursing were in *National Geographic*. The mom and her daughters made a much more appealing picture, all in all, but Gracie knew she could never have endured being pawed like that—not well into the toddler years anyway— by those charming creatures acting so territorial about their mother's body. There was something untamed about their splayed limbs, their hands milking each breast expertly, greedily. Gracie loved her own children with her whole being. But why did every generation have to figure out a new way to make motherhood an exercise in complete selflessness? Just when infant formula freed women to order their days with a bit more regularity and to sleep through the night, breastfeeding had come back into fashion. As soon as they came up with drugs to make labor go easier, women had started talking about natural childbirth. And now there was even the "stay at home mom" movement, with women fighting for the right to do the very thing that they had fought against twenty-five years earlier. Gracie had gone back to school to finish her degree when other moms were doing it, but she didn't feel liberated. She felt she had better get ready to support herself in case one of Wayne's affairs turned into something serious or in case she herself got so fed up with him that she finally kicked him out.

The young woman had taken the opposing wingback on the other side of the fireplace, head bowed over her suckling babes. But she kept looking up now and again as though she intended to carry on a conversation while trying to hold two squirming toddlers in her lap. When she ventured a full look in the woman's direction, however, she saw that the squirming toddlers were now asleep.

"I'm Lina Murillo," the woman said in a pointed, but quiet, way. "You must be Eileen's friend Grace Teller."

Grace found herself responding to the woman warmly. Lina reminded her of her own daughter, Evie, with the edges softened. And the more opportunity she had to observe her, the more convinced she became that the woman's down to earth quality went deeper than her 100 percent cotton clothing and Birkenstocks. She asked Lina how she felt about having twins, knowing it was a subject that wouldn't require too much conversational effort on her part. Lina had explained that all the books on twins stressed the importance of helping each child to achieve a separate identity, starting with their names and their clothing. She confessed that she couldn't help herself on special occasions like this one, when she dressed them alike, "like little dolls," she said a bit sheepishly, but in their daily life she worked hard to treat them as individuals. Catherina was the more assertive of the two, the one who had always weighed more and seemed to dominate her sister. Francesca was gentlehearted, the sensitive one.

And so on. Gracie remembered murmuring a question or comment now and again, but mostly, she recalled the feeling of just letting the woman's soothing, low-toned voice wash over her as she sank, dreamy and warm, ever deeper into her chair while experiencing the uncommon sensation of not knowing where her skin ended and the chair began, and of feeling too utterly comfortable in any case to become alarmed. Finally, she began dozing off in short intervals. A couple of times she started awake and had to sneak her hand up to wipe a bit of drool from the corner of her mouth. Every time she woke, she heard Lina's voice and wondered vaguely what mother had raised her.

Gracie now recalled other things she had learned about Lina, although she couldn't remember at what point in the evening she learned them. The twins' mother was from Schenectady and had gone to Vassar College and married her biology professor, one Hector Chou. After many happy years of marriage (widows always remembered their marriages as happy, Gracie had noticed), they had Catherina and Francesca. But soon after, her husband died of lymphoma. Lina found herself a job as a seed technician for an organic farming operation looking to get a foothold in the valley. She was new to the West and spending her first Christmas without her family or her husband's family, just her and the girls and Daro, the man she had come with. Daro. Now she remembered. She had fallen into conversation with him at some later point in the evening. He was the one who had told her more about Lina when she had asked.

"Daro Tagura," he had said to her when he pulled up a chair closer to the fire to shake her hand. He had that kind but ubiquitous smile, bordering on indiscriminate. He did seem sincerely kind and not merely polite. Gracie couldn't help wondering, though, if he had only felt obliged to finally come to speak to her since she was the only other Asian in the room. To whom could she express such an opinion? She wouldn't say this kind of thing to any of her neighbors or coworkers most of whom were

White, in any case. Her sisters would look at her blankly: What do you mean you were the only Asian in the room? Her children would give her a pained half smile that meant their tolerance was being strained, which would then make her aware that they had been practicing their tolerance with her when she thought they were simply having a conversation. Evie, especially, would feel provoked by the comment, would probably even conclude that her mother was being racist. She knew how to throw words around, that girl—conk you over the head with them, even cut you now and then.

But this Daro person wasn't just Asian, of course, he was Japanese. A Jap, people had called them during the war. Had her father been alive, he would have forbidden her to speak with Daro.

The son of Japanese immigrants, born and raised in the valley, Daro explained that his unusual name was owing to the fact that his parents had wanted him to have an American name—Dale—but spelled it phonetically for Japanese speakers—Daro. Gracie couldn't help laughing and told him about her own father, the Korean immigrant who voted YES on every proposition that ever appeared on a ballot once he had become an American citizen because he believed he was saying "yes" to the American way.

Daro had an easy laugh, with small, good teeth and crinkly eyes. His salt-and-pepper hair brushed the top of his collar, longish but neatly styled. She had a nephew his age. Had he been part of the sixties? That wide smile indicated something she couldn't quite read, it being just slightly too open. She could see how he would be friends with Lina. He wasn't wearing Birkenstocks; in fact, he was wearing rather dusty field boots. He looked like a comfortable person. Comfortable in himself, in his dark green shirt and wide-wale corduroy trousers. He smelled good, too, and was clean-shaven. But he was just a little odd. For one thing, he had kept referring to Lina's daughters as Click and Clack, after their mother had gone to the trouble of giving them such dignified names. For another, his only interaction with them involved sending them into hysterics of laughter, tickling and tumbling with them until something was going to get broken. Lina hadn't seemed to mind. Eileen and Vic certainly didn't mind. Even poised young Amanda wanted in on the action. Normally, Gracie would have had an opinion about all of the noise and roughhousing on this kind of occasion, which she would use up calories trying to keep to herself. But that night she lacked the energy to express an opinion about much of anything. Instead, she smiled to herself remembering when her own kids were little. Wayne would hoist them, squealing and delighted, inside a blanket over his shoulder. "Here's my sack 'o toys!" he'd roar. "My great, big sack 'o toys!"

She watched Daro and Lina, trying to discern exactly what they were to one another. At first, she had thought they were married, Daro father to her brown, part-Asian-looking twins. Now she wondered if they were merely friends. He wasn't attentive to her in more than what appeared a friendly way, and he never touched her, except to help her on with her coat when they were leaving. He did look a good fifteen or twenty years older than Lina, who must have been in her thirties but that didn't mean anything. It hadn't stopped Wayne. Now she found herself wondering why in the world she had thought about her father forbidding her to talk to Daro because he was Japanese. Gracie smiled to herself: a senior citizen and forbidden to talk to a man. He was part owner of a Japanese farming cooperative based near Sanger, never married.

"Lucky, I guess," he laughed when she had asked boldly how he had managed to avoid marriage. It was very unusual, an Asian bachelor. Then she had cringed inside, realizing that, after all, he could be gay. Her children had taught her to think of this kind of possibility. It was a subject about which she felt more or less neutral, mostly because she preferred not to think about a subject people simply never used to talk about. What did occur to her was that she and Wayne had somehow raised children who were remarkably tolerant and open-minded about such things. She admired this quality in each of them quite apart from their opinions, themselves, with which she did often disagree.

Twice before the end of the evening, a log fell, sending sparks crackling from the hearth, starting her awake. Both times, someone sat sharing silently in that circle of dying firelight with her as she nodded off in earnest. Once, Eileen's husband, Vic, made a big show of sweeping the ashes off her blanket and asking if she was all right. And once, Daro Tagura simply lifted his eyebrows at her in a kind but curious way, as though she had just uttered something slightly ridiculous in her sleep. Gracie couldn't account for her behavior of the night before, falling asleep midconversation with people she hardly knew. Having to be woken by Eileen who handed her a towel and a packaged toothbrush and steered her in the direction of the guestroom. It was no wonder some people drank all the time, what blissful oblivion.

Gracie sat up straight and pulled her bathrobe a little tighter around her waist. She had woken just before dawn and literally sneaked out of the house, cold started her car, and drove back down the mountain highway without meeting a single vehicle until she hit town. How strange it had felt, lurking around before sunrise like a thief. Or a woman having an affair. Once home, she changed into her flannel nightgown and lay her head on her pillow, blinking, breathing, until she felt normal again. Hours later, she opened her eyes, sensing even before she drew the curtains, the brightness of the day.

Now she sat and looked at the fireplace, which housed a cold, gnarled log. There had always been a fire on Christmas morning. After Wayne was gone, Ben or Mitchell had seen to it. It was ironic how all of her kids had always been such sticklers for family traditions and now they weren't even here. Christmas morning just wasn't Christmas morning without a wood fire. You got up early, you made a crackling fire, you started the coffee and the sausage or orange juice, and you went in and opened presents. A huge and leisurely breakfast followed, always with hot biscuits or scones served with the gold-plated flatware and the Christmas napkins that Evie folded just so. Once, Gracie had skimped and bought regular vanilla ice cream rather than the coconut-covered Christmas "snow-balls" everyone was used to but nobody actually liked. Such protests had ensued from grown people, people with minivans and weed whackers and insurance plans.

Gracie sighed. She might as well face it. Living alone was as hard as living with other people had ever been. You had to maintain a relationship with your solitude; you couldn't just expect solitude to fend for itself. That was how you ended up babbling, with newspapers stacked to the tops of your cupboards all around your kitchen and people giving you wide berth as you made your way, a neighborhood legend, down the grocery aisle. Not Gracie, not as long as she could see the snowcaps from her kitchen window. She owned her old beige stucco and the three acres it sat on outright. Two thin junipers stood sentinel at the front drive, which let out close to a walled housing development under construction called Sierra Lakes Village on its own county road. That road, which gave her an address separate from the annexation, was the only reason Gracie still lived in her own place and not some clapboard condo across from a strip mall. She had enjoyed her status as last holdout in the neighborhood. For what it was worth, she had roots in this place. It wasn't where she had come from. It certainly wasn't what she had dreamt for herself. But this house and the postage stamp of land on which it sat in the little blip of a township called Navelencia had been Wayne's dream, the star to which once upon a time she had hitched her wagon.

The five-acres of dead trees, brush, and the carcass of a chimney hearth had been part of Wayne's inheritance from his father along with a check to purchase land and the two-story stucco they had built. They had been Gracie's outright for years, since the divorce. Now all the developers were dying to get their hands on it so they could compete with Sierra Lakes Village. Only Isaac Garabedian, who owned the surrounding fig orchards, had land worth more. Some day Sierra Lakes Village clones would cover every last fig tree and grapevine and dusty fruit stand from here all the way up to Kings Canyon National Park. Gracie had always intended to be permanently horizontal before that happened here. But she had recently decided that a small, new, white condo with no dust, nor storage capacity to speak of and no history was exactly what she needed.

After a day spent on the back patio up to her arms in potting soil and surrounded by pots of various sizes, Gracie lifted a white teakettle from the stove just before it burst into song. She measured a scant teaspoonful of coffee crystals into a mug and sipped her coffee standing at her kitchen counter. Its clean gleam made her feel at peace. On most winter days in the valley, there wasn't any point to having a view, as there was nothing much to look out at except rain or fog. It was a rare December day when the sun did burn through the fog, and this morning was one of them. When Gracie and Wayne had moved in thirty-some years ago, they had looked out onto neighboring fig orchards, where dark, gnarled branches pierced the tule fog like the arms of desperate beasts. Back when the children had been young, Gracie sometimes caught sight of them climbing into the limbs of those beasts or later spied a child's bright scarf or winter cap left dangling behind. Muffled by the fog, their shouts and laughter, even back then, had sounded to her like the voices of memory.

When they got older, her children mumbled rather than shouted and slipped off beyond the reach of her voice, the fog a convenient blanket within which to experiment in that orchard with all of the things that promised to ruin them and nearly did ruin them for a time. They would return to the kitchen, furtive, cigarette smoke clinging to their jackets, harboring their separate and pointed miseries. Sometimes, Grace would look up from the cutting board where she stood preparing the same evening meal she had prepared ten years earlier and have the sensation that the past two decades had been nothing but a flash of light. Poof. There they were, all grown. A long string of drizzly, foggy days did that to you, wore at the edges of your sense of self until you felt gray, unarticulated. Once she retired, of course, it would either get worse or she would be so good at being alone she wouldn't give it another thought.

That pork cutlet with a little bit of applesauce, a half hour or so of television, and a shower, and it would be time for bed. In the manner of that prayer she had taught in Sunday school, Gracie would slip between her sheets, weary, content, and undishonored. She had missed her children this holiday, even ached for them. But her decision to sell the house felt as right as ever, even if her children did not see it this way. They had a right to feel so strongly against it that they stayed away for Christmas.

They could stay away next Christmas if that was what they needed to do. It didn't change a thing. Gracie was not being stubborn in the least. And if she stirred in the middle of the night, her heart pounding, her face heavy with the pillow's warmth, the fear would be only the most ordinary of fears: a tree branch tapping against the pane in a brisk night wind, the floor heater ticking on or off again, Eartha Kitten aggravating some tomcat from her perch in the windowsill. Or some other noise, difficult to place, but not persistent enough, or alarming enough, to coax her from her sleep.

## Daro

Sometimes, recalling the summer day when she had first appeared at the fruit stand, Daro Tagura couldn't believe he had let a woman like Lina go. She had stepped out of her white Jeep, and even before he noticed that she was pretty, he noticed she was a woman with a very strong back. Two tiny heads nodded toward one another from their car seats inside the Jeep, forming an arch. The woman harnessed herself with a complicated-looking cloth carrier featuring front and back pouches, ducked inside, and extracted a chubby sweaty female in a denim hat topped by a fake sunflower. After inserting the child's sausage legs into the carrier's leg holes, she somehow twisted the thing around so that the first baby was at her back while she hoisted another infant in an identical drooping sunflower hat, its legs dangling, onto her front and facing forward. Most amazingly of all, both infants had woken without a peep blinking and serene as though it would take more than roadside dust and valley heat to get them going.

The woman crunched across the gravel in a faded sundress and sandals, came up into the shade and just stood with her hands on her hips. Calm as a pastured animal, she stood there sniffing, letting her eyes adjust to the change in light. Her face shone with sweat, and all three of them appeared flushed, but clear-eyed, neither flustered nor tired. Her hair, long and a rich shade of brown, was twisted up off her neck with one of those hair claws. Daro wondered if he should have helped her with those babies instead of watching her from his perch in front of the fan, his book open on his lap, his glass of iced tea sweating atop the particle board over two sawhorses that served as the counter. When the woman turned to the nectarines, the quiet, alert backside baby reached toward the bright smells and colors with no success. The front side child looked delighted, agog.

"Do you grow this fruit?" the woman asked him. Her bangs were almost perfectly tidy and straight, the color of wet bark, and her lips were full and slightly waxy-looking, as though she'd slathered on Chapstick. Part Latina, or Polynesian, he wondered? The backside baby grabbed a plum as her mother bent to pick up a bag of oranges. She sucked, patient and earnest, unable to pierce the taut skin.

"I'm a Tagura, but the Tagura Orchards is my uncle's. I'm filling in today."

"It's nice. I've always heard this part of California is the place for fruit."

"The world's produce basket, they say. I've sold fruit here every summer since I was about their age." He nodded at the girls. "Where're you all from?"

Lina squinted when the squished plum slid down her back. He liked the way she simply reached her arm up and behind, fished for the plum, pulled it out, and tossed it in the wastebasket at the side of the counter. "Add that one to our total," she said. She didn't shave her underarms, but on her it looked good, natural. "Originally? From a decaying industrial city in upstate New York."

"I took geography," he said.

"Schenectady. But now you have to spell it."

He did. And then he said, looking at the girls, "Don't tell me—Click and Clack?"

Tiny hands with purple-stained fingers encircled her neck. "Close enough. Meet Catherine and her baby sister by two minutes, Francesca."

"Ah, I get it. No identity crisis for your girls—nice distinct names."

She smiled at him in a way that let him know he had said the right thing. "And mine's Lina Murillo."

"Daro," he replied and wiped his hand off on a counter rag to reach it out to her. "Daro Tagura. You coming up or going down?" he asked. She looked at him, clear-eyed as ever, and blinked. "The mountain," he added.

She laughed and shook her head. "Do you know that I was just about to tell you my life story? I thought you were asking if I was coming up or going down in life."

"And?"

"Down the mountain. I'm learning pottery and firing from a friend up in Coarsegold." She paused a beat. "So I guess that means up in life. Doing something for your soul again should count for that, don't you think?"

Daro noted the "again." He wanted to tell her she didn't seem like someone who had experienced many lapses in the soul-nurturing department. Instead, he asked, "Anyone along for the ride with you three?"

"Down this mountain, no. In life, well, not anymore."

He looked at her kindly, carefully. "Won't be for long, I'm sure."

He had invited them home to see the orchards and let the girls run around and play. It meant she would meet everyone, and he didn't know how to tell her that no one would think a thing of it since they were used to his bringing women home, even women with kids. Plenty of women had spent the night in his little place back of the main house. He wouldn't tell her that. He was just helping a transplanted New Yorker adjust to life in the valley, someone who could stand making a new friend or two.

For the rest of the summer, they were just friends, Catherine and Francesca playing the biggest part in their relationship. They took to him naturally; children always did. The trick was to treat kids like dogs, letting them sniff you first, not getting into their space until they invited you in.

Sleeping together was no accident. It ended up being, literally, just sleep, all of them, girls included and even a cat or two, on the floor of Lina's second-story apartment. He and Lina had been drinking wine to celebrate her landing a position as a part-time cook at a natural foods lunch place in Fresno, a job that provided a cushion in case the soft money on the organic growing cooperative ran out. She had brought home whole wheat pasta primavera in Chinese food containers—no Styrofoam—paid the babysitter, nursed each of the girls, and then started in on the food like she wasn't going to eat again for a week. Daro suddenly wanted to braid her hair, a single plait down her back, thick and loose, that he could undo later. She asked him where he had learned to do that.

"I did my own, for years and years." He could feel her smile, although her face was not to him. "You know, a Chinaman's queue."

"I do know. My husband wore one too. I go by Murillo again, my maiden name." She turned her face slightly to him. "I was Lina Murillo-Chou. The girls are." He braided, the heft and smoothness of her hair a sensation containing the possibility of arousal. The dark wave of it caused a tickling across his groin. He tugged a handful of it, pulling her face toward his. He maintained vigilance with himself, even though it was something of a waste. Later, when he wanted it, he'd embarrass himself, there'd be nothing.

"You're not Chinese though. Was it solidarity? Yellow power?"

Daro chuckled at phrases he hadn't heard in a while. "That was before your time."

"Hector was a full professor when I met him."

"Uh-oh. An older man?"

"Not as a rule," she smiled. "So don't get your hopes up. But fill me in on your sordid sixties past."

"There isn't one to speak of. I was in high school when Vietnam ended, more troublemaker than radical. I got swept up in the times, I suppose. There were the years when acting White was all that mattered. Then came the years when not being White was all that mattered."

"And now?"

He shrugged. "We had our say. Change takes, you know, time." He wondered what caused Lina's lack of reply but not enough to get into further discussion about any of it. So he added, "I wore the queue because I thought it looked good. Women loved it."

Her head tilted up with a playful smile. The feel of her hair in his hands caused a ready stir that he couldn't help feeling a little proud of. "So, they stopped loving it?" When he didn't answer right away, she tried, contritely, "Or just time for a change?"

"I cut it off for a woman I loved. She left. I never grew it back."

Lina nodded. "Hector lost his from the lymphoma of course."

He tilted her head back gently, as if to kiss her, but laid a palm against her cheek, cupped part of her chin. "I am sorry. You're young for so much loss."

The girls were whiny and clingy that night—all sorts of teeth were coming in—and he offered to take them out in the double stroller until the sun went down so Lina could have an hour or so to herself. By the time he returned, she was asleep on the sofa and the girls were out cold. Leaving didn't feel quite right, although Daro realized it wasn't up to him to decide to stay. The right thing to do would be to leave this family in peace. Carefully, he lifted the girls from the stroller, kissed the top of each sleep-damp, fragrant head and set them in their respective bean bag chairs, whereupon they rolled toward each other in the middle and entwined their bare legs, settling in for some serious sleep. He couldn't resist pretending to himself this was his wife with her arm flung across her face, chest rising and falling soundlessly, that these were his own daughters. His couch, his television. It wasn't that he wanted a wife; he'd have managed that by now if he'd wanted it bad enough. But Lina had that womanly quality of making you want to take care of her, independent as she was. He knew her enough now to know it would have appalled her to hear this said of her. She thought of herself as the last woman to inspire either protectiveness or possessiveness in a man. And, in fact, it was her very resourcefulness and self-reliance—worn with a kind of urgency due to her being a single mother of twins, he supposed—that drew him in. You had to be careful; women knew what was going on even when they appeared not to. Half the time, you eventually realized that what you thought was pursuit was nothing more than your unwitting fulfillment of a well-laid plan. But when it was genuine, there was nothing more attractive than a woman who had neither her guard up nor her line cast, probably just because it was so rare.

He couldn't help himself. He switched on the evening news so low that he could hear the hum of the set better than he could hear the football scores. Just for a little while, he wanted the blue glow to fall on somebody's face besides his own, to fall on the faces of people he loved, people who needed him.

The curtain of the conscious world had just let fall when Lina sat up, bringing him back from sleep. She was a clean waker, no fuzzy edges.

She suggested that they each take a child, put her in her crib, and then go in and lie down in her bedroom. Her sheets were a well-washed bright yellow-and-white striped pattern that made his mouth almost water from the faint suggestion of lemon. She slipped out of everything but her panties and loose-fitting lavender T-shirt, somehow getting the bra off her shoulders with the shirt still on. What did that effort at modesty suggest? Or was it modesty? He found it sexier than her simply taking the shirt off. He got undressed as well, got in, and she turned her back to him. Then she scooted backward. He had always loved these wordless transactions between bodies. His arm fit so neatly into the curve of her hip, the top of his knee snug against the back of her own. Not all women fit like that. He grew hard with the sensation of that old newness, of age-old motions with an unfamiliar body, the intimacy always surprisingly sudden to him as he breathed in a new scent, cupped a new belly, kissed a new neck. She pressed back against him, willing, wanting. But he whispered, "Sleep, in the morning," because he knew sleep was what she needed but also because, lovely as she was to him, he probably wouldn't stay hard having had so much wine and it being so late. Erections lasted a little longer in the morning. He hoped to wake with one.

When Daro woke again, he was alone in Lina's bed. Blue dark, faintest morning seeped through the half-drawn curtains. He felt around for his glasses and then lifted his head to look around for a clock. He let his head fall back to the pillow. Pointless, disjointed dreams had disturbed his rest, the familiar beginnings of depression. He lay and watched for where it would pool inside him. Neck? Lower back? Shoulders? Groin? But he found that he couldn't attend to his awareness while lying in a woman's yellow sheets, a woman that he hadn't made love to when she had asked him to and whose whereabouts were not even, at the moment, clear to him. And, of course, all of these thoughts annoyed him further. He tried to gauge the silence of the household, whether it was weighted with sleep (had she gone in to check on the girls and decided to sleep in their room?) or felt empty (had she—they—gone somewhere?).

He sat up. He lacked information, a feeling he didn't like at all. Draped across the foot of the bed was her white bathrobe. Out for a morning jog? There must be some sort of note then. Suddenly aware of the beating in his chest, he pulled the chain on the bedside lamp but nothing happened. Either it was a three-way switch or she hadn't bothered to fix or replace the bulb. Where was the wall switch then? He groped along the wall where it was reasonable to expect to find a light switch and then gave up, fumbling around amid piles of laundry that hadn't been there before. He had to urinate but didn't want to wander around half dressed in case a female came out. What he wanted very much right now was just to find his goddamned jeans and get them on. He sat down in a stuffed chair, on them he realized, much relieved. There. He sat back down in order to think about what was next. He was getting too old for this.

Where exactly Lina and her daughters were right now was Lina's business, he decided. To a younger man or a man more smitten—she was beguiling, truly, but his heart wasn't in it—this little mystery would be worth solving. Daro just wanted the smell of his own sheets, the weight of a presidential biography teetering on the rise and fall of his belly, Ranger snoring at the foot of the bed, chin on tail.

He stood and stepped his way to the hallway, where he finally found a functional light switch. The door to what he recalled was the girls' room stood ajar, the only light coming in from where he stood. He peeked in long enough to discern three slumbering heads. So much for Lina's thing for older men, Daro thought wryly. He felt for his keys and wallet, stuck his Giants cap on his head, and stepped out into the near-pink dawn. Her next-door neighbor had left his sprinkler on; the water in his patch of lawn was pooled and rising. Lina's front door had a knob lock, but he felt bad that he wouldn't be able to deadbolt it or chain it for her. Should he go back in and wake her, bother with explanations and goodbyes, thereby risking enhancing the drama of a situation he wanted to de-emphasize, if not forget? He half-turned, but no. That was probably the reason he was alone at his age. He lacked that extra something that husbands and fathers had or were supposed to have. This lack wasn't noticeable. To most people, he was a great guy. Hell, he *was* a great guy. In fact, Daro couldn't remember the last time his conscience had stepped into his path, fingers twitching and ready to draw.

Of course, that night had been his only chance to sleep with Lina. He hadn't been able to admit that at the moment, but his refusal stood like a curtain between them that he was unable to sweep aside, and before he knew it, they had become pals. If he wanted to know whether there was any possibility of ever upgrading (re-upgrading?) to the status of lovers, he could always ask her. But there it was again, that bit of stubbornness he'd somehow acquired that didn't want to take the trouble.

Just as he had expected, the morning he rose from her yellow sheets and went home, he sat in his green recliner and watched his mood lower itself link by link into a bleakness that engulfed him for days. After two days of take-out pizza and TNT accompanied by lite beer, a can of cling peaches, then deviled ham spread, and then canned water chestnuts, it was back to the shrink he'd seen on and off for a decade, who gave him the same lecture about just staying on the pills. This time she gave him a dose that kicked him in the ass, and the next thing he knew, his uncle was cosigning on a string of new condos that were being built near Reedley on land that wasn't exactly cheap but that his uncle wanted in the family before it became worth even more in the future. The first units sold so fast he was able to purchase a nearby development on his own, this time in Navelencia. He didn't miss the fruit business in the least. Didn't mind no longer being just one of many Taguras in his uncle's employ. Once the old man had decided that he could buy into development just as easily as he could resist it, Daro's life suddenly had new, if somewhat artificial, purpose. He moved out of the little place behind his uncle's and into his own spanking new condo on a man-made lake in an upscale section of north Fresno. He showed up at wine and cheese fundraisers for children's diseases and art festivals, where deeply tanned women with frosted hair and bedecked with clunky turquoise jewelry dragged him around the pavilion introducing him to their friends.

There was just the small problem of sometimes finding himself home alone, his head more or less reeling from what had become of his life.

Days like these, he resigned himself to performing useless but occupying tasks. Armor Alled the dashboard of the truck, watered the lone philodendron from Lina in the snug little bay window off the breakfast nook, picked up dog chow, a rubber door mat, and a pound of salmon on sale at the Costco. When he returned lugging the twenty-pound sack over his shoulder, the pool guy behind the gated fence glanced his way. Daro called out a friendly hello but got no response. His fingers itched to deadhead the tiny rosebushes or to water the shrubs that someone else took care of. New house smell was unnerving. He'd just read an article they'd included in his sack at the health food store: new houses were chock full of toxins. Carpets, fresh paint, poly-laminate floors, synthetic upholstery, varnish—all gave off outgases—and the door and windows on the new models were often so snug and well-insulated that it was poisonous just to hang out at home. So he did very little of it. The place had long been as bare as the surface of the moon, save for an unyielding new futon, a rustic-look TV hutch in knobby pine, and his old leather recliner from home, the kind of furniture piece that, Lina assured him, most women found offensive. Daro had argued that the chair was in perfectly good condition and that it would probably only be a few more years before avocado came back into style as an acceptable designer color. Besides, it was the only thing in the house that didn't smell like it was fresh from a factory warehouse. "Avocado will never come back as a color," Lina assured him. "Guacamole will be its next incarnation."

Lina, good woman, had decided to remain his friend throughout the changes of the past months. He and Francesca and Catherine had a movie night once a week, while Lina got out for the evening, sometimes with a date. In exchange, she brought meals from the restaurant or cooked for him once or twice a week. She brought him items she had found at estate sales—cross-stitched kitchen curtains of Dutch children playing leapfrog, milk glass pieces, funky old hand tools or cameras as decoration. She had even found some posters from old packing crates—an old Sunkist label of a fresh-cheeked brown-haired beauty, the Unrivalled label with mighty Atlas wielding an orange, and the Golden Globe label with the brightly colored hummingbirds. She had them framed with boldly contrasting matting and hung them in the dining alcove. She was so good at coming and going, her ponytail flipping behind as she rushed out to work, or clicking off in heels and a short, swishy skirt with a man on her arm that it took Daro by surprise when "pals" was suddenly supposed to be over. He thought it might have something to do with the girls starting a half day twice a week at the Boulevard Children's Center. For the hands-on mom that Lina was, this was a very big deal, for Lina more than the girls of course. She was getting to that age of waning possibility when it came to having more babies, whether or not she actually wanted more babies being a different issue altogether. How women could leap from a trivial change like starting daycare to wanting to get married and have babies was among the least charming (and most enduring) of their mysteries.

They had had a great morning at the Floating World festival downtown. Catherina and Francesca had done the traditional Oban dance holding their mom's and Daro's hands. Then they had sat together under a canopy hung with streamers where the sunshine jutted in at bright angles, scooping udon noodles off little plastic plates with little plastic forks as children sang in bright costumes on a set of risers. The way she held him lightly at the elbow or leaned into his side told Daro that Lina had been pretending he was her spouse. Since he was either related to or an acquaintance of most of the people there, what people saw was generally referred to as "Daro's latest." He really didn't mind when she did this—it had happened before, even when she announced she was serious about whoever she was dating.

Blame it on springtime igniting thoughts of romance, but it didn't stop when they got back to his place, including her ordering him around once or twice about dishes or stuff on the floor—in his own home—and in a tone of voice that reminded him why he lived alone. But he didn't hold that against her, precisely because she didn't live with him and wasn't his wife. So it wasn't resentment he felt when she started kissing his neck as they sat behind the girls on the couch, watching their previously taped PBS special. And she could get him hard—thoughts of her had done so plenty of times in the past months—so it wasn't that either. He ended up having to fake concern that the girls would see them going at it. Later, in the dark, with music playing and candles lit (he shouldn't have let her go to that length, he admitted), there was no good excuse. He was a cad at best for leading her on that night. His only explanation, not good enough for a woman, was that he had had so little of being chased in his life. The sex encounters he had enjoyed (as opposed to the far fewer enduring romantic relationships) were, with one or two notable exceptions that gave him a taste of what he was missing, almost always with women who wanted to be pursued, especially if they were cheating on a husband or boyfriend, and then it was pretty much required. So he enjoyed Lina's ardent purposefulness, the more so because she was so appealing and such a good friend. And he didn't know what he felt when he made her stop, whether he was being high-minded or coy or what.

"I'm sorry for myself more than anything," he told her. "You're so lovely. I guess I didn't know wild oats were something a guy could run low on. God knows I used up my share. But I just don't have the energy for the whole package. The girls are great, you're great. I just—God, where were you twenty years ago?"

"At about your knee. But I'm sure you must have had plenty of 1970 versions of me—without kids—to choose from."

"Ah, life before AIDS."

"I'm licking some wounds here. Aren't you supposed to say something comforting or at least face-saving?"

He gave her the half hug that signaled "just friends." "I'm sorry. I'm trying to be light. I'm trying not to lose a great pal." He peered under the wall of her hair. More words were not the solution, at least not any that were going to come from his mouth. But that was what she seemed to need right now. "You're half my age, dear," he tried. "Don't underestimate that things look different from this edge of life, especially when it comes to your energy reserves. In a couple of years, I've got free coffee for life at McDonald's. I qualify for discounts at National Parks. I need someone more my speed."

Lina squeezed her eyes shut. "Jesus. I think that hurts worse than any of this. In general, you do want someone, just not me."

He waited that one out, the observation being one worth considering. She took the cartons of pasta out of the brown paper bag. "You want lunch then? I'm not hungry." Then she shook herself, as if trying to stave off tears. "I feel like I'll do something undignified." She didn't appear to be faking those tears. Daro looked at the floor as she pulled her jacket back on, her shoulder bag up, got her keys in hand. "I'll call you when I feel ready to be just friends. But, um, don't hold your breath." She hid her face in his neck for the longest moment she could. What class, not even using real tears as a weapon. His high-mindedness felt cheap. The scent of her alone made him want to snap his idealism in two over his knee and pull Lina by the hand to the bedroom. He didn't understand what kept him from it, what gave him the strength aside from the desire not to repeat a pattern. Wasn't he just putting himself first, like he always had, to try to hold himself above his wanting her? That's a good one, his conscience answered. You almost had me with that one.

## *Grace*

It was a wild, clanging, utterly alarming pain like sirens going off inside her feet until the meds kicked in. Really, Grace hadn't expected anything like it. The meds caused a heaviness that made her feel slightly unhinged, but the trade-off was a delicious surrender to the moment that usually meant sleep or something close enough to it to count. Vaguely, she wondered if Evie was giving her more than the recommended dosage. She found she cared less to stop thoughts like these when they wafted by, unbidden. Often, her grandson Adam was in the room playing quietly at the foot of the bed, singing along with a muted but brightly colored picture on the television screen or making sound effects for his toys. Several times a day she had the intention of lifting her head to observe him. She was curious about him; he had turned into a little boy. She dreamed about him on and off, saw him stepping from the thick fog of Garabedian's orchard into the backyard clearing, pausing to consider the out-of-place chimney hearth, the rusted but still-sturdy swing set and sandbox that had been there since his own mother was his age. A strange, knowing sense flooded her when he came into sight. She already knew the small cups of his shoulders, the tender curls of his ears, the half smile at his lips. What was he doing there, and where was Evie? She felt so blanketed by dope, so heavy, so thirstily drinking up this time to do nothing but be a body trying to ward off the pain that she couldn't muster the energy to say something. And in a way she liked it, Adam nearby. His needs were obviously being met somehow—weren't they? By someone. He demanded nothing of her, although sometimes he would creep close, lean down, and press his nose up against hers. He wasn't above sticking his finger in her ear and, once, up her nostril. This is what they will do to me when I am dead, thought Gracie with a muffled concern. Sometimes he turned into Mitchell as a boy, who had always been good at occupying himself at that age too. She would open her eyes and realize her heart ached from free-floating memory and regret.

Her leg became a train track one afternoon. As the cars Evel-Knievelled from her knees to her feet she awoke, screaming out loud. That was the way it was with the medication; the pain was just suddenly, alarmingly there. Adam stood wide-eyed for a moment and then bounded out of the room calling for his mother, who rushed down the long hallway and into the room, cloaked with the smell of cigarettes and the outside chill.

"I was going to check on you as soon as I had finished that cigarette," Evie said contritely.

Adam blinked at his grandmother. "I'm sorry I vroomed on your leg." Once his apology was accepted, he intended to make the most of her awake time. "Why did they have to cut your feet?" he asked, with more curiosity than sympathy for this old woman he didn't know well.

"When I was growing up, I didn't have shoes that fit right. It made my feet grow funny. The doctor made my feet better though. So don't worry. It only hurts right now."

"You gonna walk another day, Grandma?"

"Yes I am, Adam."

"But not today?"

"Not today."

He turned back to his dragons. "My grandpa will walk today." The dragon alighted on her stomach. "They didn't have to cut his feet." Self-pity suddenly whooshed in as though she had sent out engraved invitations. "No, Adam. You're right. No one ever cut his feet."

He seemed to consider this thoughtfully. Then he asked, "Did they bind the feet of the Chinese ladies?"

Gracie shot her daughter a look. Evie merely poked her pen behind her ear, drained the last of her can of Pepsi, and shut her books with a thud. "Remember when you called and asked me to come take care of you? We had joked on the phone about your having your feet bound, you know, with bandages? Adam wanted to know what that was, so I told him."

"Told him what, Evie? Does a six-year-old really need all the details?"

"He didn't get all the details, Mother," Evie shot back. "He got the facts. Come on, guy. Daddy's gonna meet us downtown." It was plain that Gracie could get her daughter from zero to sixty in less time than ever.

"I wanna stay with Grandma."

"Well, you can't. Grandma needs to rest now."

"If you make me go, I will be really sad."

"You be however you want, just get your jacket on. And where are your shoes?"

"Can I take Rhince?"

Evie sighed and gathered the dragon parts scattered over her bed. "Here."

"Do you need help with that sash?" Gracie asked out loud.

"What, Mom?"

Gracie shook herself. "Nothing." She'd been dreaming Evie was trying on dresses to wear to a school dance. Once, she had tried to tie a Korean-style bow with the sash at her waist. Evie promptly undid the tie and refashioned it back into a regular bow.

Evie paused, Gracie was sure, as a way of wrestling her irritation under wraps. "Can we bring you back anything, Mother?"

There was a SmartMeal with marinara sauce in the freezer. She shook her head no. "But I'll take that frozen pasta dinner when you get back." There it was again, Evie's summoning of her patience. But never mind. She had to ask for what she needed, and Evie had agreed to do this. She wasn't asking for spa treatment. She just wanted to goddamned well eat some dinner like anybody else.

"Mom, can I have meatballs?" Adam asked, obviously prompted by the idea of spaghetti.

Evie did not say yes or no to anybody. Imagine being so uptight or upset or whatever she was that you couldn't answer a simple question. "We'll be back by 7:00," was all she said. And goodbye. In a moment, she heard Adam running back down the hallway toward the room. He burst in on the shut door, dragging the furry pinto throw from the living room. He draped it awkwardly over her, tugging it up to her chin. Gracie pretended to be sleeping. Then he pulled something from his coat and tucked it in on the pillow beside her head. Gracie opened one eye after he left with his mom. "Night, Rhince," she said.

❋   ❋   ❋

Before she returned to work, Grace had found time to venture into the garage, sorting through the kids' boxes of stuff from previous eras of their lives. There were Mitchell's books that had never made it to Ontario, where he was living with his Taiwanese wife who was teaching English to immigrant children and writing textbooks about it in Mandarin. Mitchell, himself, did not earn money. He conjured it. He stayed at home and (Gracie hoped) looked after her granddaughter, but she was pretty certain that most of the day he sat in front of a computer screen and moved his wife's money from one place to another, watched the financial figures go up and down, and experienced various emotions due to the rising and falling of those figures that never registered on his face but that Gracie was sure were having an effect on his vital organs in some irreversible way. There was Ben's motorcycle parked at a jaunty angle in the far corner of the garage and looking like an overgrown Schwinn lacking the red and white tassels dangling from the handlebars. Leftover from Ben's hippie carpenter phase were various boxes of saws, tools and parts and a planer hulking at the opposite end of the garage from the motorcycle. He had finally come back for his yellow Karmann Ghia that had sat out at the side of the house since he'd returned home at twenty-five, broke, his band split up (Rachel and the Elders they had called themselves), and the young woman vocalist he had thought he was going to marry had gotten engaged to a cop. He got in that car again at the age of twenty-six and drove it all the way to New Mexico to herd sheep with some back-to-the-landers. That had been a year ago. He had called and written since he left, but Gracie hadn't seen him since.

Benjamin was Gracie's dear, her baby. It wasn't that she loved him more than Mitchell and Evie, it was simply that Ben was the only one of her children Gracie would have chosen for a friend in a different life. Ben liked people. People liked Ben. Gracie would never have expected she would have the pleasure of knowing someone who had this much charisma, although she had admired people like this from afar. If you measured love by its intensity, however, it was her daughter who had commanded the most of it. Ben had been such a relief after her second child, the girl, the one she was going to dress up in little handmade outfits, the one who would just naturally want to be well-mannered, and tidy, compliant, easy. When Evie had left, she hadn't looked back. The things Gracie kept relating to Evie were things her daughter didn't even remember. The tortured entries in a diary from junior high school complaining bitterly at the betrayal of a girl who had promised to be her best friend. The letters beginning "Dear Mom and Dad," apologizing profusely for receiving a less-than-perfect grade on her report card, then launching into blame of her and Wayne for not helping, for not seeing the problem, and then ending with self-castigation for all of her faults and a promise to try harder than ever. It was as though she had been born with the volume turned way up inside her head, had always lived more intensely than other people and, Gracie thought, unnecessarily so. Dear God, not every situation required such emotional fervor, not unless you wanted to die young.

At least the house was clean. A clean house was a pleasure something like a dentist must feel, thought Grace, after the teeth are flossed and polished, the gums a gleaming bumpy pink. With the proper attitude, January could be a decent month after all, Gracie decided, which is how she found herself on her back trying to imitate the yoga pose on the video when Evie walked into the rec room.

"Just look at it this way, Mom, be glad I'm not a meth freak or strung out in detox."

From upside down and backward between her spread legs, it was clear to Grace her form looked nothing like Solomon Yin's. But yoga took the ache out of her lower back after all those weeks of bed rest. And no one knew it, but she was missing the false peace of her medication; yoga seemed to help with that too. She sat back up and looked hard at Evie. Her daughter's jaw had a familiar set to it. Gracie breathed—navel to nose, navel to nose—Solomon would say from his perch on some Hawaiian beachscape. "You have something to tell me, don't you? Which I am not going to like." She hit the remote.

"To ask you."

"You need detox?"

Evie squinted in puzzlement. "Okay, let's start over. I've been accepted into law school, and—I'm going, Mom."

Gracie picked herself up off the floor to give her daughter a hug and to buy herself some time.

"Great," Evie said. "You're not even happy for me."

Gracie kissed the hair over Evie's ear. "Of course I am. When? Where?" Her mind searched the possibilities about what Evie could want—money? A car?

"Mom, they gave me this huge scholarship at the University of Iowa. Practically a full ride."

Gracie squeezed Evie tighter and smiled so big her chin pressed into her shoulder. "Is that great or what? Did you tell your Dad? He'll be thrilled." She waited for the asking part, the bad news. "And?" Gracie finally asked.

Evie stepped away from her and went to the window looking into the backyard. People only did that in movies, crossed the room before delivering a line. Little Miss Perry Mason. "Lance doesn't want me to take Adam out of state," she explained. "But there's no way I'm letting him live with Lance."

Gracie got it, but she wasn't letting on. Besides, the answer was no. Let her ask, but the answer was—had to be—no no no no no. "Isn't four years of the Midwest enough for any Californian? There's so many good law schools here. And what about your son?"

Evie sighed, ready for this. "I don't have to pay for this school, Muther." She paused a beat. "He'll be fine. Here with you. We can keep Lance's visitation just like it is. He's already agreed to it."

Gracie plopped down on the couch. "He's staying here? He's the Iowan."

"He just got into the union, remember?"

"Oh, for God's sake. I am sixty-four years old, Evelyn. Not to mention crippled."

"And doing yoga."

"Don't."

"With the best of them."

"I'm serious. I'm happy for you, but I'm not one of those grandparents. You know, doting."

"You make it sound like a dirty word. You've known Adam—what—a fraction of his life? I brought him back here and you didn't even recognize him."

"I was medicated, for God's sake."

"Well, now's your chance to catch up for lost time."

"You're doing me the favor?"

"You know, Mom, there are some grandparents who would see it exactly that way."

"But not Lance's folks, I take it?"

"His mother's already raising his brother's kids, three of them. Messed up family."

"Oh, well good thing we're perfect," said Grace. "I don't know, Evie. It's like you expect me to take care of your son. Like my agreeing to this is the only thing standing between you and your plans."

Evie must have practiced not reacting, Grace decided. All she said was, "Lance would take him every single weekend." And then added, "Please just try it for one semester? A trial basis."

"I don't owe you this, Evie."

"Of course you don't."

"You'll say anything right now."

"I want what I want, Mom. I'm not going to pretend otherwise. But this is a good thing. And you can help. I need your help." She came to her and draped her arms around her neck from behind in a bad imitation of an affectionate daughter. "You'll love him," she whispered.

"I put your father through law school and look where that got me."

"I can't divorce you, Mom. Believe me, I've tried."

Gracie sighed. It was true she didn't know her grandson well. She could regard it as an investment in his future. "One semester," Grace said. "And you'll pay me child support, both of you."

Her daughter kissed her on each cheek. "Just watch, Mom. You won't regret doing this for Adam, for us."

"I'd better not."

"By the way, you should probably know—Lance calls him Chink."

"My God, Evie."

"He means it affectionately."

"Evelyn, what the hell is wrong with you? I don't need to give you a history lesson."

"Mom mom mom, calm down. He does it ironically."

"How is that possible? Lance is not capable of irony."

"Very funny. Look, just think of it as a reclaiming of the word."

"Like nigger?" Gracie shot back. "See, I made you wince."

She was awoken by a low whirring from afar that could have passed for World War II fighter planes. She sat up a little in bed, parting the curtains and looking out past the fig orchards under a cold, clear moon. The stars in a clear winter sky always seemed to contribute to its icy silence. Frost. So late? It was March. Besides, when she'd gone to bed only a few hours earlier, she could hardly see the tops of the trees in the orchards for the fog. The moonlight revealed Adam's sleeping form. He was on his back, legs splayed out over the comforter leaving him completely uncovered but thankfully in his footed polar bear sleeper. He slept like it was good, hard work, flush cheeked and slightly sweaty, and hovering around him the irresistible, hushed, animal aura of a slumbering innocent. She thought of all the faces that would gaze upon his sleeping form in his lifetime. A child of his, perhaps, wondering whether she dared try to wake him. A wife, reading beside him or perhaps wiping the tears from her cheeks as she pondered how to tell him the thing she could not tell him. Surely Gracie underestimated his parents Evelyn and Lance. In the early days, when it was just Evie alone, she must have gazed upon her infant, filled with amazement, gratitude, love. And once his father had come round to the idea that he had a son, he, too, must have watched his sleeping baby with that tender arch in the neck of a young parent learning the depths of love.

The smoke from the smudge pots began to lift above the orchards, almost hanging in the air despite the wind machines. She hoped her neighbor Isaac had a chance tonight. She put her hand on the windowpane, cold almost aching in her pressed palm. He was going to lose some oranges tonight, even running those wind machines. Poor Isaac.

She watched Adam's sleeping form nearly upside down to her. She hoped he would be outrageously handsome, that those blond locks and blue slanted eyes would be considered exotic and cool by all the girls. In truth, he was what they used to call a throwback, like a black Irish, someone whose features reveal an almost all but forgotten racial past. Now with that still-round face of childhood, the tiniest pudge under his chin, and the half smile at his lips, he really did look like a sleeping Buddha. Buddha with hair. Blond-haired blue-eyed Buddha child. Forget it, thought Gracie. He's too hard to wake and too heavy to lift. I'm not bringing him back to his own bed. Suddenly, the fear descended sharply upon her that she was going to have this child with her forever. As though concurring with her thought, the child turned, snorted in his sleep, and brought his arm smack against her side.

Too soon, it was morning. He sat up, yawned, and then confirming Gracie was awake by shoving his nose into her face. Once he had her attention, he turned to the collection of small toys he had gathered about him the night before. He asked her what catnip was.

"Oh, well it's a small plant that cats like to eat. It makes them feel really good."

"No, a cat nap. A catnap."

"I see, yes. That's a short nap." She saw Eartha Kitten at her feet. "Cats like to sleep, and they're good at taking short naps as well as long ones. We could have one right now, if you want."

"No, thanks," he told her. "I just woke up."

She was still getting used to the daily-ness of living with a small child again. He would have chores, just like her other grandkids did when they were visiting and just like all her own kids had from a very young age. And she would be going back to work soon, so it would be time to find a good daycare.

"Adam, you may set the table now." The child seemed absorbed in his play, but something told Gracie he was faking it. "Adam," she tried again. Still nothing. She gritted her teeth. "Chink!" He looked up at her, a wooden puzzle piece in each hand. God, thought Gracie. This is sick.

"My dad and mom call me Chink," Adam announced. Gracie couldn't hear the word without her gut turning.

"Yes, I know that, child. But I will not."

"Why not? It's one of my names."

"Adam is your name. Adam Bidden. I want you to prefer to be called that." She liked that her grandson never simply burst into reaction before considering his words, unlike his mother. He was calculating something, arriving at some sort of conclusion. "You don't like my name because that's what they call me."

"What do you mean they? Your mommy is my little girl." She dumped vegetable peels into the trash and scraped the remainder off the cutting board with a knife. "I love her as much as you do, you know." She watched her grandson consider his image in the black glass of the oven door. It was hard to say whether he was, like most children, simply fascinated with his reflection or whether he was contemplating the origin of the term his father used with him in his physical features. The child did not, thank god, seem to get it yet.

"Do you know what it means, Adam, the word 'Chink?'"

He shrugged.

"Do we shrug at our grandmothers? A shrug is not an answer, child." Still, she hesitated about going into definitions, as there was no way to explain why, if it was such a bad word, his parents sometimes called him by it. "Adam, you call me Halmoni, right?"

"Hall-money?" He seemed to consider the word in its three syllables, a new word when you said it more carefully like that.

"Which means grandmother, did you know that?"

"In your language?"

"In my mother and father's language, Korean. Halmoni is what your mom used to call her own grandmother, my mother, you see how that works?"

Adam seemed to start tuning her out, suddenly very interested in his writing things and in securing a piece of paper from the tray she had set out for him on the low counter.

"So I was thinking, Adam. Adam? I was thinking we might give you a Korean name to be called, in case you really don't want me to call you Adam anymore. What do you think?"

He was writing out the letters he had heard, having never considered the word as a word before. H-O-M.

"I want to tell you something," he said. "I am six years old."

If she waited until she had his complete attention, she might never speak. "You know, the Korean word for grandson is a pretty good word. It's Son-ja. How about we call you Son-ja?"

He made a face but kept writing. When he finished, he held the paper up to her. HOMINY it read, with letters getting larger as they marched across the page. He seemed pleased that he had made her laugh. "That's just how it sounds, yes. I am your hominy."

"Okay, I'll be Adam," he consented.

"No Son-ja, then?"

He slid a glance from one end of the room to the other. "That's gonna be my other secret name," he decided.

"And how many secret names do you have?"

"Two. The one you call me that only you and me know, and the one I call myself that only I know."

She nodded sagely. "Except even I don't know that one yet," he said.

The more she thought about how to explain herself to the child, the more indignant she became about the situation. It was unconscionable that she would be put in this position because of the ignorance of his father. Grace decided this warranted her breaking her agreement to Evie not to contact Lance for any reason between scheduled visits unless absolutely necessary. Well, this was absolutely necessary. She would put a stop to anyone's referring to her grandson with this derogatory term.

That Lance Bidden would call his son by this name was only fitting given the young man's general uncouthness and ignorance. Her own daughter had no such excuse. That "reappropriation" remark was so Evie. Nothing was ever just what it was. There was always an explanation that she couldn't be expected to understand. No, as Grace saw it, her daughter who spouted feminism and pierced and tattooed herself in places her clothing only partially hid, went along with "Chink" because she had gone along with whatever Lance did or wanted. Oh, she understood the trade-off. That a woman would submit so entirely to a male had something to do with what she was getting in return. It wasn't necessarily pretty on the outside, but it met some of her deepest needs. Evie would be shocked and downright angry with Grace if she dared to reveal that she understood her daughter as well as that.

If you went for the rugged type, she supposed Lance was a decent specimen, a skinnier version of the lumberjack on the paper towels, only shiftier looking, as though the lumberjack had to do something demeaning like sell drugs to supplement his income from appearing on paper towel packages. His hands were perpetually dirty, calloused, bandaged from some wound or another. He wore layers of things, like a bum. A dead sweatshirt over a tired turtleneck over the filthiest Carhartt she had ever seen. It looked as though he had been dragged through a mechanic's garage and then behind a dirt bike. To be fair, she had seen him cleaned up a few times, and she always had the same reaction: now there's what soap and water can do for a person. Then she was able at least to understand what Evie might have seen in him once upon a time. Fridays Lance came to get Adam right from work, always in a stocking cap and thick and dirty sherpa-lined mud boots. Despite his overall appearance, the one thing he apologized for was his hair, about which he must be vain, judging from the lovingly framed high school graduation portrait Evie kept of the young man with shining golden hair parted down the middle and falling down past his shoulders. He wore a hard hat all day, which made his now considerably browner and shorter haircut poke out around the ears, while the top was matted.

Evie had always had to have a bad boy. They weren't very nice to her, but then, she wasn't very nice to them either. Nice didn't seem to enter into the picture, but if it didn't, then for God's sake why drag things out with each other? Lance didn't strike Grace as being the tender sort. She could imagine that Evie longed for tenderness—who didn't?—but, to hell with it. A mother couldn't get far in being critical of her children; all paths seemed to lead back to her: Unable to achieve intimacy. Lacking access to her emotional side. All those jargony descriptions, all of them, were the fault of her child-rearing. She had never heard a single complaint from Evie's lips about Wayne. Wayne, who brought the female clients he was screwing home as dinner guests out of some twisted sense of guilt about what he was doing.

It was with something of a drunkard's remorse that Gracie watched Daro Tagura make his way up her walk in his blazer, blue jeans, and casual tie. His briefcase was a worn leather schoolboy's satchel. It had been months, but the man's first impression of her came only after she had sipped one too many cups of mulled wine in front of the fire. Her heart pulsed blood to her face, although she wasn't yet sure whether it was embarrassment about Christmas Eve, anxiety about having taken this step with a developer thereby ushering in huge changes to her small, quiet life, or something else.

She let him ring the bell and watched through the peep hole as Daro appeared to rummage through his satchel for something. Adam leaped to the front door and yanked it open, revealing a man bearing a cellophane-wrapped basket of a few pretty pears and nectarines.

Gracie more or less blocked the doorway. "I didn't do anything to deserve this, so you must be trying to get on my good side."

He laughed heartily. He had a movie star's smile, which you couldn't tell until he did smile. Gracie couldn't believe his response was genuine good humor, even though this was the beginning of a business transaction. Grace didn't finesse things with people; she was too old for that. Life was okay, sometimes downright pleasant, but rarely was it worth charm's exertion.

"This?" Daro replied, releasing the basket into Adam's grip. "Don't worry. If I needed on your good side, it'd be a much bigger basket."

"Well thank you. This is my grandson Adam Bidden. We're working on waiting our turn. And gentlemen shake hands when they are introduced to others." Daro raised his eyebrows at her like he had on Christmas Eve. Gracie blushed. "Listen to me. I sound like a kindergarten teacher."

"That's your grandson?" Daro asked. "He's so . . . blonde."

"Well, his father calls him 'Chink,' and his mother allows it."

Daro looked at Grace. "What the hell's wrong with them?" Gracie couldn't help a smile. "That's a refreshing response. You mean you don't automatically blame me?"

"I don't know you well enough yet." Daro grinned. "Perhaps we'll get to that." He gamely played along as Adam grabbed his hands and began walking up the stranger's legs. "Look at me, being walked all over by a six-year-old."

Gracie sighed. "I'm a bit out of practice, although I've been through this three times. Plus, kids are different now. Or this one is anyway." They looked at Adam as each tried to figure out the next thing to say.

"Do you only see the blonde?" she asked him. "Look at him."

"He's a gorgeous child."

"I mean the eyes. They're as blue as can be. But you can see why anyway."

"Why they call him Chink?"

She squinted. "Ugh, don't keep saying the word."

Daro laughed. "You and your daughter don't get along, I take it?"

"That's none of your business," Gracie told him and rose to bring her mug to the counter. "And yes, he is a gorgeous child."

"I'd apologize for the lived-in look of the place and the grime of country living, but I won't since it's not my house you're after." She showed him the acreage, its border ending where Garabedian's old figs began. "This used to all be oranges, I hear," she told him. "No offense, but how many condos can displace agricultural land before you reach a point of no return?"

"Not to dodge your question, but I was raised not far from here. There was a hotel where the Santa Fe came through. Maybe that old chimney in your yard was the very heart of it, once upon a time. There was even a postal office. It was quite the orange boom, which lasted until a wipe-out drought about the time of the First World War."

"My in-laws founded this town—the Tellers—but they were all cleared out of here by the end of the war. Their investment was about profit, and temporary. Your family built its fortune off of produce. How could you develop it now for such a . . . finite purpose?"

"Finite, eh? You're going easy on me. But I thought that's why you asked me out here."

At the Christmas party, she had opened her eyes and there he was. Now she had made him appear before her, had summoned him on this piece of business she was still unsure about. He did not take bait; he did not respond to provocation. She wondered what it would be like to be interested in a man again, if she had the energy to learn a whole new set of rules. And for what?

"My own dad lived somewhere in this valley for a time," Gracie told him. "He was a fruit picker, I believe, and a cook. None of us knew much about that period of his life. What I'd like is to see where he was born."

"I could never live in Japan; I have no interest in going back."

"Going back?"

"I was actually born in Yokohama. My father married a picture bride and had to travel back home to meet her. There were delays, and they ended up staying for a couple of years before being allowed to return."

"Restrictions, right?"

"Every time they turned around. The Japanese American Citizens

League finally got my parents back into the country, arguing that my father had farming techniques that were indispensable for peaches and cherries. He built up what you might call a small fruit empire and then, of course, came the war. I was born after the camps, and it was so strange because it was like there was no way to get a sense of what my family history was like before Manzanar. No one would talk about it. When I was a kid—I had a sick sense of humor—I'd go around with a flashlight I used as a fake mike and ask my mom and dad and my auntie and uncles and anyone who hadn't just tuned me out questions that I'd thought up, things I really did want the answer to even though I got very few answers. 'Where did they put you when you had a baby? Did they have a prom for the high school graduates?' On my wall at home, I have this exit form, this questionnaire that they gave out, one per family. Very few of my family's things survived from the camp, but this was one of them in a folder of paperwork, along with a copy of the deed to Dad's home and land signed over to a buddy of his who had promised to take care of things until they got out. That was one thing, my father did have friends in the area. I'd go around asking the questions from this exit form just to keep things lively, not expecting any real answers. Questions like 'Where do you plan to reside?' and 'How will you support yourself and your family?' that were beyond ridiculous since they had lost their homes and incomes to the people who were asking the questions.

"One day my father told me to get the strap from the nail on the wall. It hung right in the kitchen next to the wall clock and the copper molding pans. Understand he had never—no one had ever—used it on me. They'd never had to; I had a healthy respect for warnings. But he took that belt in his hand, doubled it up, snapped it tight, and smacked me but good. Just once. Once in my whole life. Then he lit the questionnaire with a match from the matchbook he always kept in his shirt pocket and threw it in the kitchen sink. It flared up, charred the porcelain, and turned to ashes. I think I understood even then that history tells us about the significance of events, but it isn't very good about consequences. Leave that to the shrinks, right?"

"Is that where you ended up?"

Daro shrugged. "Who doesn't, eventually? I went off to college. A lot of us got very active in the Asian version of La Raza and all that. But, I don't know what it was with me. I didn't have the character, the staying power, I dunno. My friends said it was because I was too comfortable being part of the owning classes and didn't really want change."

Gracie waited for more. The sixties hadn't happened to her and they had changed everything and this man was speaking to her from the other side of history. "Owning classes," Daro shook his head. "A few Japanese growing peaches out of the dry dirt." She liked that he seemed to be working things through. He wasn't young; he could live with that about himself.

When the grass became damp, she called to Adam. She was wearing sandals for the first time since her surgery. Her scars were pink and fading, and she sported a toe ring, one of several sent from Evie in a little satin pull-string bag. Adam took the opportunity to admire her toe ring, which reminded him of her former bunions. He told Daro all about the surgery, opining that he believed bunions had to do with food and with his halmoni's improper hygiene. He reminded Daro of the story of the little girl who refused to take a bath and eventually spouted radishes in her hair. His halmoni had sprouted onions in her feet—that explained the bulges—and they, the "bunions," had to be cut out. He further explained to Daro that he didn't see why he had to brush his teeth every day if his own halmoni didn't keep herself clean.

"That'd be between you and your halmoni," replied Daro. Always game, he added, "But wouldn't they be funions? You know, foot onions?"

"No," Adam insisted, "they were not fun at all." He rolled his eyes, incredulous that it wasn't perfectly sensible to these two, "Bumpy onions is bunions, get it?"

"Now that you promise to make me rich, the least I can do is invite you to stay for dinner. I hadn't been expecting company, but we can manage." Now, hearing the two of them laughing together at the table (she never would have invited Daro without Adam there as buffer and distraction) made Gracie feel like she was playing house. Like a single mother must feel when a man she likes is getting along with the other part of the package, the crucial part. She thought of Evie, whether she was dating anyone new out there in grad school, hoping she wouldn't hook up with another Iowan, for God's sake. It hurt to think of Evie and Lance—what a mistake they had been.

She found herself wondering whether she should have "dressed for dinner," as it were. Changed out of those filthy comfort waistband slacks she wore around the house and into that darted skirt that accentuated the fact that she still actually had a waist. Good Lord, not for enchilada casserole. That was the crazy part. That she might seek to do something that would enhance her appearance in this man's presence meant—what? Desirable men of any age did not, as a rule, inspire much of anything in her. She encountered any number of good-looking younger men in her classrooms at the Adult Ed building, but they didn't inspire butterflies and certainly not romantic fantasies. Perhaps that was her problem. Why shouldn't they, after all?

According to Daro, she didn't stand to make nearly so much as her neighbors, given something called easement junctures and water table parcel codes involving the nearby Copper Pond, but in his professional opinion, she'd make enough to be comfortable. "I'd like to do this again," Daro added.

"Do you get a lot of free meals this way?"

Adam crawled onto a chair, then the counter, so that he could maneuver his way onto Daro's back. "Eartha Kitten has a worm in her heart," Adam said. "Can you fix it?"

"That only happens to dogs, Adam, and then only some of them. Now please climb down from our guest." She wanted this man gone. And Adam in bed. She wanted to be alone, to get familiar with the enticing possibility that Daro Tagura presented in her life. As soon as Adam was out for the night, she was going to go into the bathroom, take off her clothes and examine her reflection in the cruel light of the full-length mirror. Then, when she had determined there was absolutely no reason why a man like Daro should be interested in her romantically—sexually—she would shower, crawl into a thick and cozy nightgown, and peruse bulb catalogs in the light of her bedside reading lamp, a cup of hot tea steaming on the table beside her.

The long, strange trip of aging wasn't what she had expected. For one thing, she hadn't realized at the age of forty, even back when forty meant forty, that forty wasn't old. Physically, she'd still been a spring chicken. She'd never done much to maintain her health, never jogged or swum a mile in her life, but she'd never really abused it either. There had been that diet-for-a-small-planet phase with her last pregnancy (Ben) when she fixed tabouleh and tahini before anyone had heard of the stuff and blended herself tiger's milk shakes made with flaxseed and brewer's yeast. Being Asian, she'd had the tofu thing down long before it had become good for you, and she had enjoyed serving elaborate pan-Asian style dinners to friends where she prepared Korean dishes and tried out passable forms of sushi and stir-fry because it worked as a dinner party theme and everyone expected her to be good at it. She was good at it. And at teaching Sunday school and home-sewn mother-daughter dresses and passing out home-made cupcakes in the kids' classrooms. She'd been good at all of it. When she thinks back to when her kids were growing, her family was intact, and at least from certain angles, she and Wayne appeared to have one of the better marriages around, she wants to step back into the picture and tap that old Grace on the shoulder and just make her freeze-frame everything. This is the good part, she wants to tell that younger Grace. The part you're flying through.

## V

you there?

>   I'm here. Thank you very much for the toe rings and the pretty little bag they came in. It's great to look down my legs to my neatly aligned, normal-looking feet and see my even (and now decorated!) little toes.

I've got a night class in a bit. what did you mean about adam's asking questions you shouldn't answer?

>   Mostly he asks me when you'll be coming back. Big surprise. And if you're going to be here for his birthday.

like I would miss his birthday. damn that lance. okay, what else?

>   Things like: are we White people? And how long are people supposed to stay married before they get their divorce? This is your job, Ev! I want to be Halmoni, not . . . this.

when you tell him the answers, could you tell me? you there?

>   Who's responsible for throwing this party, Evelyn?

uh-oh, i'm getting evelyned. me, of course. and lance. and his new girlfriend, if she wants to help, i guess.

>   So you know.

shit. i guess i do now.

>   I'm sorry.

You there?

>   going to class. more tomorrow. nite.

"When is it my turn on the computer?" Adam announced from the floor where he was erecting a tower from a package of windmill cookies he had commandeered.

"As soon as your penmanship improves."

"But I'm six."

"Some six-year-olds have already taken their college entrance exams."

His cookie tower collapsed; almond slivers slid across the linoleum. "Miss Lina is a Black person," said Adam. Declaratives were his mode of asking questions lately. Grace started a Word file titled *Adam ???* right then and there and typed in the comment about Lina and an earlier declaration about where babies come from (Adam's reply: a place called The Farm—?).

"Not black, honey. You might say brown."

"What color are we?"

"Ask your mom, honey."

"You always say that," Adam replied.

The first morning Grace brought Adam to his new daycare, Lina Murillo, the woman from Eileen's Christmas party, was busy duct-taping huge squares of contact paper, sticky side up, to the linoleum. Adam leapt right onto a square and began laying down and picking up his hand with satisfying thwacks. "Sensory integration," Lina had smiled. Another day when Grace came to pick him up, they were tossing rolls of toilet paper around the room and letting them unravel across the furniture and from the light fixtures, all of them in such a frenzy of joy that Grace stood there two minutes before Adam even noticed her. Then there was beach day, when Lina laid out a huge tarp and let the kids splash in their bright swimsuits and scuba gear in a wading pool on the floor. Really, Lina was almost too much fun. The child would never put up with normal life and responsibilities if he spent the day "fingerpainting," up to his arms in whipped cream and mini marshmallows or making solar energy s'mores atop squares of foil on the front sidewalk. And it gave her a pang to think of poor Adam's faraway tort-reform-on-the-prairie mother who was missing all of this.

To her credit, Evelyn had been fiercely maternal in Adam's early years, even a bit holier-than-thou, which of course wasn't hard for Evie. Grace had not particularly wanted to know it, but she heard from her all the same about her biweekly massages from a male massage therapist and how she did guided meditations in which she communicated with her baby in the womb or danced naked to African world beat as she rubbed herself up with shea butter and conditioned her nipples for breastfeeding with purified lanolin. She had a midwife and a doula, the latter of which Gracie had never even heard of, and further revealed that the only reason she wasn't having her baby in the water right in the middle of her own living room was because her student health insurance plan wouldn't cover it. And that was just the pregnancy. After the baby was born, she wore him everywhere, including into the shower, to class, and on campus protest marches for better student health insurance coverage. And, of course, to bed, where she nursed him "on command" until he was three, which she reported was on the early side when you compared it to weaning age in many cultures. Grace never knew what to say to such statements from Evelyn; they did not seem to invite either inquiry or agreement.

It was probably best that at that early stage of the game Lance was driving drunk and smoking drugs and whatever else he was up to, enough trouble to land him in jail and then into a halfway house, where Evie visited him once a month, baby in tow, and where classes with titles such as "Getting Real" and "Rid Yourself of Stinkin' Thinkin'" somehow took. The next thing she knew the three of them were a family. They headed back to California and took up residence at Otter's Cove trailer park on the Kings River, where Lance went to work fixing restaurant coffeemakers and other indirect heat-sourced appliances, and Evie got on as shipping and accounts receivable manager at an orthopedic supply warehouse out near the airport. No one ever says, "When I grow up I want to be a shipping and accounts receivable manager at an orthopedic supply warehouse"— and so much for that degree in biomedical ethics and the three expensive months spent in acupressure school—but at least they were both steadily employed.

Of course it wasn't enough for Evie, who got itchy for a change about the time other people were just settling in. Grace sincerely hoped that her pursuit of a law degree was about trying to make something of herself for real this time. She had started and abandoned three different undergraduate degrees. Had gone away for a semester abroad and wasn't seen again for a year and a half. Had slept with enough men to populate a small army. Dear God let it be time for her to get herself figured out, instead of dragging her would-be husband and son through the part that most people had gotten out of their system in their twenties.

❀  ❀  ❀

On Friday when Adam was waiting for Lance to arrive, he announced, "My dad is married to a different lady now."

"I didn't know your dad had ever been married, Adam."

"She's a pistol worker. I forgot her name. I don't like it."

"Do you mean a postal worker?"

He shrugged.

"Why do you say they are married, sweetheart? Did they get married?"

"Because she sleeps where my mom used to sleep. She has yellow hair like me and Dad. Do you know her?"

Gracie and Daro looked at one another.

Some weeks Adam ran to Lance and leaped up into his arms. Other weeks he gave an almost world-weary "hi, Dad" as though he could hardly be troubled with the formality. Lance was cleaned up and brought in a nice outdoor smell with him. "Don't you look handsome," Grace offered.

And in a rare good mood, to boot. "Well, thanks, Grace." He rubbed his chin and nodded at Daro. "Evening."

"Lance, meet Daro Tagura." The men shook hands, and then Daro discreetly busied himself with retying an action figure dangling on a shoestring from Adam's backpack.

"I have an aunt who married someone by the name of Tagura," Lance offered conversationally. "I never met her. She moved to Japan with him."

Daro sat up straight trying to work the kinks out of his back from bending over Adam's toy. "She probably had to back then. They might even have been chased out of town."

"No kidding?"

"I think there were laws against intermarriage right up til probably about the time you and Adam's mother were born."

"Jeez, I thought that was all back in the Dark Ages."

Daro was starting to formulate a thought that would get them much too deep into this conversation, so Gracie interrupted, "Adam said something about a pistol worker?"

Lance's good-natured demeanor collapsed into a frown.

"I mean I assume he meant postal worker, but I just thought I'd check whether firearms might be involved, that's all." Gracie peered out the window at the darkened car. Yellow hair. The three of them would look like a family together at the pizza place. "Did you want to invite her in?"

"Maybe Sunday. And it's not serious, Grace. You don't need to bring it up."

"You mean with Evie? It's been brought up."

Lance rubbed his face in exasperation and took a half step involuntarily toward the door. "Here we go." He started snatching together Adam's things. "Let's go, Chink. Tell your grandma and Mr. Tagura goodbye." At the door, Adam saw the woman in the car and shouted the name he'd said he couldn't recall earlier, running out to her with his shoelaces flapping.

Lance paused, his hand on the doorknob. "Let's get one thing straight, Grace. It's me that's waiting for Evie, not the other way around." He stuck a thumb at his chest. "I'm the one that got left behind. In the meantime, I don't think I owe anyone an explanation about my personal life."

"Would you just remember that I can watch Adam, you know, any time?"

Lance put his hands up. "Grace, we both know that kid's got a hell of an imagination."

Grace paused and looked at Daro before she began, deciding whether to let him witness this little scene or save it for later. "I'm cooler than Evie probably makes me out to be, Lance, but I'm not that cool."

"Say goodbye, son."

"And please no cable in his room, Lance," she called.

Daro put his arm lightly around Gracie's shoulder. Then he shut the door behind Lance and walked her to the kitchen table, where he sat her down and dug his fingers into her shoulder muscles, working them with just the right touch—not so hard as to feel intrusive, not so tentative as to make her wonder why he had bothered. She let escape an involuntary sigh. If she wasn't careful, she was going to become confessional. "Sometimes I just want to go home."

His fingers stayed busy. "Where's home?"

"This isn't where I'm from, you know. I want to be with my people."

"Your people, eh? I think I've rubbed off on you already."

"Sometimes I think that was the whole problem, leaving my family, leaving the city. I felt like I could never go back, once I left. Even though they are my own flesh and blood. You'd think I was crossing an ocean, marrying my White husband and moving out here." The massage brought tears to her eyes. "Is it possible to feel displaced for forty years?"

"You're talking to the son of internment camp victims."

"Koreans have a word for the feeling—*han*. Maybe it's how I was meant to feel."

"Fatalist," Daro accused her. "Why not just take a trip to South Korea, where it really started?"

"My sisters went ten years ago. They took my mother. Everybody she had not seen for sixty years—imagine—who was still alive was so happy to see her. But do you know what they wanted? American things. For her to send American things, and money, and to take their kids with her."

"She didn't think she was ever going back, right?"

"To where? The DMZ?" Gracie shot him a look. "Sorry, I'm not up on Asian American decorum here. What's proper between historical enemies?"

165

Daro laughed. "We're all the same color to White folks. Where were you during the sixties and seventies, woman?"

"Raising my children."

"So were lots of folks, Grace. We were yellow and proud, our race— La Raza as the Latinos say—was what mattered. We weren't going to let divisive U.S. policies create our national identities. It turns out that inability to distinguish us from one another is our strength. Strength in numbers."

"Which is where I wouldn't have fit in."

"Because?"

"Because I married a White man."

"You think that makes you unique? Lots of us married White folks."

"Us? You said you never married."

Daro smiled. "I mean the race. You and me might not be any example, but lots of those marriages lasted."

"It sure felt unique back in my day. But we were happy; we thought we were creating a new society."

He nodded to the photo of Adam on the fridge. "You were."

She smiled. "You make me feel like I can breathe." The truth was that his touch felt sure and healing, and she feared she would begin to weep. He stroked her on the sides of the arms and then began to massage her head, working methodically around her hairline, at the base of her skull, behind her ears, at her temples. She felt at once electric and serene, and sighed again, "I don't know if I can do this."

"Let's just take it step by step, shall we?"

Gracie's breath caught. "I meant Adam, raising my grandson for who knows how long."

"Oh, I'm sorry. I didn't know we were still on the subject of Adam."

She had to laugh. "You can't mean you think I'm—interested in you?"

"I can't speak for you. I guess I was hoping something along those lines. Forgive me if I've picked up on something that isn't there."

"Daro, I'm sure I'm closer to your mother's age than your own."

He shrugged. "My mother's cool."

"Wouldn't you be getting the raw end of the deal? You could have anyone—Lina, Evie, for that matter."

Another hearty laugh but no comment.

"You have. Lina, I mean. Right?"

"Lina's a pal now. A great pal but just that."

"Well, it's absurd to move from a beautiful young woman like that to . . . How can you expect me to take you seriously? You don't know a thing about women my age. I could introduce you to my daughter however. She's attractive, if a tad prickly." Daro merely sucked his lips together in an amused expression. "I see you've been trained," Grace continued. "You know when it's better to keep your mouth shut. But really, everyone you know will ask why you chose, you know, the vanilla."

He laughed out loud. "The RC cola?"

"The four-door sedan. The creamed corn. The sensible shoes."

"Just think how you'll make out. Asian men are the new sex symbol."

"Even if that were true, what's in it for you?"

Daro kept his smile but said nothing.

"Don't tell me—pursuit is its own reward, quite apart from the object."

"On the contrary, it tires me. What I'd really like, Grace, is not to have to work so hard, at pursuit, I mean. So that there's energy for other things, you know?"

"So, 'I'm attracted to you but don't tax me?' I'm supposed to make this easy for you?"

"How about, 'I'm attracted to you,' period? It already is easy."

"Uh-oh, you're using lines on me. And don't pour me more wine. Your strategies do nothing but amuse me." She let out an almost guttural breath when he found a spot in her right shoulder blade and worked it expertly.

"Liar," he mused. She breathed out again. Her hands went limp in her lap. "Fine," Grace managed to utter. "But I don't know the rules here."

"I have a feeling they'll kick in. Watch," he said and kissed her.

In class the next day, Grace tried to determine which of her studly looking male students might be a candidate for a sexual fantasy, but there were so many to choose from if you were just going on appearance that the effort seemed beside the point. At lunch, she asked her friend Eileen if she ever fantasized about any of her male students. "Are you kidding me? My students are potters. Talk about good with their hands." Eileen sounded disconcertingly knowledgeable on that score. And when she picked up Adam that evening, she told Lina flat out that Daro was interested in her because she figured the incredulous look on Lina's face would bring her to her senses. It came out wrong, however, and Gracie ended up making Daro sound like the kook for expressing interest in her.

"My God, Grace," Lina had replied. "You are so hard on him—and on yourself. Why does he have to be a perfect human being in order to like you no matter your age?"

"That's your generation talking, dear. I know nothing about sleeping around, and I don't see why I should be enticed into something risky and, well, uncharacteristic unless it really is worth it. Besides, you're hardly one to speak on his behalf—right?"

Lina smiled sadly. "That hurts some, Grace. He's the one who jilted me, in case he didn't share that with you."

"God, he's an idiot," Grace told her. And she meant it. Nevertheless, the next evening she found herself peering in through the plate glass at the dining room wall with three attractive framed orange crate labels, one of them of the pretty brown-haired Sunkist girl. Above the sink, an embroidered ruffle valance hung. She couldn't make out the cross-stitched decorative figures in red and blue. From a distance, they looked almost like the copulating figures of East Indian mythology. She squinted. Kama sutra curtains? Surely not.

An hour later, Grace eyed her empty wine glass and cleared her throat. Daro sat up straight and looked at the wall. "Um, the nibbling on your ear thing is kind of my specialty."

Gracie winced at the casual allusion to Daro's lifetime of lovers—that sort of loose comment made him seem even more unsuitable as her lover.

That he didn't have the sensitivity to see that now was only another point against him.

"Daro, look, I can't . . . some people aren't . . ."

"Bullshit, Grace. That's bullshit. Some people have accepted less. That doesn't mean their substitutes are working."

"Well, Daro, I hate to disappoint you, but I suspect I may qualify as one of those people. You don't know me that well, you know."

"As an empty shell? Did you aspire to that or did it just come naturally?"

"Look, Daro, I'm not your project. You don't have to save me from my sexual wasteland, which is what I'll admit it is. I manage just fine, thank you."

"I don't want a project, Grace, I want to get laid!"

"That was a joke, right? See, there you go again. You just don't get that I don't think that's funny. I'm too old to find that funny, I just would never use that phrase. Daro, I wear polyester striped things that went out of fashion so long ago they're back in fashion. I own a pair of shoes from the McCarthy era, for God's sake. That is why we cannot do this."

"Hang on to those shoes, girl, they could be worth money."

"I like to watch those pathetic British comedies on PBS. In bed. Bill Moyers is my standard for a stimulating evening. I scruff around in ter-rycloth house slippers, Daro. You don't want to watch me eat a chicken wing."

"Hey, now that's going too far. Don't you try to out-Asian me. The whole thing disappears, right?"

"There's not just an age difference. I was an adult when Kennedy was assassinated."

"Kennedy was assassinated?"

"I wear white cotton underwear, Daro, because I prefer it. Don't un-derestimate the turnoff that will be."

He ignored her use of the future tense, but noted it, she could tell.

They looked at one another. "This is all just foreplay to you, isn't it?" she said.

He grinned.

"I'll disappoint you."

"Grace, have some self-respect."

"See? Already I have."

"Look, what sort of kinkiness did you have in mind? All I want to do is make love to you. We don't even have to do that right away. Or we could just, I dunno, touch, relax together. It doesn't have to lead anywhere in particular—welcome to sex in middle age."

"I have scars . . ."

"That's scraping the bottom of the excuse bucket, now."

She did feel ridiculously girlish, her elbows locked at her waist. Surely there was a more grown-up way to do this.

"Look, this isn't exactly the summer of love. Why me? Why now? No man has even cast a glance my way for fifteen years."

"I don't know about the last fifteen years, but I'm damned sure they're looking now, all the way from those sexy little toes of yours to the top of your head. Be with me, Grace. I'm not twenty-seven. This is not a conquest."

Oddly enough, she thought about Wayne a lot more now. What Wayne had needed, what she had been unable to give him, was affection—kisses in public, squeezes of the hand, smiling glances across the room at a dinner party. She might have given these things to some other husband, but Wayne needed it too badly from her. She was raising his children and keeping his house; must she also demonstrate to him that he was loved? Then again, she knew that she had a touch deficit. She had started from too far back in life, with a mother whose touch she couldn't remember in the least. The grown-up result, in shorthand, was frigid, for most people, certainly in Wayne's view. But there was a history behind frigid, and while frigid was not Wayne's fault, a lover with more patience to go along with that desire to experiment, that itch to scratch that was just this side of kinky (that he finally, and to Gracie's relief, dammit, began to satisfy with magazines—not your average *Playboy* or *Penthouse* but raunchier stuff—

*JUGS, CUM, OUI*). Tenderness now and then he could muster, but it never seemed to grow into skill. And then, of course, came that fateful year, long before the marriage died, when it became too late to be the kind of woman he needed, when she only recognized any second chances she had been handed as such when it was too late to avail herself of them. Grace would have stayed with Wayne happy or not, satisfied or not, because her people simply did not get divorced. That's what putting up with his affairs had been about, and there'd been no awards for that, no credit in the I've-been-persecuted-so-be-nice-to-me department from any of her family members, immediate or extended. Just a flat-lipped grimace from her mother as though it had just been a matter of time before this happened because she had married the *hajukin*, the White man.

One night Grace wore some lingerie she'd picked out, lacy, not racy. The dragons Daro would have had to slay to be what she wanted when Grace was feeling that vulnerable were too much for the most valiant of men. He kissed her on each cheek and went home.

"Just hold me—that was a mixed message given my choice of underwear," she told him on the phone a half hour later. "I'm a grown-up, really I am. Have I ruined my chance?"

"Grace," he said. "Who put me in charge?" He hung up the phone. To Grace, he felt endless, like if she decided to trust that body, that voice, those lips and hands, there'd be no end to the fall.

Later, they had more time to talk it out. "I think you're just hiding behind your modesty because you don't think it's okay to be an out-and-out coquette."

"A coquette? I've never heard anyone actually use that word. And on me! Imagine! But I am modest."

"You are a grown woman in nothing but a pair of panties that do no justice to the sweet curve of your hips, making choices. Just be naked, Grace. Enjoy the way the tips of your nipples pucker, inviting my lips."

"I feel like I'm in bed with a sex therapist."

"Don't knock it. Sex is therapy."

"Oh, God. You're going to make me groan, but not from pleasure." He kept at it. "Okay, with pleasure."

His hands spread and wandered where she let them. "Feel free to participate," he managed to say without making it come off like an insult. How self-evident was his comment. And kind. Simply permitting some-one to give her sensation or pleasure was no longer participation enough, and she had not been updated on this news.

She cupped his head in her hands and thought how disembodied a person's head felt in that position. His coarse black-white hair, the warmth of his lips. He was round muscled but taut, his back narrowed to slim hips and a bit of a paunch. He had the thick, squat legs she expected to see, but they were perfectly in proportion with his body, and smooth, so smooth. She felt an old pain in the fleshy part behind her knee that started to ache again. Such an old sensation it made her laugh. It was a quirky little body tick but as reliable as her little sewing machine; it meant she was aroused. Then a wild, bleating thought came to mind. By God, she was going to be reminded of what all the fuss was about. As though he'd heard and understood, he whispered into the underside of her breast, the crook of her elbow, her armpit. "Use me, Grace. Use me up."

Grace pulled the bedsheet over her scar, a motion Daro gently countered. He placed a palm over it. She exhaled.

"You're so soft here on your belly," he observed on one of their after-noons. "There's a lot of give."

"That's because I'm short one uterus, Daro."

His hand lifted almost involuntarily. "I get it. When did you have that done?"

"It's okay to say the word."

"Your hysterectomy. It doesn't bother me, Grace."

"Tell me something that makes you vulnerable," she asked another day. "I'm tired of being the only one."

"Once upon a time I got into a hot tub with two beautiful, willing women. I couldn't achieve an erection. Every man's dream, right? I sat there feeling like, I dunno, feeling like my parents' son."

"They were White women?"

"In that time of my life, they always were."

"I can't believe you told me that. You call this tit for tat?"

"I'm trying to impress you with my willingness to be vulnerable. It's all part of your seduction."

"I can't keep up with this banter, especially when you distract me with . . . sensation."

"Don't. The last thing on earth you want to have is an ironic orgasm."

"I disagree. I'll take any kind you've got."

"See how my bicep looks against your breasts? We look like the cover of one of those novels. Watch how my hand covers the flesh of your inner thigh. Oh, that's warm. That's nice."

"You're beautiful," said Grace.

"You are beautiful. Say it."

"Don't. Don't touch me like that."

"Why is that not for you? And this? And this? As much as it is any woman's right?"

She inhaled his scent in the sheets, in the room, in the crook of his elbow or cap of his shoulder. Outside, children screamed and shouted on the playground of the nearby schoolyard. A ball thwopped against the wall, repeatedly. She saw that image of Adam again, stepping from the dark of the orchard, looking solemn, puzzled, and she squinted until a bright light flashed at the edges of her sight.

"Show me with your hand what you like," he said. They were like a ship pushed out into quiet waters. Fog shrouded the shore. Then there was no shore.

For God's sake, thought Gracie. Why, if I'm going to get something so outlandishly beyond what I could hope to expect—why can't I get what I really want? She stood at the counter mincing garlic, julienning carrots, just the sort of task that allowed her thoughts to flit. What would that be, at your age, some part of her countered. Winning the lottery? Honey, this is the lottery. She kissed the back of her hand and shook her head. What the hell was happening? It's like you're sleeping with one of your students. That was Evie-speak, only she would use a different verb. Gracie did not intend for Evie to find out about her and Daro, but if she did that's how Evie would describe it.

"Teach me about you," he had said. Your body, your mind. What kind of movie was that? This was not happening. Such a simple question, but a question she had never once been asked, certainly not in bed. "If you don't know," he had said, "let me explore. But talk to me. I can stop. I can start again. Let me know." Unbelievable.

Adam had his set of cardboard bricks out, building a wall around himself and leaving little peepholes here and there. He watched her at the counter through a peephole and told her knock-knock jokes. Grace was so used to Adam's being close by that when he went out the sliding glass door to pick dandelions, she expected he'd be right back in to decorate his castle.

Something even better than the fact of being desired had occurred to Grace, and it felt delicious to contemplate: she felt desirable to him. What pleasure to think that the trouble she took with her bath, with her hair, with her scent, meant something beyond self-care or the social obligation to maintain one's physical dignity through hygiene. She was getting ready to spend an evening with a man, and every trouble she took might contribute to his pleasure. Had she ever felt that? Being in his hands made it difficult to maintain her sense of reasonableness, her sense of the Gracie she knew at all. How beyond the rules pleasure could transport you! That's how she felt—that she was living a lifted, higher version of her own life. Because she did feel like herself, but a self to whom such things did not happen. And she wanted to tell Daro all about it, this jumble of things that did not make sense, because he would listen, which was a huge part of his sexiness, or at least pretend to listen as his head moved beneath her hands. How indulgent it would be to talk and talk to him, but she could not talk, her attention being so distracted by new sensations, not all of which she was sure she liked, and many of which sometimes whipped up a storm of resistance inside her that eventually gave way. Trust of him was like being in a bright white room, her soul laid so clean and bare by him that it nearly squeaked.

She smiled to herself. She finally understood that other advantage of doing daily Kegel exercises that the pamphlets in the doctor's office talked about. The truth was that she had enjoyed herself in bed years ago, far more than Wayne had ever given her credit for. When she let Wayne do the things he asked her to do, she did them, and she often did enjoy them. But afterward Wayne wouldn't speak to her, sometimes for days. He'd shut off like a faucet and not even look at her over the heads of their children across the dinner table. But then the next thing she knew, he was leaving crumpled Weinstocks charge slips in his dresser caddy and asking her if she'd ever considered having an "open marriage."

"Adam," Gracie called, a little irritated that he'd left open the patio door. She'd spied his blond head bobbing up and down as he darted around the lawn picking the flowers. When she called his name again and got no response, she wiped her hands on a towel and went to the door. The swing on the playset lifted gently in the early evening breeze. She padded out in her terrycloth slippers around the side of the house. "Adam." Still life with cranes and bulldozers was the scene across the gravel road, where development had approached the foundation-laying stage of the new side of Sierra Lakes Village North. Like any little boy, Adam loved watching the builders at work. She pictured him slipping into the seat of a Bobcat and trying to work the controls. Nothing in the area was blocked off, which was certainly irresponsible of them, if not illegal. Fortunately, there was lots of mud and mucky pits from recent rains. Adam disliked getting muddy. She hurried across the front lawn back around the other side of the house. Calling Adam's given name didn't seem to be working. She peered down the lanes of Garabedian's orchard, her feet sinking a little in the soil and slowing her steps. "Son-ja!" she called. She hurried back into the house, checking his brick castle, his bedroom. He wasn't merely hiding because he made a big show of where he was when he did that.

"Son-ja!" She was going to smack his little bottom when she found him. She made another trip around the house, this time crossing the road and calling into the construction site, then back over into the orchard. It was like a magical word now, the thing she had to say to make this not be real: "Chink!" She was a step away from panic, cops, search parties. How had this happened? Weeks ago she was a woman living her small, quiet life. "Chink!" Once she found him, that was absolutely it, she decided. She was too old for this. Then she heard sirens. She raced into the house to call Daro. Her breathing was stuck high in her throat. She placed a hand there to calm herself. There was no need to call Lance or Evie. Or the police. This was not going to be any sort of crisis. He was lost, that was all. He had wandered off, lost in his thoughts and looked up and discovered he didn't quite recognize the way back. Daro was on his way. The child was somewhere. The child was somewhere.

And then there he stood quietly at the orchard's edge, where a moment ago he had not been. At the sight of him, Gracie sank onto a patio chair and clamped her hand over her mouth. Adam ran to her and climbed into her lap. "I cannot do this," she said into his hair, her tears hot and unstoppable and genuine. "I'm sorry, child. I have tried, and I simply cannot."

"I'm sorry, Halmoni. Please don't be mad. Please don't tell my mom or she won't come back home. Please, Halmoni."

"I don't owe her this. I don't. Did you hear those sirens? I thought they were for you. I thought something happened to you. Where have you been?"

Daro arrived and stepped out onto the back patio.

"I'm one of those people who shakes children now," Gracie told him.

"You look pretty shaken yourself."

"I found these things from Somebody's Grandpa," Adam said, showing Daro and Gracie his yellow plastic bucket. Inside were a pair of wire-rim spectacles that looked like they could be antique, a used green plastic spoon, a wilted spiral pocket-sized notebook with all the pages torn out save a few damp sheets with lists of ratios in a column, and a lidless can of orange spray paint.

"What do you mean 'Somebody's Grandpa'?"

"He died a long time ago. He is a very sad man."

"Were you in the orchard, Adam?" Daro asked. "Your grandma doesn't ever want you to go out there by yourself. "Did you see anyone out there, buddy?"

Adam looked at Daro straight on and nodded his head.

"Who did you see?"

"I'm shaking my head yes because yes I was in the orchard. Please don't be mad at me, you guys." The child was not going to give a straight answer, and it occurred to Grace that she might not be ready to hear it in any case. She went and lay down with a cool cloth on her forehead while Daro took over for a while.

That night Adam asked, "Halmoni, does every boy get to be a grandpa someday?"

"Boys cannot be grandpas, Son-ja. Some men are. The ones with children who have children."

"But not the dead ones."

The next morning two police officers knocked on the door. The body of a young man had been found on the north side of Isaac's orchard, cause of death as yet to be determined. Isaac had reported he had seen a white Lincoln with suicide doors full of kids going past several times around 1:00 a.m. Had they seen anyone?

"Adam, honey, why didn't you tell us there was a man out there?"

"I did tell you. I said Somebody's Grandpa was out there, but he didn't talk to me."

"Did you see somebody or not, honey?"

Adam nodded.

"Was he an old man, Adam? Or a young man? Did he look like Somebody's Grandpa to you? How old is a grandpa, Adam?"

"All right, that's enough. Please try not to overwhelm him. And we should get a lawyer." Gracie looked at Daro.

"You said boys become grandpas and girls become grandmothers. Well, this was a boy."

"A boy and not a man?"

"Kind of a man."

The officers looked at one another. "All right, you will need to retain counsel on the boy's behalf. And we'll need to finish this down at the station. Are you the legal guardian?"

"I'm his grandmother. He's visiting; his father lives in Fresno. But what are you suggesting? A six-year-old boy could not be mixed up in this. You only want to ask him some questions, right? He doesn't know anything."

"That's right, ma'am. His parents should be notified, and they have the right to remain with him throughout the questioning."

Why had he called the man Somebody's Grandpa if he was too young to be anyone's grandpa? Why were the items he found under the trees seemingly more important to him than the actual body? The investigators had a right to those questions; she just didn't have the answers. Adam certainly didn't.

His name was Bin Pham. He was twenty-two years old, a Laotian born in the United States. Worked at Jiffy Lube part-time while caring for grandparents. The parents worked eighty hours a week each. A good-looking young man, high school wrestling champion and homecoming king. Had a girlfriend who attended Reedley High, Cassandra Harcomb. Had been interested in street racing until his love of music won out, then became a bass player in a hip-hop band that had begun getting gigs in the area. Had gotten into a fight with some members of a country-and-western band that played at the same location in Reedley, a renovated building people called the Chatterbox. The members of the country-and-western band resented the young man's dating an ex-girlfriend of the lead singer. The girlfriend, Cassie Harcomb, had not been injured. There had been talk of roughing him up somehow, but evidence pointed to suicide. The investigation continued. If it got classified as a homicide investigation, it would be months before they were through with Adam.

i never asked a dime from you for college, you know. i'm not saying you owe me, but i do feel like this is the least you can do so that i can get through grad school. Don't you want me to have a better life? Don't you at least want your own grandson to have a better life? This is my chance, Mom. It's not that much longer.

Tell Adam I got the giraffe picture he sent and both math tests (way to go, babe!) will phone Tuesday but not before. Am out of town at a conference.

The top of Adam's head, his scalp, always smelled slightly sour when Lance dropped him off on Sunday evenings. Either he wasn't bathing the child, or he'd worn a sweaty cap all weekend. Grace was more than ready to be annoyed with Lance, but he lingered in her kitchen and helped himself to a plate of frosted lemon bars.

"Let me ask you something, Grace. Did anyone ever tell you to ask for more?"

"Once."

"Who was that?"

"A sister."

"One of those aunties Evie talks about?"

"No, it was a different sister. She died before I was born." Grace loved watching Lance trying to digest information that took him a beat or two more than most people. "Grace, you're spookin' me."

"I'm perfectly serious. I dream about her maybe once or twice a year, and she tells me exactly that—that I should ask for all that is my right."

Lance appeared to think this over. "We should all have somebody reminding us of that."

"Some people feel pretty entitled already, don't you think?"

Lance studied her face to see if this was an accusation. She hadn't actually meant it as such, but if the shoe fit.

"I lost a big brother. Desert Storm."

"I'm sorry," said Grace, although she felt an ever-ready irritation with him for being so persistently self-referential. "What was his name?"

"Jack. Jacky Bidden."

"Tell me something he liked to do."

"He liked to hunt. He would feed his dog, Circe, chocolate bars, which

179

is supposed to kill dogs, but not Circe. He wasn't trying to kill her or anything. She liked them."

Gracie gave him a napkin and poured him a glass of milk.

"I'd wanted him gone so badly, you know? We used to fistfight in the backyard. Tough fights, like sometimes it felt like he wanted me dead. And then he was gone." For a moment, he seemed lost in recollections he had no intention of sharing with his sort of mother-in-law. "My family's been military from way back. My dad's been in and out of a vet's hospital since Vietnam. It's all a big mistake." He shook his head but didn't offer more. Instead he asked, "So what this sister tells you—do you listen? I mean does it ever occur to you to ask for more, Grace?"

Gracie smiled, partly because Lance had just foiled her theory about him and partly because she realized even a week ago her answer would have been very different. The old answer was the one she gave, however, as she wasn't about to jinx the good, new things in her life by letting Lance in on anything, even obliquely. "When you're older, you stop yearning quite so much for things. You don't have the energy."

Lance shrugged. "I bet I stopped long before you ever did."

"Hey now," Grace offered charitably. The two of them shared custody, after all. "I don't know you very well, but I'm sure you have a lot going for you—youth, strength, a good job, a beautiful son." When her list petered out, Lance stole a glance at her to make sure no more was coming. Clearly, he was unused to simple bucking up; it almost made Gracie sorry there really wasn't more to say.

In the heat of the first days of June, they rode their bicycles out to Copper Pond. "Halmoni, why do you have brown bumps all over you?" Her neck and upper chest and shoulders were covered with skin tags.

"I wish I knew." She looked down at herself and shook her head. "They don't hurt."

He touched them with his fingertips like he was doing a gentle dot-to-dot. "Do you want to hear the inside of the world?" he asked her.

"It's green and quiet, but only sort of quiet. Like something is going vruuuuuuuuum."

She laughed and floated on her back as Adam did. She heard the green, felt the quiet, the murky stillness. "I wish I could go there," he called out so that she would be able to hear him with her ears submerged. Gracie quickly righted herself, her toes grabbing the silty bottom. Adam did the same, then paddled to her and attached himself to her side, in the crook of her hip, where her body responded with an ache of memory, so many small bodies on that hip in past years. He moved to her front, embraced her with arms and legs wrapping her torso, eel-skin slick against her bathing suit and glistening, his neck and dripping hair fragrant with pond scum and heat on skin and strawberry scented shampoo. "I would miss you very much. Don't go there," she said into his neck.

"Is that where the sad man went?"

"I don't think that's where the sad man went."

Adam paused to consider her slant answer. Then he said, a child mimicking some adult's certainty, "Heaven is not a place, you know."

When they were drying off on the comforter she had thrown over the spiky grass, Gracie lay on her back, blinking and at peace. Which adult, she wondered—Evelyn? Lina? Lance? A warm breeze smoothed itself over them. Even though she was helping it to happen, it would be too bad when the condos spread as far as Copper Pond. From his pocket, Adam pulled a spyglass and a tarnished tube of lipstick with a stub of antique red. Lately, his bed had become littered with objects: a pearl-handled comb, a pocket mirror. He brought them home from his visits to the bunkhouses where Grace had consented to let him roam because there was nothing out that direction but fields, foothills, mountains, and sky. Grace often wondered why no local history buff had considered the site a historic treasure; she figured the items might be worth something someday. The funny thing was, her kids had used to play out there all the time and they never came home with this stuff. One day, Adam had even come home and started writing imitations of ideographs on a piece of paper and primitive-looking sketches that looked like cave drawings—a tiger with jagged bones, a large-winged raptor, a man urinating onto the top of a mountain.

At school, she thinks she sees Bin Pham in the halls. He might have been her student, might have brushed past her in the halls. At night she dreams of his face, one that could have been any of the hundreds she has seen in Adult Ed. Although she has probably never seen Bin Pham alive and certainly not dead, in her dream she sees him in detail. It is a blue-gray face, lips blanched, cheeks bloated, the eyes puffy slits with reddened, somewhat chafed-looking eyelids and faint eyebrows. He wears an expression of mild amusement, as though someone had cracked a decent joke but not a knee-slapper. She wakes from the dream, often thirsty, although that is partly due to the season, and feels compelled to go in and check on Adam. Adam had decided that he wanted to go solely by the name "Chink," which Grace still refused to call him. But when she checked in on him at night, she smoothed the hair from his forehead, pulled the sheet back up to his chin, and said the name because he wanted her to, just once, not ironically, not with appropriation in mind, not bitterly, just once, whispered with a kiss, because it was how he was known.

"I don't get it," Daro says. "The kid was an American success story—son of immigrants who can't read or write English becomes an athletic star off to college with a wrestling scholarship, fucking prom king, blond cheerleader girlfriend, plays in a band. What went wrong? Was he really still an outsider after all that just because he's Asian? Will this country never get over itself? Will we never be assimilated?"

"But who do you mean by we, Daro? What do I have in common with people from a country I've never been to who came here eighty or ninety years after my own father? I mean, I sympathize with them, but not more or less than I sympathize with families from Bosnia or Sierra Leone."

"Chink," Daro called her.

Gracie bristled.

"The day no one can call you that, or me, or Adam is the day I keep my mouth shut."

"Look at how many White kids commit suicide."

"What's that supposed to mean?"

"And how many Asian kids don't."

"You mean that maybe it's actually a sign of his assimilation that he killed himself?"

"It's bleak, I know."

"Except for that pesky little detail of the hate crime, you've almost got a point."

"Technically not a hate crime though, right? Because it originated in a romantic feud."

"That's bullshit, Grace. There wouldn't have been a feud if Bin Pham had been White."

"Over Cassandra Harcomb? I've seen pictures of her. She could inspire a feud or two among men of any color. Not everything is about race, Daro."

"Don't be White, Grace."

"That word is sure easy to throw around."

"The Man can't stand to see the beautiful ones go to men of color."

"The Man? Don't provoke me, Daro. I'm not young enough to be thrown into worrying about what gorgeous blondes lurk in your own past, even though I think you'd like me to be." She looked at him carefully. "You're fuming, I can see that. Look, even if everything did come down to race, a person can't live like that."

"Maybe you can't. I don't see that I ever had a choice."

"Oh, please."

"Now you're going to pull the generation gap on me again, aren't you?"

"My, I've become predictable. But in any case, it's true. How did we survive all of last century? Not by maximizing the race issue, but by proceeding in spite of it, Daro. And don't look at me like that. I married Wayne because I loved him. Think what it cost me in terms of my own family. After the sixties, that may seem quaint."

She couldn't tell whether he'd been softened or defeated. He started putting his things back into his overnight bag. "Just like that? Can't we have a conversation anymore, Daro?"

"You know what's sadder than anything? That race would come between us. And don't give me that crap about Japs and Koreans. We're yellow, Grace. Yellow. I've got to go. I'll call you."

They were miles out. No shore. She was going to let him drift out of sight. At least she knew where to find him; according to Lina, he'd be at home sinking into his green leather recliner.

Once a year, Wayne would explode. Objects, sometimes even small animals or people, would go flying. In a jaw-clenched red-faced fury, he would unleash a year's worth of foiled tolerance, unappreciated attempts at placation, well-timed walks around the block, guilt riddled into a sense of persecution, and the usual frustrated ambition, desire, and longing of a domesticated, socially harnessed, middle-aged family man. Scared the hell out of everyone, including Wayne himself Grace felt sure. But she had to admit, it cleared the air. She wouldn't go so far as to say she preferred it to Daro's disappearance, but she understood a whole lot better where she stood.

She gave him what she was forever telling Adam to give her—space—but quickly discovered that a body gets used to pleasure just as easily as it gets used to its denial. "Masturbation" was such a drawn-out and heavily enunciated word there was no wonder you felt guilt for doing it. Guys had their terms for it, but equivalent terms for women did not exist, so far as she knew; she would have to ask Eileen. Then along came *Our Bodies, Ourselves*, by that bra-burning women's collective, to liberate women from cold steel foot stirrups and speculums at the gynecologist's office and encourage them to dance naked before mirrors. Grace found that she was just a shade too old (and too uptight) for things like self-examination with speculums and hand mirrors or menstrual dripping. In a way, she was sorry she had missed that boat because that door in her remained at least slightly ajar. But mostly she was content to watch with one eye squinted as women did away with every last shred of mystery they possessed. Then Grace recalled that the book had indeed given a better name for masturbation—self-pleasuring, they called it, and much to her astonishment, Grace was finding it to be a useful, workable term.

"Don't tell me," Lina said when she came in with the twins to fetch Adam for a playdate. "Daro?"

"Does it show that easily?" Francesca and Catherina encircled Grace's waist with hugs.

"I admit Lance had said he was starting to wonder about you. He didn't want to ask you directly."

"Oh, well, I'm all right."

"Is that why your African violets are crispy?"

For some reason, she cannot bring herself to venture back out there. She herself had never actually done what each of her children and now her grandson had done—walk in the orchards in the fog, after dark. She had walked through them a few times but only in the daytime to get through to Garabedian's on some neighborly errand.

A cloak of stillness, of soaking quiet. Fig trees had to be really the ugliest trees on Earth, so dark and craggy in this season. She slid her back against a tree to scratch her back, then slid all the way down the bark until her bottom hit the exposed roots. These trees were so old; Garabedian had got all the fruit off them he could possibly be expected to get. Time to raze these terrific creatures for some nice, tidy Cape Cods featuring their little balconies and grill style windows in pastels of blue and peach. He'd make such a bundle; his kids and grandkids would be set for life, she supposed.

But then, she thought morbidly, where would people go to kill themselves? Where would teenagers go to have sex? Where would you go if you

wanted to sit at the base of a scarred, fruitless tree and worry that your
lover had just picked a fight with you in order to get out of a relationship
that wasn't what he'd hoped it would be (never mind what you hoped it
might be) and have a good cry and be left utterly alone?

❀ ❀ ❀

you there? there's a tornado watch here in johnson county. kind of a thrill.
Evie! Take cover! Better sign out NOW.


it's only a watch, mother. Warnings are when you want to start thinking about heading to the basement.
Even so, let's keep this short. Should your computer even be on during
a storm? Let me just say this—I think you should come home as soon as
you can.
i thought you said the investigation wasn't a big deal. adam won't talk
about it. that bugs me.
This isn't about Adam, not directly. And there's nothing more going on
with the investigation. We've told them everything we know. I just think a
month is too long to wait right now.
too long for what???? what the hell is going on?
Call it a Lance watch, with possibility of upgrading to a Lance
warning.
he started drinking again? got busted for something?
Nothing like that, at least not that I know of. Evie, this is the
only warning you're going to get from me. If you ever thought you and
Lance could make it work, better come now.
you're killing me, Mom. why won't tell me WHAT?
Because I think you know WHAT. Come home.

❀ ❀ ❀

Gracie had gotten to where she recognized Officer Svoboda's knock.
Randall Svoboda, who just missed being handsome, compensated by being very nice. Or maybe he was just nice. But, still, he was not a man she

wanted to see daily, and she told him as much when she opened the door. It was a Saturday.

"Hey, buddy. I like those jammies," he said, lifting his hand to Adam.

"They're not jammies. It's my jamos. That's Korean for pj's."

"Adam, don't talk back to grown-ups for one thing. For another thing, it's time to brush your teeth. Scoot." Grace smiled at Officer Svoboda. "You'd think my grandson was a suspect, you're here so often."

"No, ma'am. But we do have a lead I thought you should know about. We think there may have been someone else out there that day. Your grandson may have been approached by an individual, possibly the 'Somebody's Grandpa,' he referred to."

"No. That's not it," Adam insisted. Gracie and the officer turned to look at Adam.

"Did you see somebody out there, or not, buddy?"

"Not the boy."

"Not the boy? Was there someone there with you?"

"No," he replied. "I didn't touch him."

Officer Svoboda looked at Grace. "Now, I don't mean anything by this, but he's a little . . . he's very. Is this maybe a little bit unusual behavior for him?"

"Personally, I think it's because he doesn't watch much television."

"One thing's clear, ma'am. The boy's statements are not consistent or credible."

"You mean he's lying?"

Adam went to his notepad and wrote: IM TRYING TO TRIK THE ~~GOATS~~GHOSTS. He brought it to Officer Svoboda. "Ghosts can't read," he whispered.

The officer looked at Grace helplessly. "Adam is learning about Chinese culture from his daycare lady. They're very multiculturally oriented, as you can see. Tell him what you've been learning, Adam."

"When the ghosts try to take Chinese babies away, the mothers will lie or hide them or put them in disguideds—"

"Disguises," Grace interrupted.

"Disguises so that they can't take the babies away."

Gracie smiled and shrugged at the officer. "It's a Jewish-owned day-care run by a Latina. Go figure."

She could tell he was wondering what kind of daycare would talk about ghosts and snatching babies away from their homes. You had to know Lina. "Look, Officer—Randy? May I call you that? Let's say we find out that the investigation is ruled a suicide, then you can shut down this case, can't you?"

"No ruling has been filed, ma'am."

"Hey, Randy. Randy, can I tell you something?" Adam tugged on the officer's striped pant leg.

"His name is Officer Svoboda to you, young man."

"Guess what, Randy? My halmoni has these scissors that are really old like about a thousand years and they're still sharp."

Officer Svoboda raised his eyebrows at Grace. "It's true they're still sharp. My father was a barber. Now, Office Svoboda, I will certainly encourage Adam to cooperate to the fullest extent. But if suicide is the determination, let's have that be the end of Adam's involvement, all right? The boy was in the wrong place at the wrong time, but he has done nothing wrong."

"With all due respect, ma'am, the exact finding has yet to be determined."

"Hey, Randy," Adam tugged again. "What do you get when you cross a cat with a flashlight?"

Officer Svoboda was already out the door. Gracie smiled apologetically at her grandson.

❋ ❋ ❋

That night, Adam woke Gracie by jostling her shoulder until she opened her eyes.

"Some people die and some people just go on and on," he said into the dark. She patted the side of the bed and he crawled in beside her. "No, I'm sorry honey but it doesn't work that way. Everybody dies."

"Where's Mr. Daro?"

"He's at home. He has some things he needs to take care of."

"But you and me. And my mom. And my dad. And Mr. Daro, and Miss Lina. We will go on and on, won't we?"

"I suppose as long as somebody remembers you, yes, you do go on and on. But everybody dies. Only don't worry because that isn't going to happen today."

"It happened to Bin Pham. He wasn't too old. He wasn't even as old as you."

"You're right, Son-ja, it did happen to Bin Pham. Sometimes it happens when it isn't really supposed to."

"But why?"

"To be very honest, Son-ja, because sometimes people want it to. But you know what? For one, you are just too little to understand more than that. For another, it is your mom and dad's job to talk to you about this, so I will let them talk to you when they see you. And for another, most of the time it doesn't happen too soon. Most people get a pretty long time. I've had a long time."

"Didn't Bin Pham want a long time too?"

"Yes, he probably did. But he was confused. And if he had known he was going to be Somebody's Grandpa one day, he might have made sure he stuck around." Saying this, she missed her friend Daro. And somehow, in missing him, she felt suddenly flooded with a rush of unfamiliar feeling. Gratitude.

❀   ❀   ❀

mom: adam told me all about "gitte" the blonde. what the hell kind of a name is that? i think she's out of the picture, or so I gather from adam. but should i be worried about this Lina person? am arriving Sunday at 4 p.m. flight #1762 from SF. lance is picking me up and bringing adam and dropping us off at your place. we leave for disneyland early monday a.m. big favor: do you think you could still send that $100 to help out with the plane fare? i didn't know if you thought you could still swing that. teaching assistants did not get the raise they were expecting, and i'm trying to stay away from any more student loans see you this weekend. love, me.

❀ ❀ ❀

"Hello, Adam. My name is Cassandra. May I come in?"

The boy stepped aside and watched the young woman as she entered. "Are you going to have a baby?" he asked.

Gracie took the young woman's hand. "I apologize, my dear. He comes from a long line of people who are very direct."

Cassie looked at him wonderingly. "As a matter of fact, I am going to have a baby girl. Do I show already?" Gracie intercepted the slightly untoward question by offering the girl a glass of juice or tea. She couldn't possibly know the sex of a fetus that hadn't even begun to show. Lord, these babies having babies. Adam had not taken his eyes off her. "Are you the Sunkist girl?"

She laughed. "Who's that? Is that from LA Live?" Adam looked rather helplessly to his grandmother. How could she not know, especially when she looked so much like her?

"He's paying you a compliment, honestly," Gracie explained. "Do you know the girl on the red raisin box? A long time ago there was an orange maiden a lot like her, only she didn't wear a bonnet. I think her hair was tied in a blue bow."

"You could come to my birthday party after we get back from Disneyland."

"Disneyland? How exciting." He was charming, standing near her so ready to be of service, setting the glass of tea down before her with a deference she didn't know he was capable of. But this young woman had come with a purpose, and she looked rather eagerly out the patio doors toward the orchard.

"Would you mind if I went out there? Just for a little ways. I just want to I guess sort of say goodbye."

"They aren't my orchards, but believe me, people go through there all the time."

"Can I go, Halmoni?"

190

"That's up to Cassandra." She took the boy's still chubby hand.

"I'll ask you both to stay within shouting distance. And please don't let go of him."

She was very young indeed. Her hair was pleasingly unfussy brown curls pulled back loosely with a silver clip. Those fresh cheeks didn't look like they had so recently suffered a loss. For a moment before they disappeared from view, Gracie's heart leapt into a tiny flurry. When the girl had called to ask if she might visit, Gracie had been so anxious to do something about the awful situation that she urged her to come over as soon as possible. Now she saw that she was letting her grandson disappear—again—holding the hand of a perfect stranger.

She set down her coffee and newspaper and went out into the orchard a ways herself. They had been truthful; they weren't far at all. When they came into view many yards ahead, Gracie stopped and watched them. They appeared not to be aware of her presence, but stood quietly holding hands, very patient and very still, looking up into the branches of a tree. From where she stood, Grace couldn't see what had captured their attention, but dear God they looked like such children, both of them. They began to walk, still hand in hand, down the orchard row making very slow time and pausing to examine things on the ground now and then. The last gesture Grace could make out was of Cassandra jutting her elbows to the side and bracing herself at the hips with her hands, that classic pregnant mother's pose to relieve the aching back. She wasn't pregnant enough; she must have been practicing. She wasn't even beyond the risk of miscarriage. They were getting out so far that Grace felt nearly compelled to shout at them to head back. But something in her told her to trust them, to allow the girl this time.

There had been a moment in the lives of each of her children when she looked at them and realized they were separate from her, there before her but gone forever from the chalk circle she had drawn around them in her mind. Each had stepped across that line at different ages, on different occasions. For Ben, it had happened at summer camp when he had lost his glasses on the very first day and endured the week able to see next to nothing. He had been furious with her even though he knew it was not her fault. And after that week, he still loved her—loved her more than ever in some ways—but the self of his own making had begun. Mitchell, her first, had been the longest holdout. He'd lived at home and attended the state university, studying Mandarin at the kitchen table rather than socializing with friends. For years, Grace thought he would never meet a girl, but he did, a student of his from Taiwan whom he assisted in the foreign language lab. And then there was Evie, whose separation from her was complete before she was out of her crib, if not the womb. And it's too bad she wasn't here to see this, thought Grace—this moment when her son was walking away from all of them hand in hand with his Sunkist girl down a lane of Valencias a breath or a sigh from bursting into bloom.

The moon was a wink above the white-blossomed blur of the orange groves flying past, filling the rushing air with the citrusy scent of the blossoms. Lance killed the headlights as they rode through the night, navigating by slicing a dark line through the luminous, fragrant groves. She threw her head back and a swirl of implacable stars washed around inside her skull. Her hair whipped her cheeks. He tucked his free hand neatly between her thighs, steered with the other. She turned to check on Adam asleep in the back seat.

"His favorite ride was the most boring ride of all," Evie said to Grace and Daro the next morning. "I don't remember the name of it; he called it the People Mover. You know that ride where you sit in those cars on that conveyor belt, and on the outside is that telescope that makes the people going in look like they're getting smaller and smaller? And you learn all about microscopic life, and in the end, you come out big again. That's what he wanted. Big, small, big. Over and over. Unbelievable."

Gracie sighed at the energy her daughter put into her reactions to things and then let it go. It had been a good weekend. Daro had called to say he was glad to have the excuse of house-buying paperwork for her to fill out because he wanted to come over and hold her in his arms the entire night. Now the kitchen streamed with sunlight, and Daro had something that smelled delicious baking in the oven. She didn't want to jeopardize their peace by venturing too close to the subject of their last argument. Still, it was an irony she would love to share with him—an article about a hate crime at the university, this time a Caucasian boy who had been downtown at the bars with an Asian girl, and they got taunted by a drunken crowd of young men. Underneath that article was an announcement about the upcoming Taidom festival, also at the university. What a country, as Lance Bidden was fond of saying. No, she wouldn't mention it until they were back on surer footing. She wasn't sure how long that would take, since she wasn't going to use sex to expedite their reconciliation. There'd been too much of that with Wayne—sex that was like poking a jellyfish to gauge its response, sex that was like changing the dressing on a wound, sex that was business as usual when really you were seething inside. Leave that to married folks.

When she had lived alone not so very long ago, Grace liked, on windy days, to leave the windows open. Muscular coastal gusts galloped across the valley a few times a year, relocating her lawn furniture to wild angles and lifting her wind chimes to a clanging horizontal fury. She loved to open the casements for a swift cross draft that sucked doors shut in empty rooms and jostled her ferns. It was as though spirits—tidy ones, nowadays—were going about their daily lives, slipping down the hallway to let the cat out, tucking into the bedroom to put away the folded socks. A loose screen door at the side of the house added to the drama as it lifted open and then slammed shut against the jamb. It was probably best that she had people in her life now who would not abide this practice. When Daro spent the night, he leapt straight up from bed at the slam of a door (which caused Gracie a lift of the eyebrows about his past), groaned awake, and went to shut windows, muttering about fixing the goddam doors. Adam, for his part, stirred in his sleep and, if awoken, would crawl into bed with Grace and Daro. So it wasn't the same sort of fun. When Grace brought this habit into the light of day and really examined it, she had to admit it was the edge of looney, a disconcerting habit to develop at this stage of the game, and Lord only knew where it might lead.

She had even gone as far as checking out the continental wind currents in the newspaper to figure out what was blowing in from where, an Alberta clipper from the Northwest Passage or an Asian wind current from the Pacific. Was this the air that, yesterday, someone had breathed in Bangor, and, a week before that, Bangkok? Someone's sighs, someone's germs swooping across her front lawn. Topsoil and dandruff and pheromones coursing in from the trees. The wing dust of alpine moths, the cumulus syllables of a prayer, the skins of balloons alighting, drifting, eddying, settling in.

She wasn't a traveler, save for, years ago, an obligatory trip to Europe with Wayne as part of a last-ditch effort to save her marriage. This was her pathetic substitute—to let the world course through her doors and windows depositing its invisible traces through her curtains and onto her couch and carpet and plate glass coffee table. Someone's past, and someone else's future pausing here, leavened now with the sweet-mouthed yawns of a child, the laughter of an aging man whose age would never catch up with hers, and the ever-present barely discernible sighs of a woman for whom adventure and travel and even delight had been a mostly interior journey whom no one, probably not even God, found remarkable. At least it wasn't an ill wind she set forth. At least that was something.

"How come we've done so little of this, you and I?" Grace asked her daughter in the postbirthday lull out in the backyard. She wanted to reach across and tuck under a stray curl of Evie's auburn hair. She wanted to tell her she had never looked more beautiful to her, with the evening sun igniting the color in her hair and cheeks.

"Because, Mother," Evie started, and then paused. "Look at how that tree bends in the wind. Just bends." She looked straight at Grace. "You're flawed, Mother," she said. "So don't take this as any sort of huge pardon for my childhood. But—I've never known how to bend. Is that your fault? Or was I born that way, or what?"

Gracie had to smile at love's distance from clarity. "When you were little we'd eat at a Chinese restaurant and you'd empty the sugar shaker into your little cup of tea. I'd be mortified."

"If you weren't supposed to do it, there wouldn't have been a sugar shaker there in the first place, right?"

"You see?"

She pulled out a cigarette and lighter but then put them away.

"Easy for me to look back and judge, isn't it, now that I'm settled and old?"

"And having the time of your life in bed?"

Gracie's squint was her normal response to Evie's frankness, she couldn't help it. But she grabbed Evie's hand to make up for the gesture, squeezed, and nodded yes.

Evie told her, looking across the lawn strewn with birthday party detritus. "I still wish we could convince you to keep this place. You don't want to mess with a condo owner's association, do you? All those bylaws and busybodies and fumbling for the pool key."

"I haven't decided anything for sure. Please remember, though, it's not up to you or your brothers."

Evie sat down in the rusted glider; Grace sat down next to her. "Adam was no accident," Evie told her. "I don't know if you realized that."

"You chose to be a single mother, Evelyn?"

She shook her head. "I don't know. I chose Adam. Lance and I had tried for a baby once, back when I was even dumber than I am now. And I did get pregnant—for thirteen weeks." She put her hand on her mother's arm. "I'd been about to tell you. So close, at which point I lost the baby. And then I just couldn't, for all sorts of reasons. I remember the day, playing Frisbee golf with a bunch of friends out at the greenway. One of those perfect spring days in Iowa, and I'd felt great. Lance was getting more and more into the idea that he was going to be—had chosen to be—a father. But I went home that night and started getting cramps and throwing up. I lost it that night. He didn't want to try again—he was sinking for other reasons, for his own reasons, and we split up not long after that. But of course we saw each other eventually like we did after the first five split-ups. And I knew it was the worst timing ever for us, but I found out I was pregnant that summer, which is why I didn't make the trip home that year to visit. And the funny thing is that I had nothing against abortion—it wasn't that. I was alone, but I knew somehow I really was ready. Maybe not ready in all the ways that would have made me a responsible, secure mother, but in enough of them to make me sure I could do it. I haven't screwed him up, yet, I don't think."

He's only seven would have been Grace's first response; barring that, she didn't know what to say. Evie added, "Law school is for Adam as much as it is for me, you believe that much, don't you?"

Grace just nodded and breathed. How did someone as safe as she was end up with a daughter so reckless with her life? They watched Lina and Daro and Lance step out onto the deck and begin gathering up small mountains of bows and wrapping paper. One mountain came alive and it turned out to be Catherine or Francesca, no one ever knew for certain except their mom. Someone had let Adam loose with his Super Blaster, which he was now filling with water from the hose. "Very few women as gorgeous as Lina are not models," Evie observed. "Do we stand a chance with these men?"

The garage door banged shut in the breeze, then lifted open again, creakingly. Gracie looked at her daughter. "You're no slouch in that department, but I'm sure you know that."

Evie choked out a sigh. "Where did you get that idea? I didn't know that. I don't know that, Mother. It would have been so easy for you to say it just once in my life."

Gracie grabbed her daughter's chin. "Stop it. Stop it. You're a beauty. I thought you knew."

Evie wiped her nose with the back of her hand, sighed again.

"Did you tell your Dad and Arlene about Daro when you visited?"

Evie nodded carefully. "Don't be mad, please? They were tickled pink for you."

"Ha! I'll just bet they were."

"Okay, so we're still working on the bitterness."

"Okay, so yeah we are."

Adam and the twins had become bored with trees and each other for targets and started in on grown-ups with the Super Blasters. Grown-ups in motion, or those protesting the loudest, were getting hit early and often. "We went to see Aunt Elin, too, up in Calgary. She put Lance to work fixing things, so he felt right at home. And she made Adam promise to be her pen pal. Man, I want to live like that someday. All alone in the high chaparral with my books and peace and quiet." Gracie looked at her doubtfully. "I said one day, Mother. Also, it helps when you've made your fortune."

"Does she still wear that god-awful red hat when she's writing her books?"

"You've gotta admit it works for her. I think she earned the life she's got."

"Who does she meet up there?"

"Ranch hands. Gardeners."

"Men?"

"Shit-boy howdy."

"Good for her." Grace put her hand on Evie's arm as Super Blasters found their way into the hands of grown-ups headed their way.

"Elin gave me a notebook of Grandmother's she kept the year she died. She'd started writing letters that she never sent. Some of them are to Dad when he was a kid. Stuff you don't even know."

"Stuff I don't need to know. How old was she when she died?"

"Ninety-something, same as Halmoni, which is great news for me." Gracie shrugged. "And me. I suppose. What's Elin's next book then?"

"Another one on angels. Angels and children, this time. The working title is something like *What Your Young Child Would Like You to Know*."

"Duck!" Gracie shouted, just in time to see a blast of water hit her daughter straight in the backside.

The pilot said the sun was shining up high where they were going and then wouldn't it be something to see. But right now, it reminded him of winter in Iowa, like the sky was about to cave in from the whiteness. It wasn't his mom's fault she was back in Iowa now. She was taking care of business, his dad explained. In Iowa, everything was puffy white with black or brown edges, like an old photograph. The puffy parts were snow, and they were everywhere. His mom had a patio chair on the little patio place that hung outside her tall apartment building, and the chair was very puffy, and the arms on the chair were very puffy. But if you sat down on it, you wouldn't feel soft, you would feel wet and cold and then you would get in trouble from your mom if you didn't have clean underpants and socks to change into right away. Even when the weather was nice, Adam wasn't allowed to sit out there because the balcony was still icy and it didn't pass the "six feet" rule.

"What's the matter with you?" his halmoni chided. He knew she meant that after getting a bag of goodies from the airline and getting his picture taken in the cockpit with the pilot and having apple juice brought to him by more than one airline hostess, there had better not be anything the matter.

"I feel sad about your mom."

"My mother? What in the world for?"

Her face was like a moon in the photograph on Halmoni's piano, round and white and shiny with some feeling he didn't have the name for. His halmoni says she was painted in next to her husband later on. A painted lady, he had asked? No! she'd shouted back, like she did sometimes. The great-grandfather part was the first picture, and then when Changmi, that was her name, came to this country to be with him they painted her in. That was what he was sad about; they had had to paint her in.

Halmoni laughed and took his hand. "But why is that a sad thing, Adam?"

"Because she had to wait all that time to be put next to him."

"Yes, she did have to wait a long time. About thirteen years."

He couldn't even imagine what it would be like to wait for something that was even longer than your whole lifetime.

As he drifted off to sleep between Halmoni and Daro, he thought about the man they called Bin Pham. That morning, he had been finding lots of stuff—a no-good balloon with white gravy in it (he knew to leave that alone), the side of a box of Frosted Flakes, a wet book that had lots of words melted together by the dripping, and a pair of glasses. The man he had seen was not just a man; he was a sad man. Maybe he could not stand to look at himself, so he took his glasses off that were bent like a giant paperclip. Adam knew the man could not talk to him. But Adam could talk to the sad man. "Somebody's Grandpa," he called him, in case that was a name the young man might know. "I'm sorry for you." He did not think he was dead or not dead. He only thought he should get away so that he could explain there was someone out there. He knew this was the right thing to do, but he had felt a little bit bad about it. The sad man really looked like what he wanted was to be left alone.

❀ ❀ ❀

The customs official was a pretty redhead in crisp teal shirtsleeves. "Good morning. Does the child have a passport?"

"We were told we wouldn't need one as long as we had his birth certificate."

The agent took the document and examined it, making quick marks and circles on a card. "You are tourists. This is your first trip to ROK. Your return date is August 17th, correct? Every member of your party has the same return date, correct?" Gracie and Daro nodded. Adam had an arm wound round Daro's leg while studying the woman behind them in the line who seemed to be talking to no one until you noticed the headset and slip-on microphone on her jacket. Even with her hands free, she seemed busy, attempting to arrange a scarf with one hand while pulling a strapped-together luggage series on wheels.

"Your relationship to the child?"

"I am his grandmother." The agent's eyes slid to Daro. "I'm just a friend of the family."

"I see. And the parents are where? Deceased?" Gracie had forgotten how much of one's personal business became the business of the state when you began crossing oceans. It wasn't just the stuff in your suitcase or on your person they wanted to know about. "No, they are not deceased," Grace retorted, "they are at home. This is nothing but a pleasure trip with my companion and my grandson."

"I understand, ma'am. My job is to ask you a few questions, and your patience is certainly appreciated." The agent from the next booth, an attractive Black woman, glanced over at them, seemed to note something about them that Gracie couldn't read.

"Now, then," the agent continued. "Do you have a letter from the child's parents giving you permission to have him travel with you?" She wore lipstick that matched the stripes in her neck scarf in an unbecoming shade of frosted rust.

"A letter? No, I don't have any letter. I had no idea I'd need something like that. We're just going on vacation, for goodness sake."

Daro put his hand on Gracie's shoulder and spoke to the agent. "What happens if we don't have a letter? Is this going to be a problem?"

They could see the agent sizing up the situation. What did she see? An Asian man and an Asian woman taking a gorgeous towheaded boy to South Korea with them. Did she see the Asian in him? "He is my biological grandson, in case you were wondering." Gracie offered. Daro squinted and scratched his temple.

The agent looked at Gracie with implacable officialness. "Halmoni," Adam said, tugging on her arm. "Halmoni, look." A swarm of reporters whooshed after some sort of celebrity, darting around a corner with cameras on shoulders, all of them attached to one another with cords and microphones. Other cameras followed on a go cart; Gracie realized that the swarm was part of a movie and the reporters were only actors. That explained the Christmas decorations hung in late August. Gracie had seen Hope Lange once in the days when she was older but still much more famous. She had been waiting in line just like everybody else at the train station of all places, getting her bags checked. She had looked Grace right in the eyes with a sort of neutral goodwill and then quickly looked away. For the rest of the day, Grace felt in good spirits. Even Hope Lange took trains. Even Hope Lange, beautiful as she was, aged.

"We'll need the full names and address of the parents, with phone contact."

A moment later, Gracie stood gasping at the price of duty-free L'Eau du Temps, Daro and Adam both now tugging on her arm.

❀ ❀ ❀

The guide announced they were approaching Chejudo, what Koreans liked to call the Island of Wind, Rocks, and Women because of the famous deep-sea diving women with incredible lung capacity, and the rocky wild wind and shore. It was a favorite destination of Korean honeymooners and vacationers. The guide repeated herself in Korean. Then she launched into history and details that became background noise for a few moments as Gracie watched the shore. Inland, the clumped tropical growth seemed to give off an almost minty scent, something fresh that competed with the smell of the sea.

Grace knew little about her father's past. She had never even met her own grandparents. But she did know that one hundred years ago, Sin Tae Song had boarded a ship to leave this place forever. She wondered about the person he was in that limbo, that traveling self that was neither the person you had been nor the person you were about to become. She thought about both the willing and unwilling traversal of distances that had made her life—and Adam's life—possible. The journey of the famous woman traveler Isabella Bird Bishop, who had passed through her mother's village with her nimble but dignified step. Of her father, crowded with hundreds of dreamers on board the *Gaelic*. Of her mother, her still hopeful heart lifted toward adventure. And of other journeys, as well. From the edge of the bed to the middle, where someone beside you sleeps with light and even breath. From the fog shrouded orchard to the clearing back of the house.

Adam looked far out over the water. Grace had a finger hooked around his back belt loop. When he thought no one was looking, he pulled a small item from his jacket pocket, kept his fist enclosed over it, and dropped it over the ferry's edge. Shiny metal, possibly ornate was all Gracie had time to discern. "What was that you just threw in, Adam?"

He shrugged. "One of my treasures. I found it."

"But why? I thought that was precious to you."

"It is precious to me. That's why I wanted Captain Hamel to have it."
The guide had told of a Hendrik Hamel, a Dutch sailor who had ship-
wrecked on this island in 1683 with forty surviving crew members. Aside
from an escape by thirteen of the men that got them thirteen miles from
shore, none of the crew ever returned home.

"But he died over three hundred years ago!"

"So? You say he was buried at sea."

Gracie can picture the sailor, that accidental immigrant, soaked and
clinging to his piece of ship, his hair and shirt stiff with the salt of the
sea. From the rocky beach, obscured by trees, a young woman watches,
squatting behind a rock on powerful legs. She is smiling because she can
see that, despite the pinkness of his skin and his red-gold beard, he is
handsome. That makes his fate more interesting. What this handsome
sailor does not know is that it is the custom of the Korean king to capture
and retain foreigners forever. Korea is not called the hermit kingdom for
nothing.

Perhaps the native girl will get a chance to see the expression on his face
when the man learns he has entered a land neither hostile nor friendly to
him but simply neutral. He and his men will be fed and provided for. At
first they will be the objects of curiosity and amusement, but eventually,
interest in them will subside. Perhaps they will father children. Perhaps
some will adopt the country as their own, becoming quite at home among
its customs and people. Perhaps some will accept their fate with a bitter
heart. But, in any case, they will always be watched and, at the same time,
invisible. Isn't that a kind of glory, to be so important for the rest of your
days? And, anyway, it wouldn't be so bad. She will lay fish and fruit and
cakes before them at their first welcome. They will not exchange a single
word. Her smile, however, will mesmerize him, telling them everything
they need to know: You will die here. But today you live. Eat.

A pocket mirror fitted inside a mother-of-pearl frame bobs in the ship's
wake. Sometimes it is mirror side down, reflecting the quick-silver glint of

a school of fish. Sometimes it floats, mirror side skyward, a rectangle of gray or blue, crisscrossed now and again by the image of a sea bird or an airplane passing overhead or the cheeks of a cloud. One day it may wash to shore, lodged between the slick stones of Kaesang Beach. Or it may sink for no known reason to the ocean floor, caught between the jaws of some scuttling bottom creature. Or one day it may be taken up into the clutch of a young diver practicing the arts of her foremothers. She will be a modern girl, one not yet dreamed into being. She will be familiar with her own reflection, and the image of her face will cause her to smile an ancient smile. This, too, could happen. Or has happened. Or all of these things. Or none.

# ACKNOWLEDGMENTS

I am deeply grateful to the University of Georgia Press for honoring my collection with this distinguished award. Thirty years ago, Don Lee pulled the title story out of the slush pile at *Ploughshares*, and DeWitt Henry and James Alan MacPherson included it in the special issue they edited, called "Confronting Racial Difference." I am grateful to these writers for giving me my start. For their encouragement and commentary at critical moments in the development of the collection, I want to thank Marie Myong-ok Lee, Vince Gotera, Barbara Camillo, Pat Stevens, JoAnn Beard, Nancy Reincke, Tracey Manson, Ann Robinson, Calla Devlin and, most of all, Lori Ostlund, the Series editor, for her sincere warmth, collaboration, and guiding hand. Thanks go to Elaine Kim for the visit to UC Berkeley and to Janet Burroway for including "Waiting for Mr. Kim" in the first edition of *Writing Fiction*. Sincere thanks to the agents and editors who helped shape my idea of what this collection could be, including Kathy Pories, Esmund Harmsworth, and Nicki Richesin. This collection would never have existed had I not discovered my *halmoni's* oral history included in Bong Youn Choy's *Koreans in America* and learned details that lit my imagination. Nearly every story got its start in one of the literary journals and collections whose prizes served as reassurance that I should keep trying. Thanks, first, for the reprints of "Waiting for Mr. Kim," in *Pushcart Annual XVI; Other Sides of Silence*, edited by Dewitt Henry; *Love Stories for the Rest of Us* from Pushcart Press; and the Harper-Collins *Literary Mosaic Series* edition on Asian American Literature edited by Shawn Wong. Deepest gratitude to Linda Swanson Davies and Susan Burmeister at *Glimmer Train* for selecting "White Fate" for second place in the Fiction Open and for the lovely visit to Portland. My sincere appreciation to *Southwest Review* for the David Nathan Meyerson Award for "A Former Citizen," *Nimrod International* for selecting "Do Us Part" for the Katherine Anne Porter Prize for fiction and to Alice Hoffman for selecting "Typesetting, 1964" for *The Ledge* fiction prize. And my gratitude to the early online literary journal, *Blood Lotus*, and *Other Voices* for taking a risk on "Day of the Swallows" and "Made You Look," respectively. Although they don't know it, the Franciscan sisters of Prairiewoods in Hiawatha, Iowa have done almost more to support my writing than anyone I know by providing gracious hospitality and retreat over the decades. But the deepest thanks go to Jonah and Tim, my beloveds, because they live with a writer and love her anyway.

C. M. Mayo, *Sky over El Nido*

Wendy Brenner, *Large Animals in Everyday Life*

Paul Rawlins, *No Lie Like Love*

Harvey Grossinger, *The Quarry*

Ha Jin, *Under the Red Flag*

Andy Plattner, *Winter Money*

Frank Soos, *Unified Field Theory*

Mary Clyde, *Survival Rates*

Hester Kaplan, *The Edge of Marriage*

Darrell Spencer, *CAUTION Men in Trees*

Robert Anderson, *Ice Age*

Bill Roorbach, *Big Bend*

Dana Johnson, *Break Any Woman Down*

Gina Ochsner, *The Necessary Grace to Fall*

Kellie Wells, *Compression Scars*

Eric Shade, *Eyesores*

Catherine Brady, *Curled in the Bed of Love*

Ed Allen, *Ate It Anyway*

Gary Fincke, *Sorry I Worried You*

Barbara Sutton, *The Send-Away Girl*

David Crouse, *Copy Cats*

Randy F. Nelson, *The Imaginary Lives of Mechanical Men*

Greg Downs, *Spit Baths*

Peter LaSalle, *Tell Borges If You See Him: Tales of Contemporary Somnambulism*

Anne Panning, *Super America*

Margot Singer, *The Pale of Settlement*

Andrew Porter, *The Theory of Light and Matter*

Peter Selgin, *Drowning Lessons*

# ANNIVERSARY ANTHOLOGIES

TENTH ANNIVERSARY

*The Flannery O'Connor Award: Selected Stories,* edited by Charles East

FIFTEENTH ANNIVERSARY

*Listening to the Voices: Stories from the Flannery O'Connor Award,* edited by Charles East

THIRTEENTH ANNIVERSARY

*Stories from the Flannery O'Connor Award: A Thirtieth Anniversary Anthology: The Early Years,* edited by Charles East

*Stories from the Flannery O'Connor Award: A Thirtieth Anniversary Anthology: The Recent Years,* edited by Nancy Zafris

THEMATIC ANTHOLOGIES

*Hold That Knowledge: Stories about Love from the Flannery O'Connor Award for Short Fiction,* edited by Ethan Laughman

*The Slow Release: Stories about Death from the Flannery O'Connor Award for Short Fiction,* edited by Ethan Laughman

*Spinning Away from the Center: Stories about Homesickness and Homecoming from the Flannery O'Connor Award for Short Fiction,* edited by Ethan Laughman

*Rituals to Observe: Stories about Holidays from the Flannery O'Connor Award for Short Fiction,* edited by Ethan Laughman

*Good and Balanced: Stories about Sports from the Flannery O'Connor Award for Short Fiction,* edited by Ethan Laughman

*Down on the Sidewalk: Stories about Children and Childhood from the Flannery O'Connor Award for Short Fiction,* edited by Ethan Laughman

*A Perfect Souvenir: Stories about Travel from the Flannery O'Connor Award for Short Fiction,* edited by Ethan Laughman

*A Day's Pay: Stories about Work from the Flannery O'Connor Award for Short Fiction,* edited by Ethan Laughman

*Growing Up: Stories about Adolescence from the Flannery O'Connor Award for Short Fiction,* edited by Ethan Laughman

*Changes: Stories about Transformation from the Flannery O'Connor Award for Short Fiction,* edited by Ethan Laughman